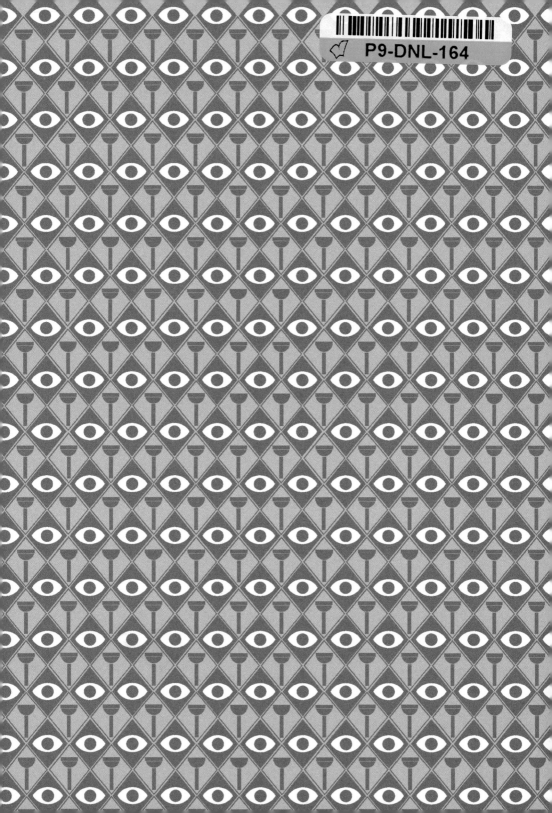

EDISON BEAKER CREATURE SEEKER

THE NIGHT DOOR

BY FRANK CAMMUSO

VIKING

For the Reverend Adrian Amaya
— F.C.

Special thanks to Ngoc Huynh, Khai Cammuso, Kathy Leonardo,
Nancy Iacovelli, Mai Huynh, Min Hong, Ai Vy Hong, Van Hong, Hart Seely,
Tom Peyer, Randy Elliot, Sheila Keenan, Denise Cronin, and Judy Hansen.

VIKING
Penguin Young Readers
An imprint of Penguin Random House LLC
375 Hudson Street
New York, New York 10014

First published in the United States of America by Viking,
an imprint of Penguin Random House LLC, 2018

Copyright © 2018 by Frank Cammuso

LIBRARY OF CONGRESS CATALOGING-IN-PUBLICATION DATA IS AVAILABLE.
ISBN 9780425291924 (hardcover); 9780425291931 (paperback)

Manufactured in China

1 3 5 7 9 10 8 6 4 2

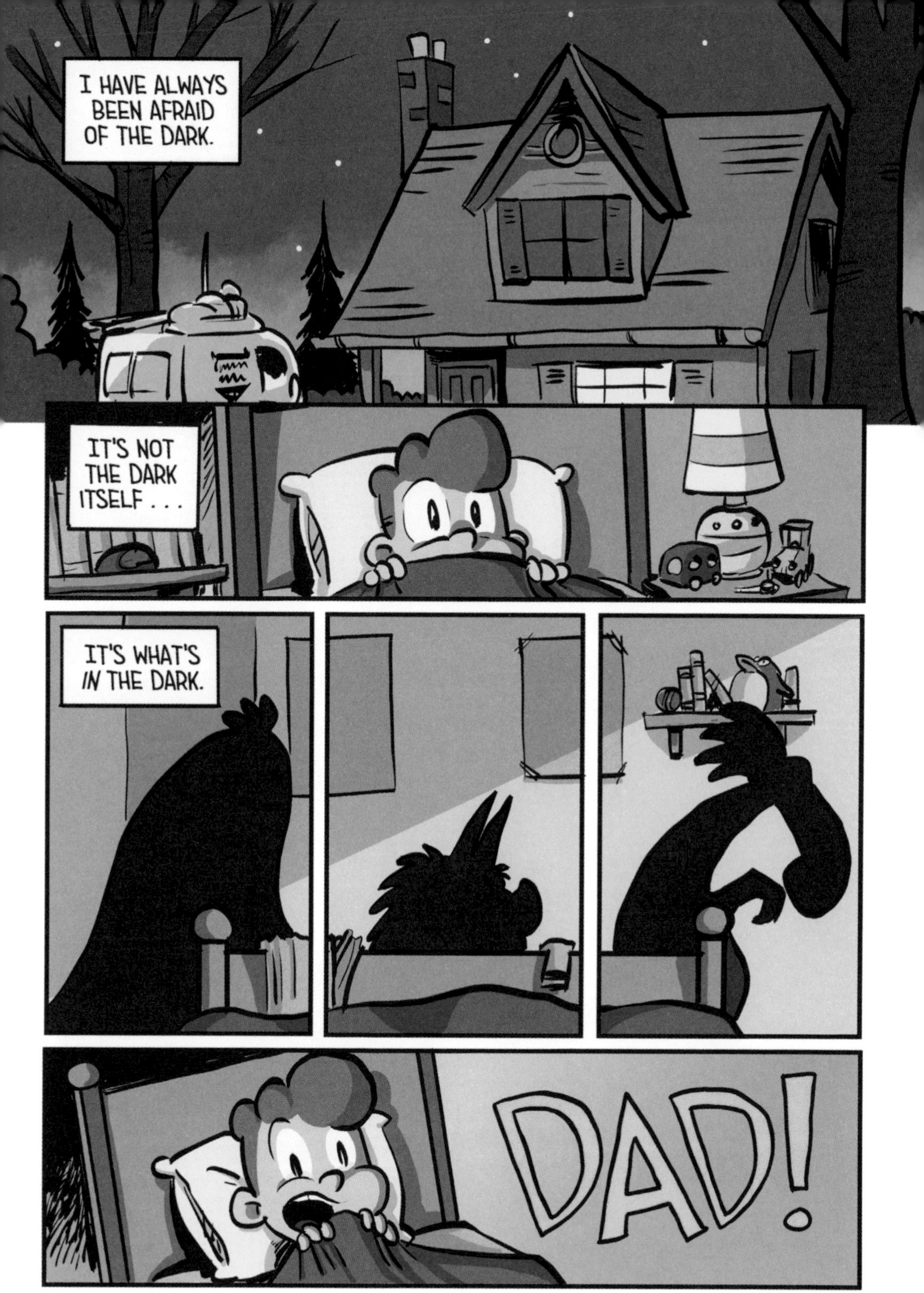
I HAVE ALWAYS BEEN AFRAID OF THE DARK.
IT'S NOT THE DARK ITSELF . . .
IT'S WHAT'S *IN* THE DARK.
DAD!

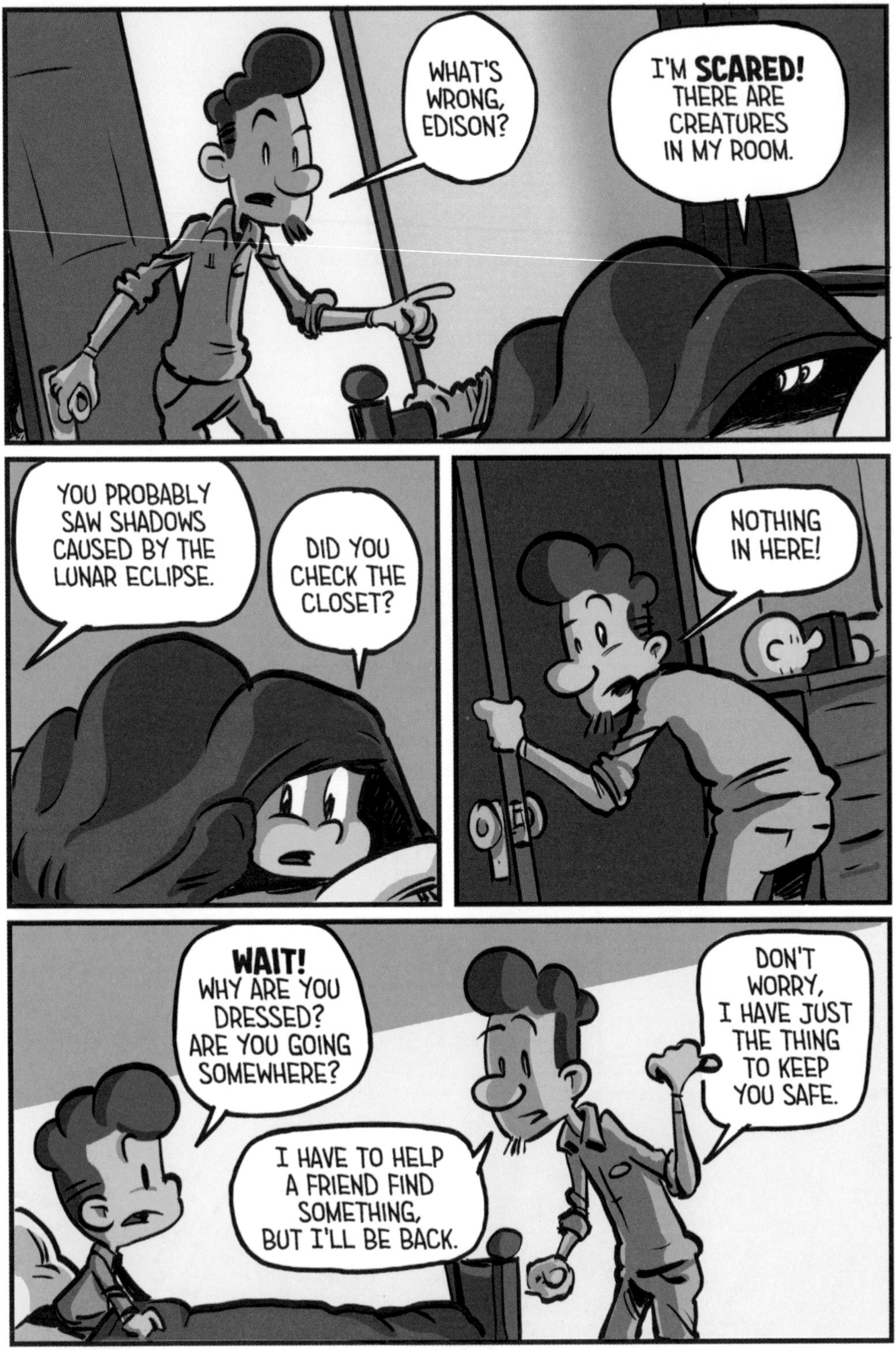
WHAT'S WRONG, EDISON?
I'M **SCARED!** THERE ARE CREATURES IN MY ROOM.
YOU PROBABLY SAW SHADOWS CAUSED BY THE LUNAR ECLIPSE.
DID YOU CHECK THE CLOSET?
NOTHING IN HERE!
WAIT! WHY ARE YOU DRESSED? ARE YOU GOING SOMEWHERE?
I HAVE TO HELP A FRIEND FIND SOMETHING, BUT I'LL BE BACK.
DON'T WORRY, I HAVE JUST THE THING TO KEEP YOU SAFE.

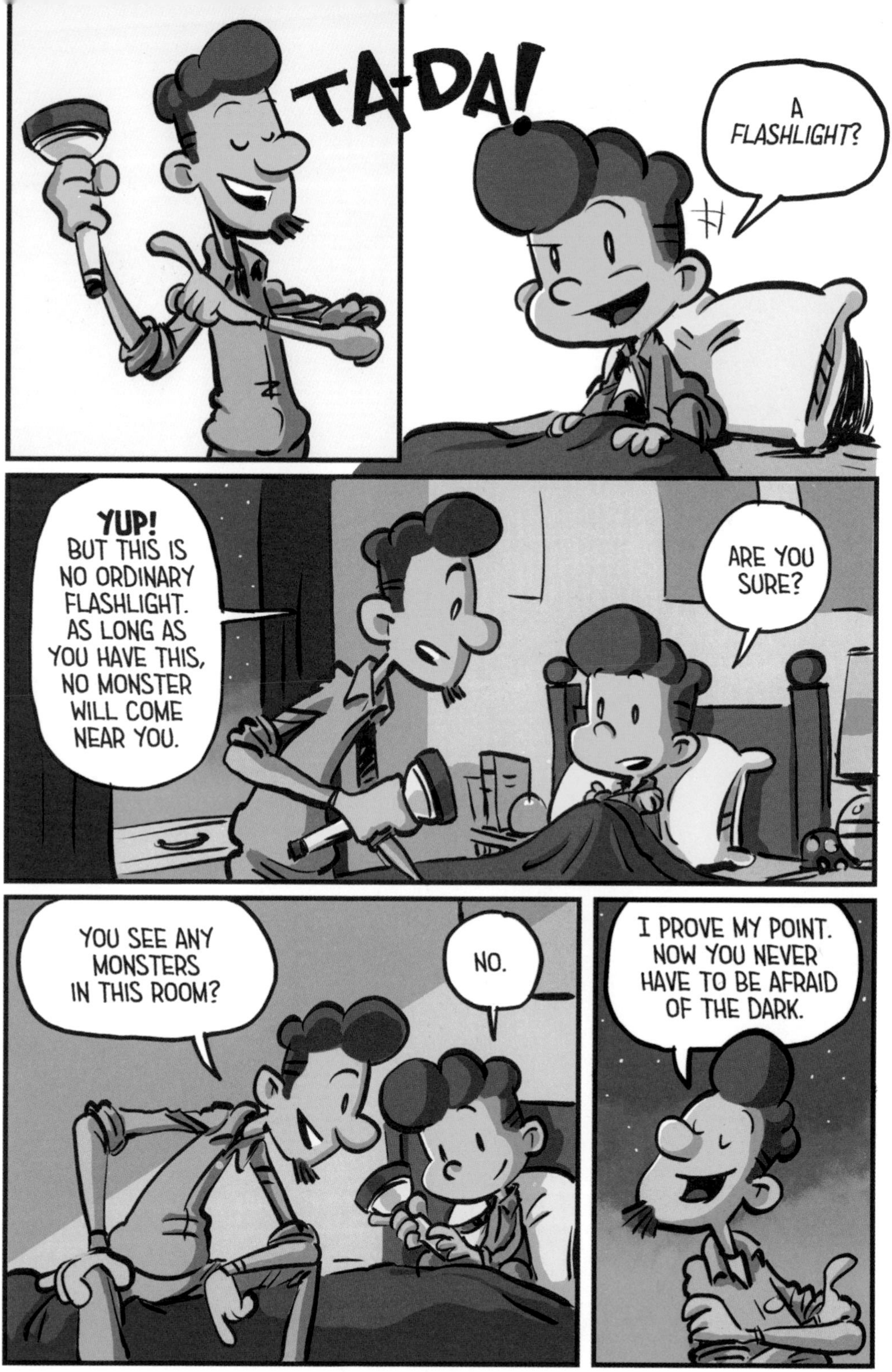
TA-DA!
A FLASHLIGHT?
YUP! BUT THIS IS NO ORDINARY FLASHLIGHT. AS LONG AS YOU HAVE THIS, NO MONSTER WILL COME NEAR YOU.
ARE YOU SURE?
YOU SEE ANY MONSTERS IN THIS ROOM?
NO.
I PROVE MY POINT. NOW YOU NEVER HAVE TO BE AFRAID OF THE DARK.

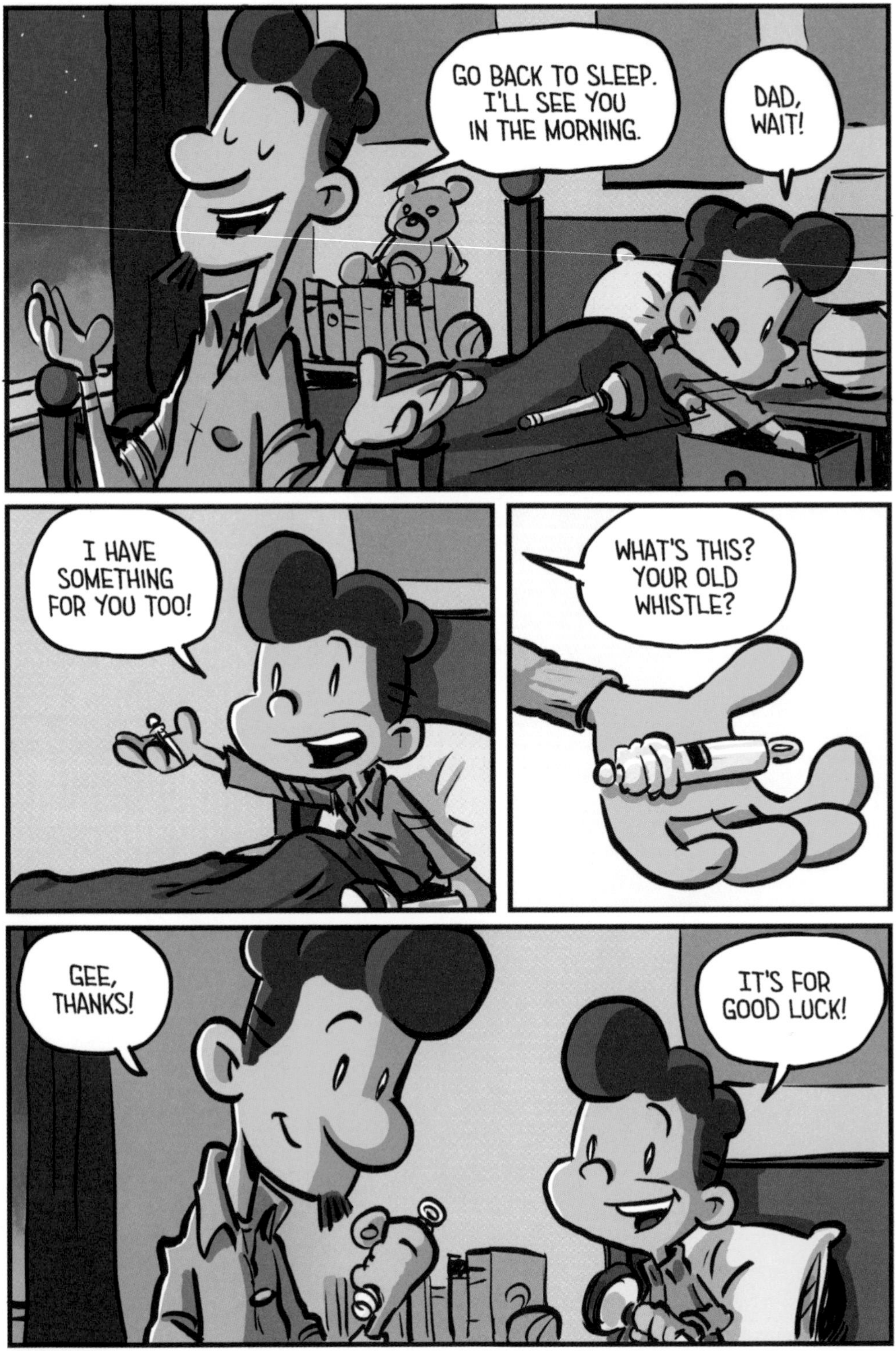
GO BACK TO SLEEP. I'LL SEE YOU IN THE MORNING.
DAD, WAIT!
I HAVE SOMETHING FOR YOU TOO!
WHAT'S THIS? YOUR OLD WHISTLE?
GEE, THANKS!
IT'S FOR GOOD LUCK!

GOOD NIGHT, BUDDY.

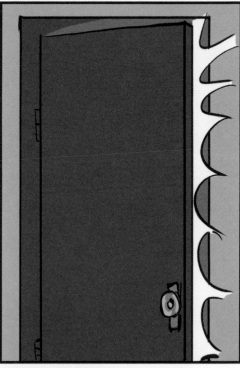

THAT WAS THE LAST TIME I SAW MY DAD.

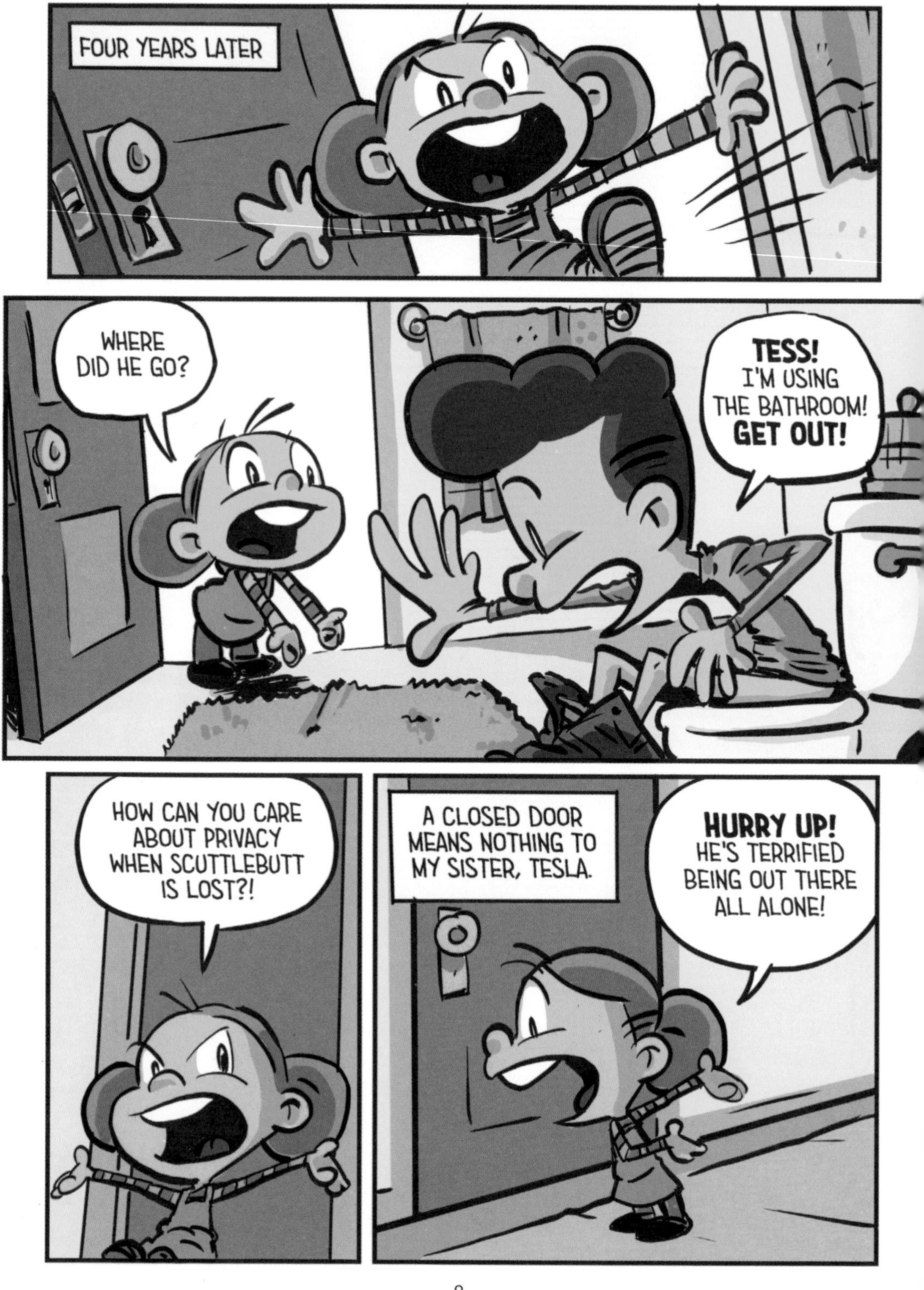
FOUR YEARS LATER
WHERE DID HE GO?
TESS! I'M USING THE BATHROOM! GET OUT!
HOW CAN YOU CARE ABOUT PRIVACY WHEN SCUTTLEBUTT IS LOST?!
A CLOSED DOOR MEANS NOTHING TO MY SISTER, TESLA.
HURRY UP! HE'S TERRIFIED BEING OUT THERE ALL ALONE!

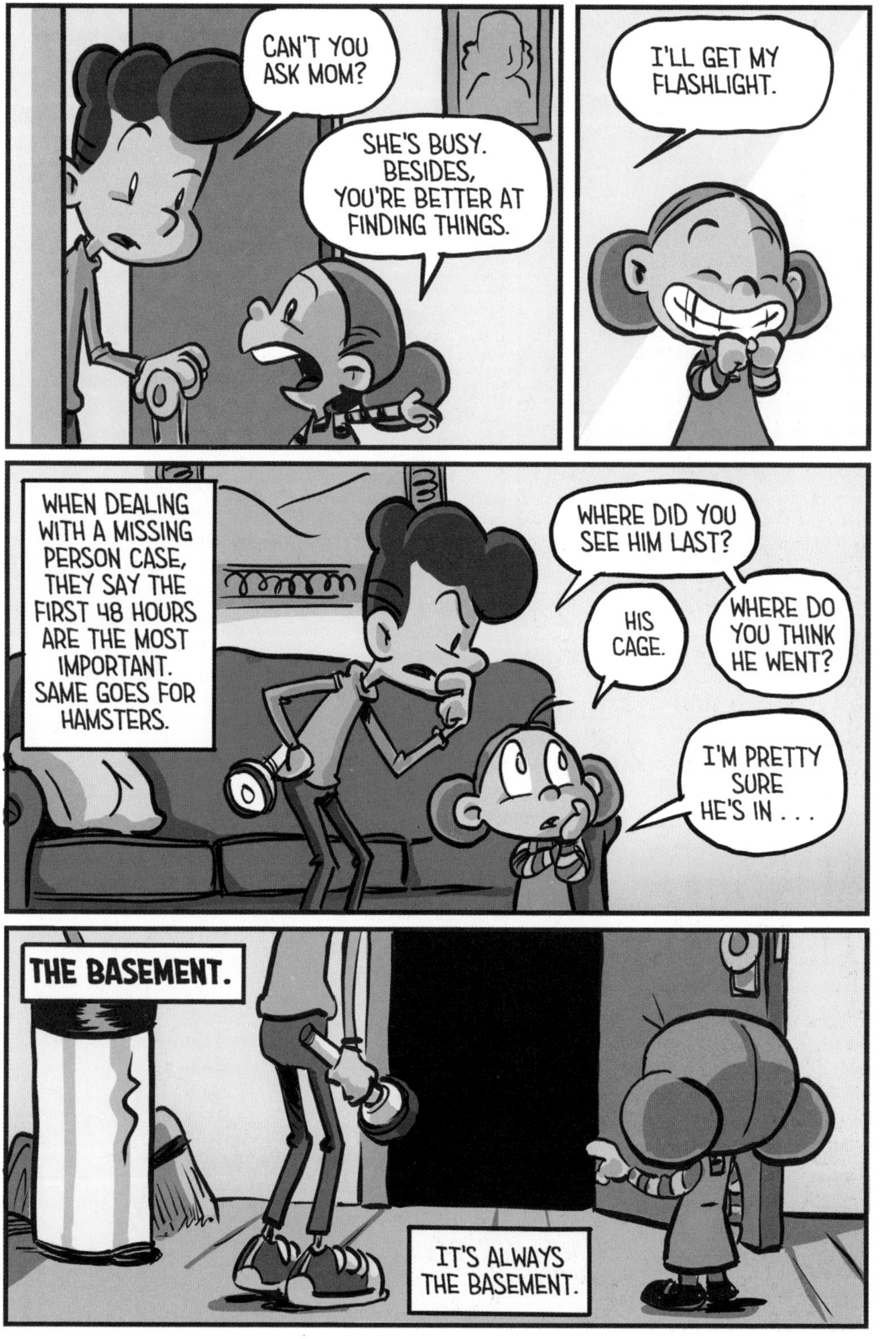
CAN'T YOU ASK MOM?
SHE'S BUSY. BESIDES, YOU'RE BETTER AT FINDING THINGS.
I'LL GET MY FLASHLIGHT.
WHEN DEALING WITH A MISSING PERSON CASE, THEY SAY THE FIRST 48 HOURS ARE THE MOST IMPORTANT. SAME GOES FOR HAMSTERS.
WHERE DID YOU SEE HIM LAST?
HIS CAGE.
WHERE DO YOU THINK HE WENT?
I'M PRETTY SURE HE'S IN . . .
THE BASEMENT.
IT'S ALWAYS THE BASEMENT.

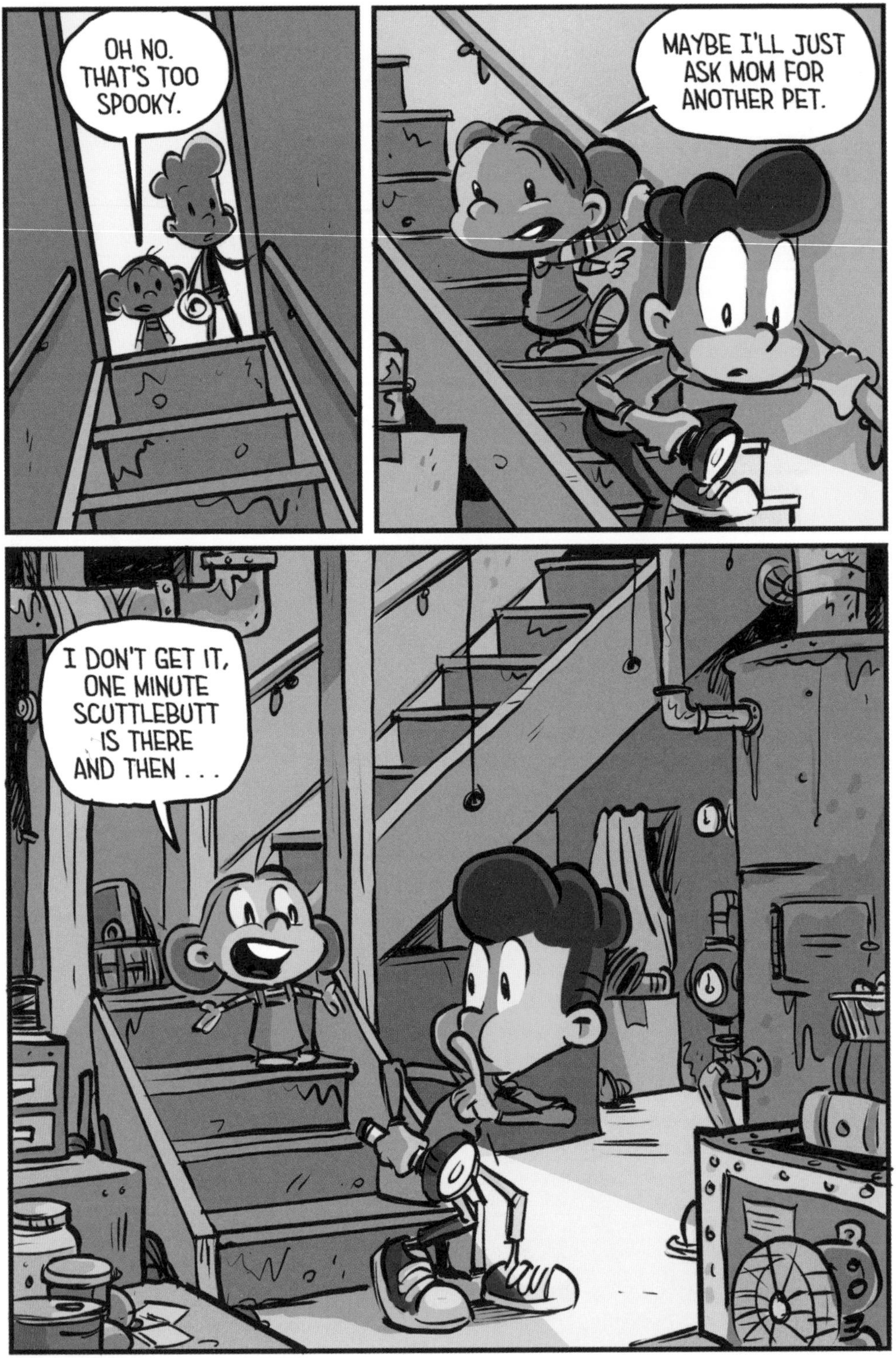
OH NO. THAT'S TOO SPOOKY.
MAYBE I'LL JUST ASK MOM FOR ANOTHER PET.
I DON'T GET IT, ONE MINUTE SCUTTLEBUTT IS THERE AND THEN . . .

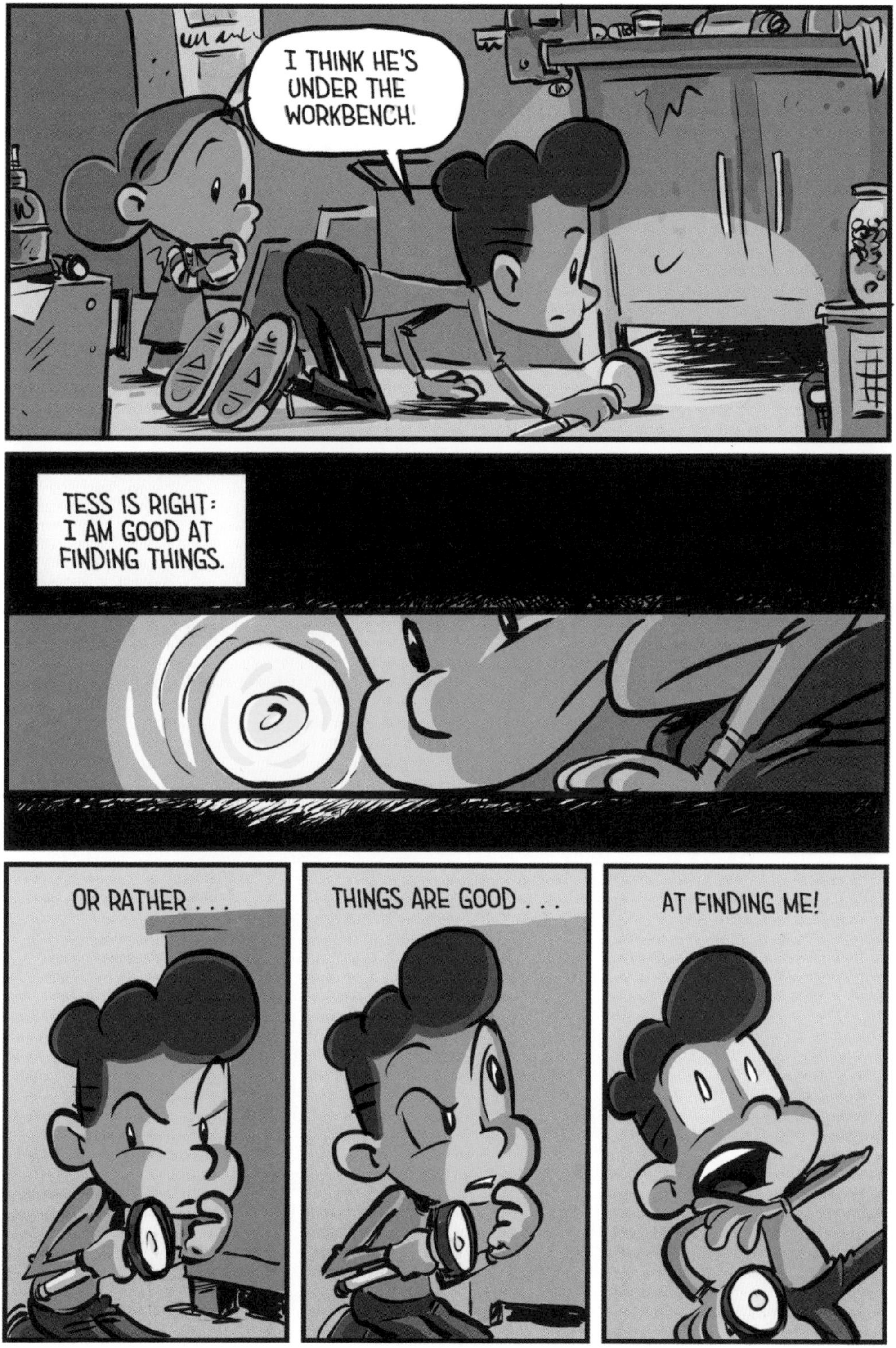
I THINK HE'S UNDER THE WORKBENCH!
TESS IS RIGHT: I AM GOOD AT FINDING THINGS.
OR RATHER . . .
THINGS ARE GOOD . . .
AT FINDING ME!

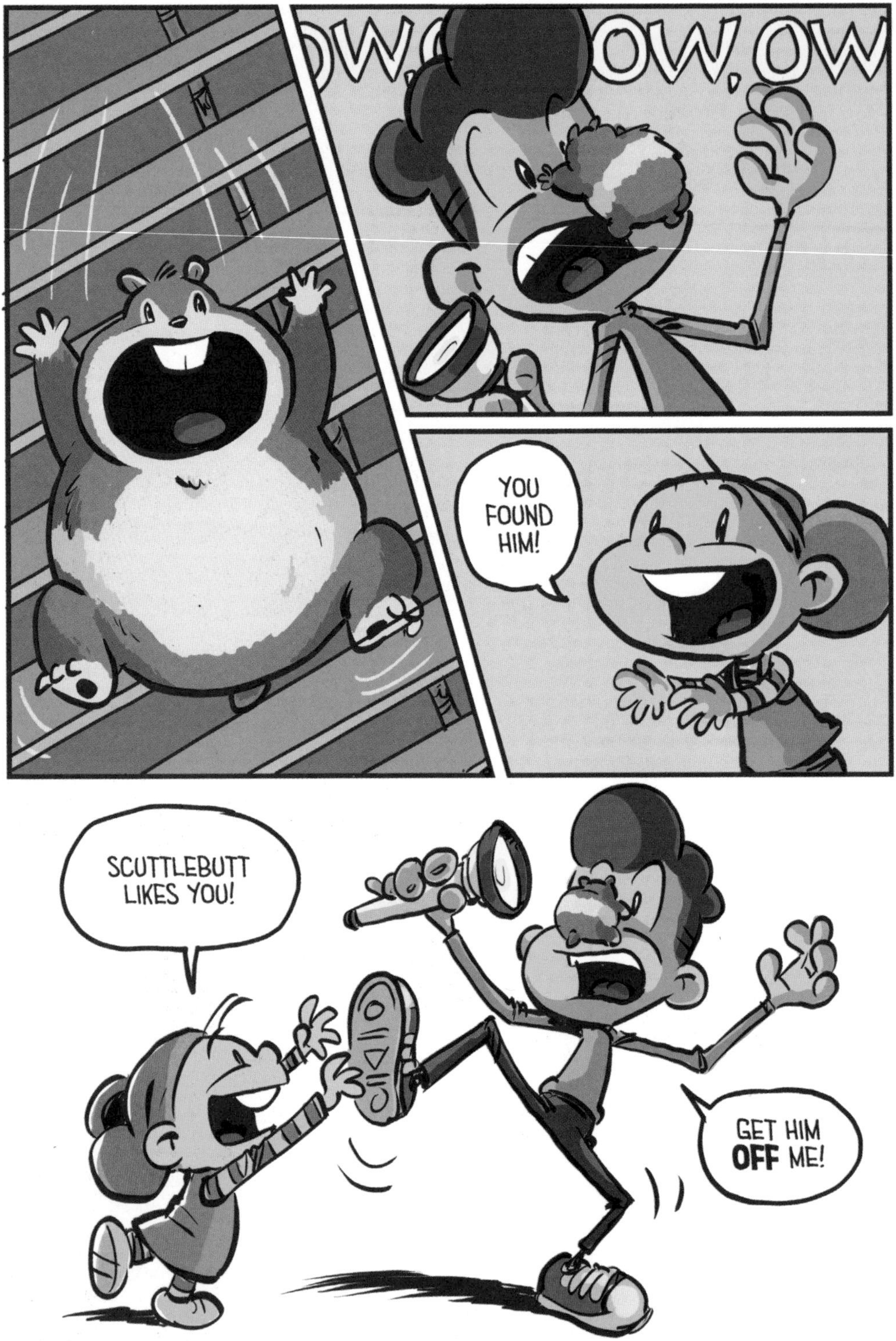
OW, OW, OW, OW
YOU FOUND HIM!
SCUTTLEBUTT LIKES YOU!
GET HIM **OFF** ME!

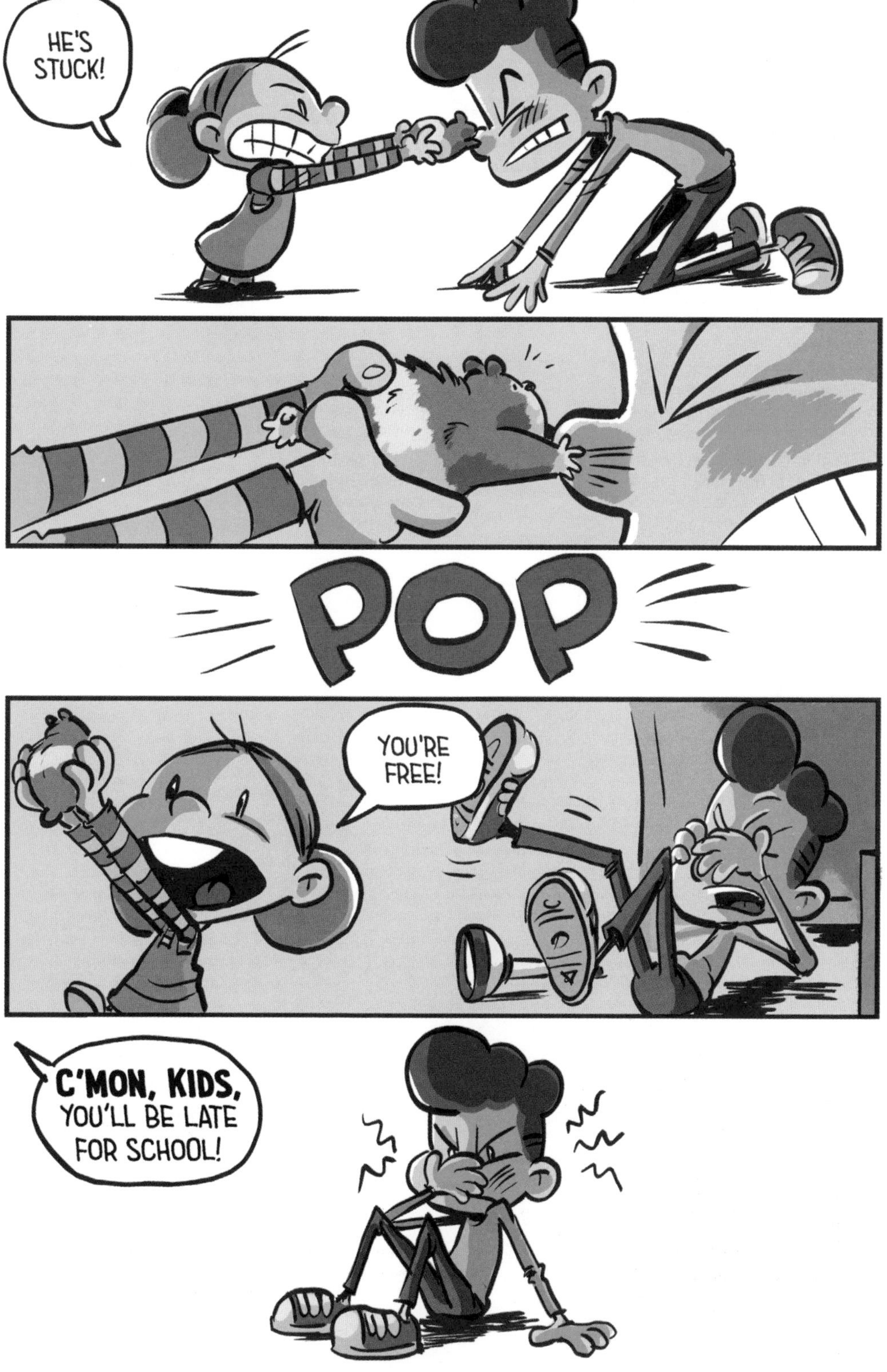
HE'S STUCK!
POP
YOU'RE FREE!
C'MON, KIDS, YOU'LL BE LATE FOR SCHOOL!

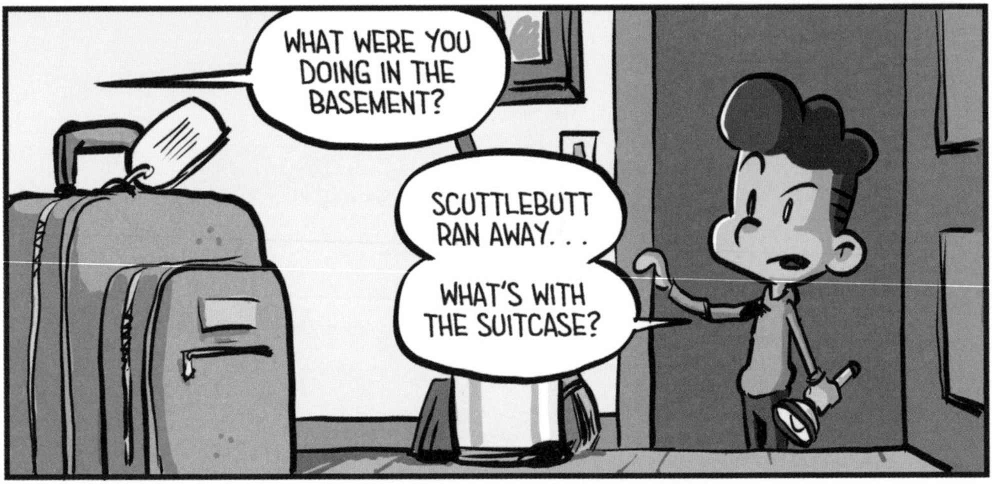
WHAT WERE YOU DOING IN THE BASEMENT?
SCUTTLEBUTT RAN AWAY. . .
WHAT'S WITH THE SUITCASE?

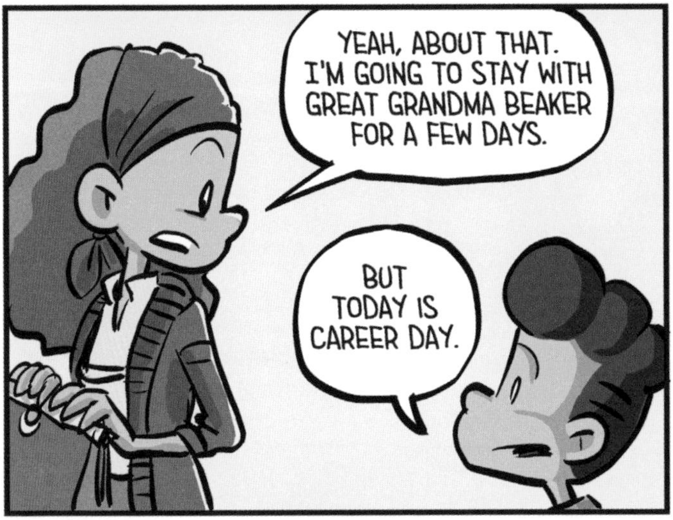
YEAH, ABOUT THAT. I'M GOING TO STAY WITH GREAT GRANDMA BEAKER FOR A FEW DAYS.
BUT TODAY IS CAREER DAY.

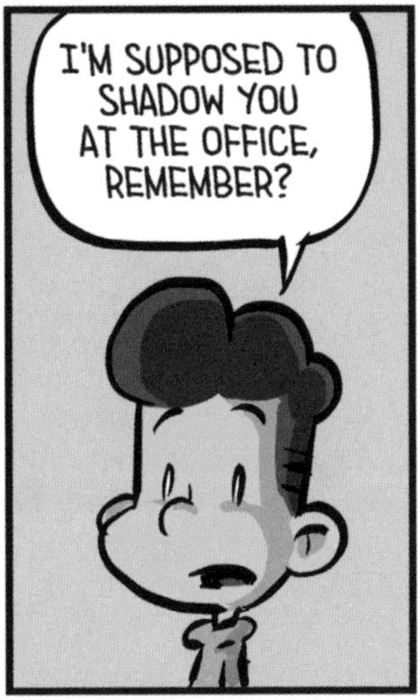
I'M SUPPOSED TO SHADOW YOU AT THE OFFICE, REMEMBER?

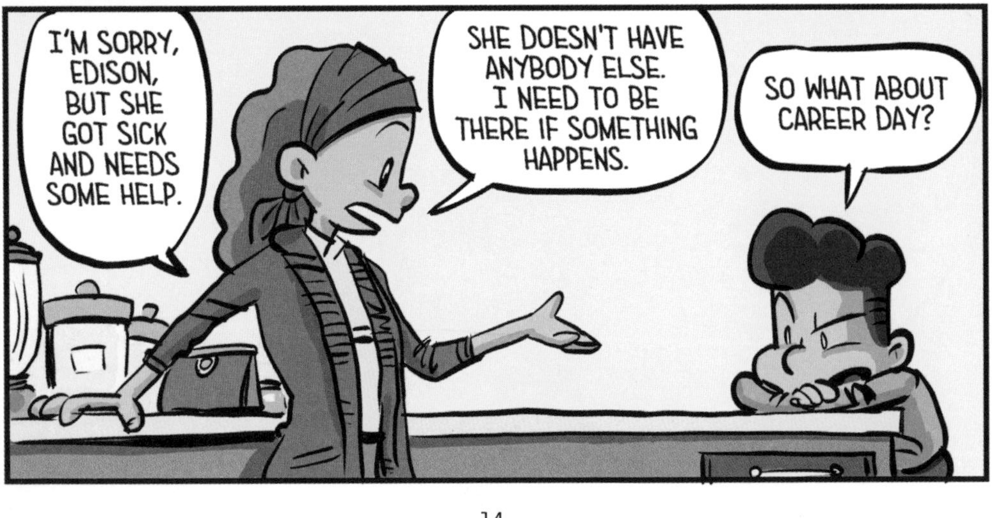
I'M SORRY, EDISON, BUT SHE GOT SICK AND NEEDS SOME HELP.
SHE DOESN'T HAVE ANYBODY ELSE. I NEED TO BE THERE IF SOMETHING HAPPENS.
SO WHAT ABOUT CAREER DAY?

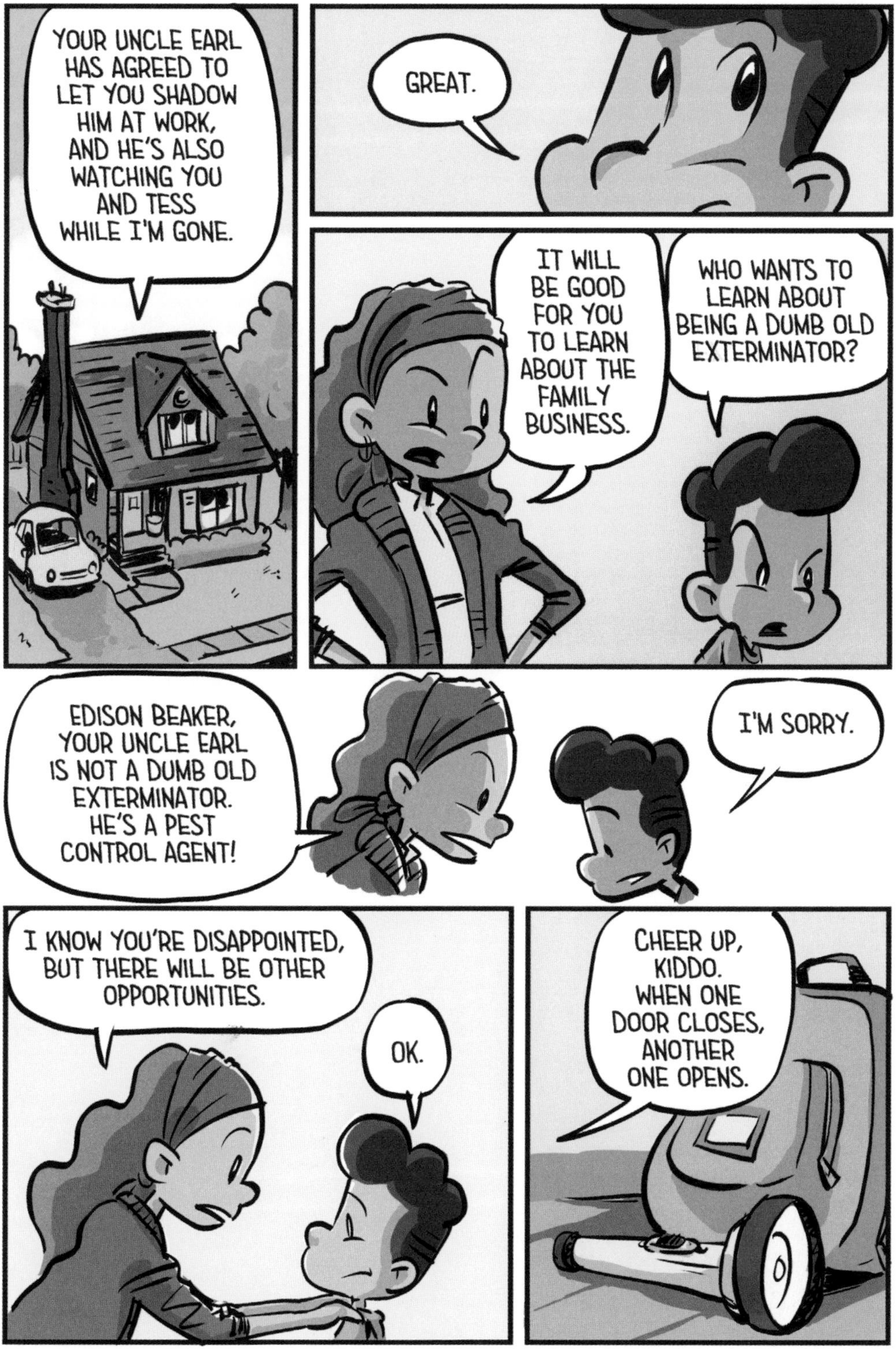
YOUR UNCLE EARL HAS AGREED TO LET YOU SHADOW HIM AT WORK, AND HE'S ALSO WATCHING YOU AND TESS WHILE I'M GONE.
GREAT.
IT WILL BE GOOD FOR YOU TO LEARN ABOUT THE FAMILY BUSINESS.
WHO WANTS TO LEARN ABOUT BEING A DUMB OLD EXTERMINATOR?
EDISON BEAKER, YOUR UNCLE EARL IS NOT A DUMB OLD EXTERMINATOR. HE'S A PEST CONTROL AGENT!
I'M SORRY.
I KNOW YOU'RE DISAPPOINTED, BUT THERE WILL BE OTHER OPPORTUNITIES.
OK.
CHEER UP, KIDDO. WHEN ONE DOOR CLOSES, ANOTHER ONE OPENS.

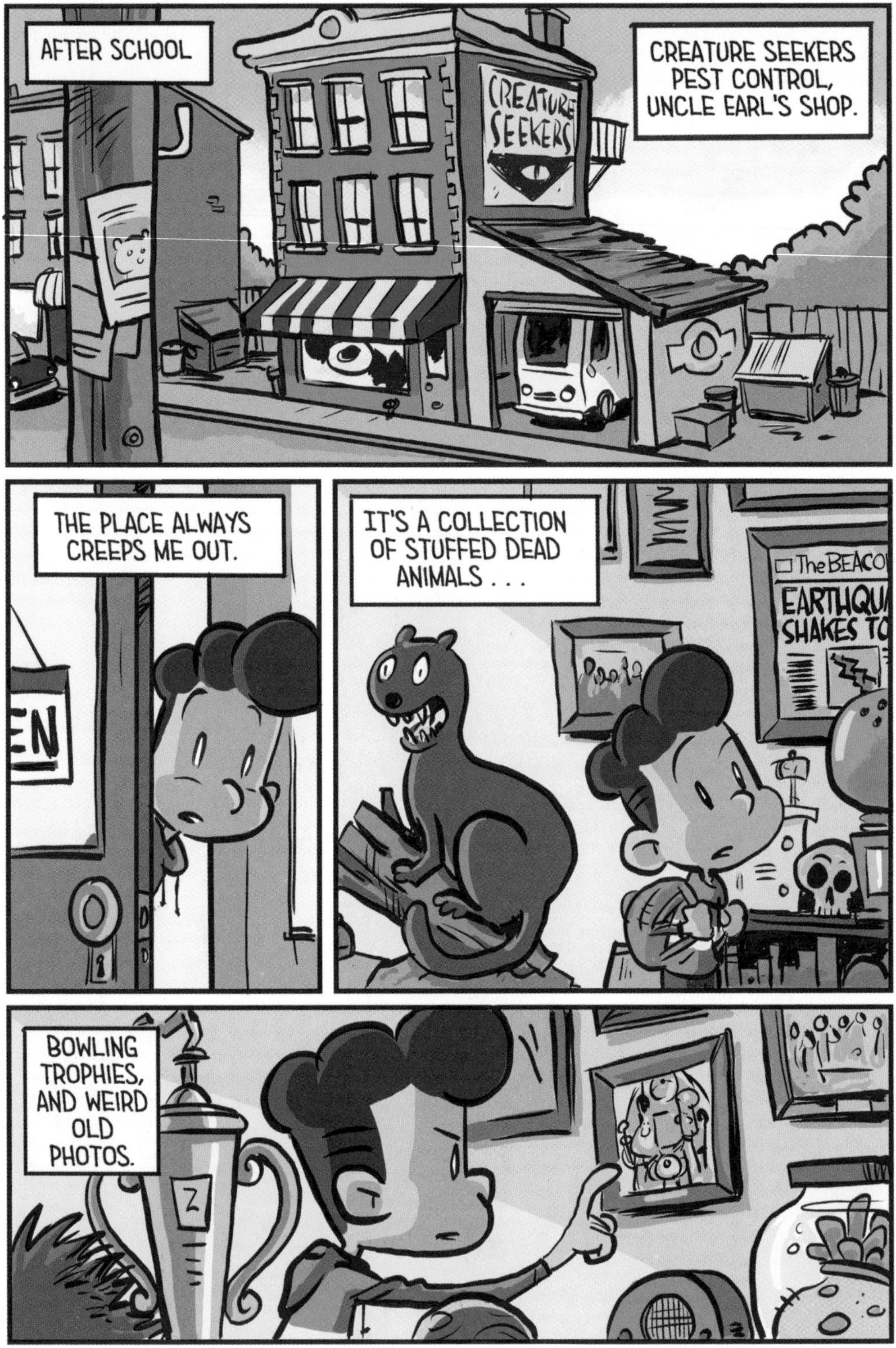

AFTER SCHOOL
CREATURE SEEKERS PEST CONTROL, UNCLE EARL'S SHOP.
CREATURE SEEKERS
THE PLACE ALWAYS CREEPS ME OUT.
IT'S A COLLECTION OF STUFFED DEAD ANIMALS . . .
BOWLING TROPHIES, AND WEIRD OLD PHOTOS.

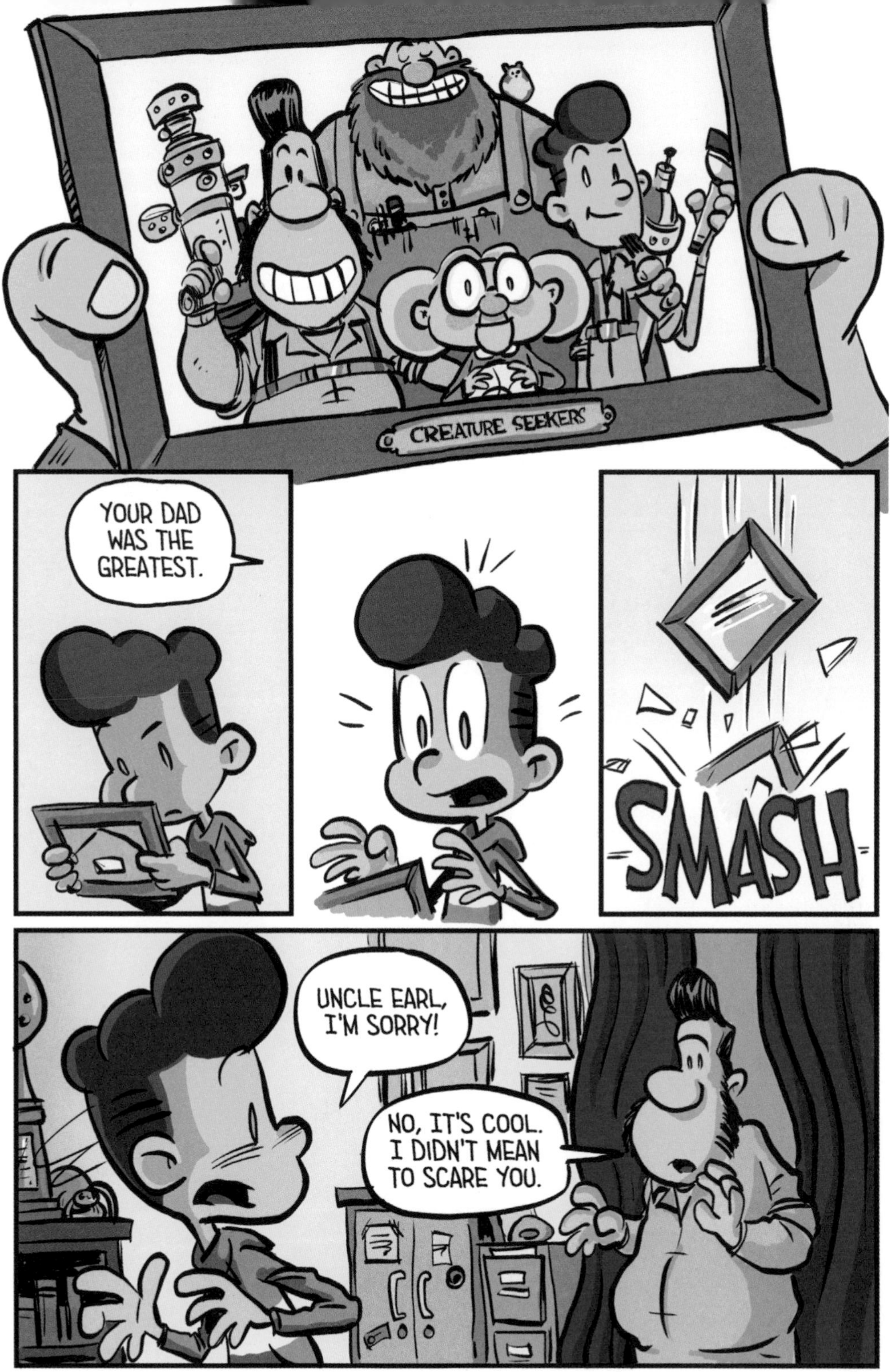
CREATURE SEEKERS
YOUR DAD WAS THE GREATEST.
SMASH
UNCLE EARL, I'M SORRY!
NO, IT'S COOL. I DIDN'T MEAN TO SCARE YOU.

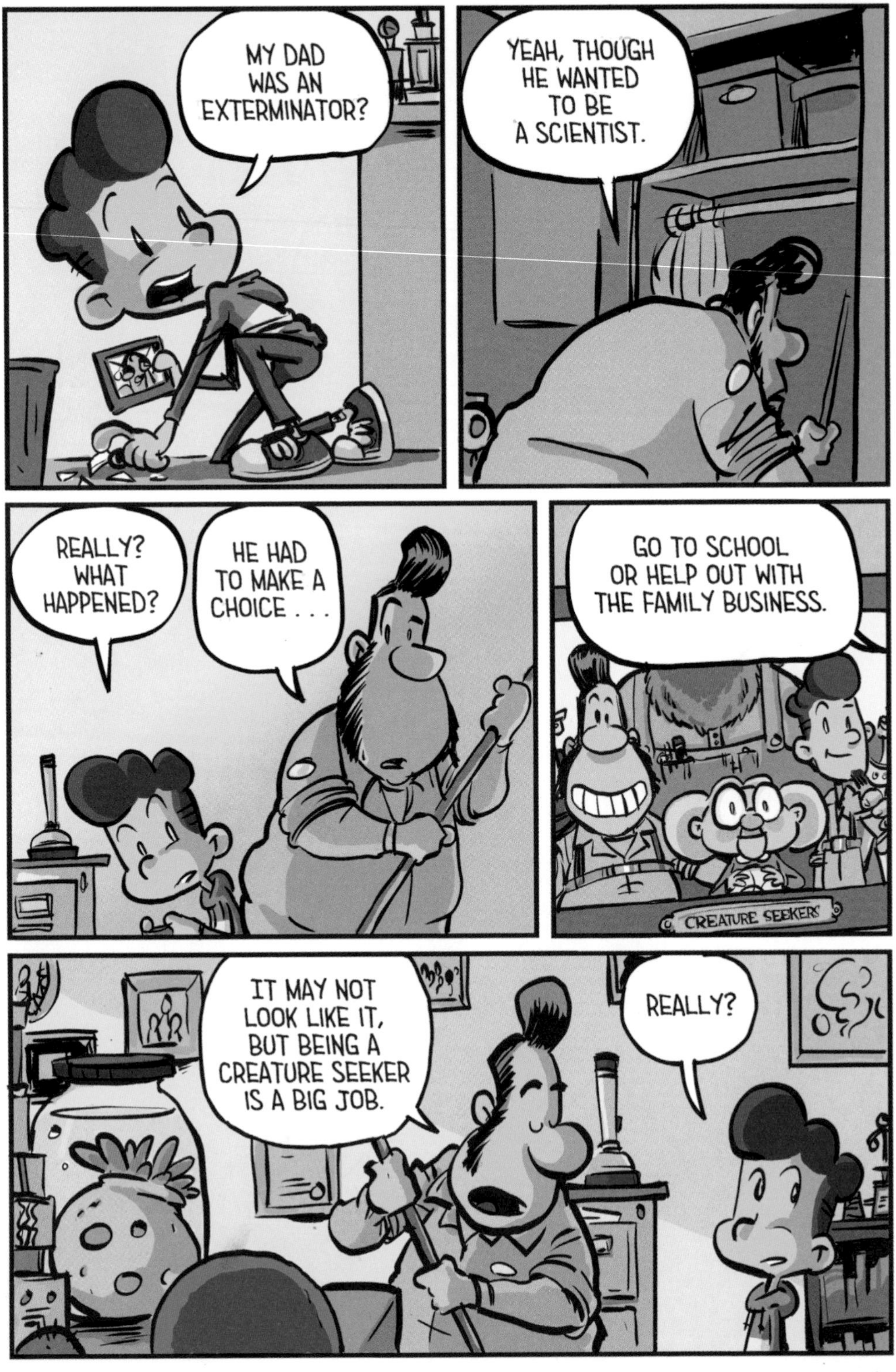
MY DAD WAS AN EXTERMINATOR?
YEAH, THOUGH HE WANTED TO BE A SCIENTIST.
REALLY? WHAT HAPPENED?
HE HAD TO MAKE A CHOICE . . .
GO TO SCHOOL OR HELP OUT WITH THE FAMILY BUSINESS.
CREATURE SEEKERS
IT MAY NOT LOOK LIKE IT, BUT BEING A CREATURE SEEKER IS A BIG JOB.
REALLY?

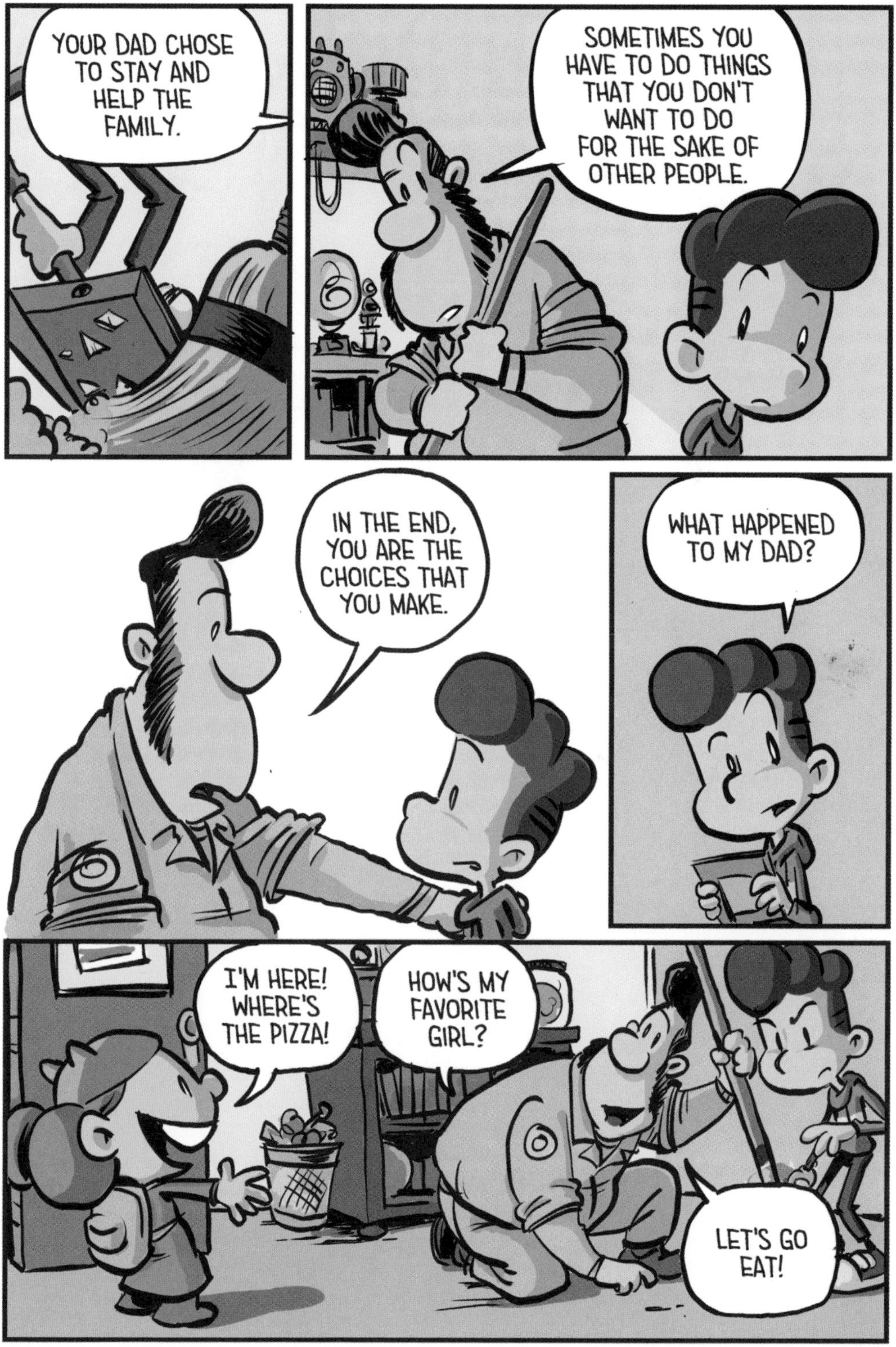
YOUR DAD CHOSE TO STAY AND HELP THE FAMILY.
SOMETIMES YOU HAVE TO DO THINGS THAT YOU DON'T WANT TO DO FOR THE SAKE OF OTHER PEOPLE.
IN THE END, YOU ARE THE CHOICES THAT YOU MAKE.
WHAT HAPPENED TO MY DAD?
I'M HERE! WHERE'S THE PIZZA!
HOW'S MY FAVORITE GIRL?
LET'S GO EAT!

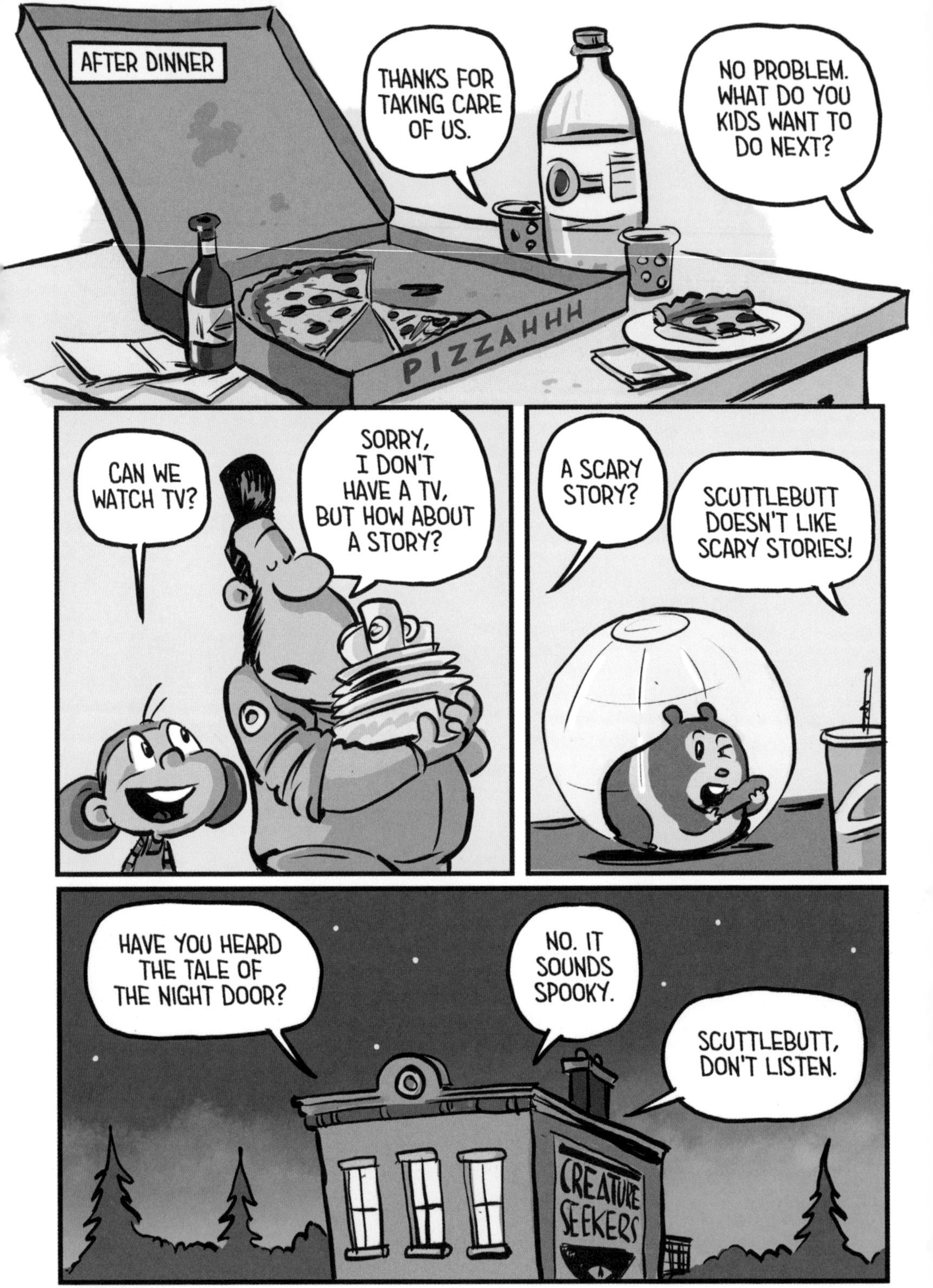
AFTER DINNER
THANKS FOR TAKING CARE OF US.
NO PROBLEM. WHAT DO YOU KIDS WANT TO DO NEXT?
PIZZAHHH
CAN WE WATCH TV?
SORRY, I DON'T HAVE A TV, BUT HOW ABOUT A STORY?
A SCARY STORY?
SCUTTLEBUTT DOESN'T LIKE SCARY STORIES!
HAVE YOU HEARD THE TALE OF THE NIGHT DOOR?
NO. IT SOUNDS SPOOKY.
SCUTTLEBUTT, DON'T LISTEN.
CREATURE SEEKERS

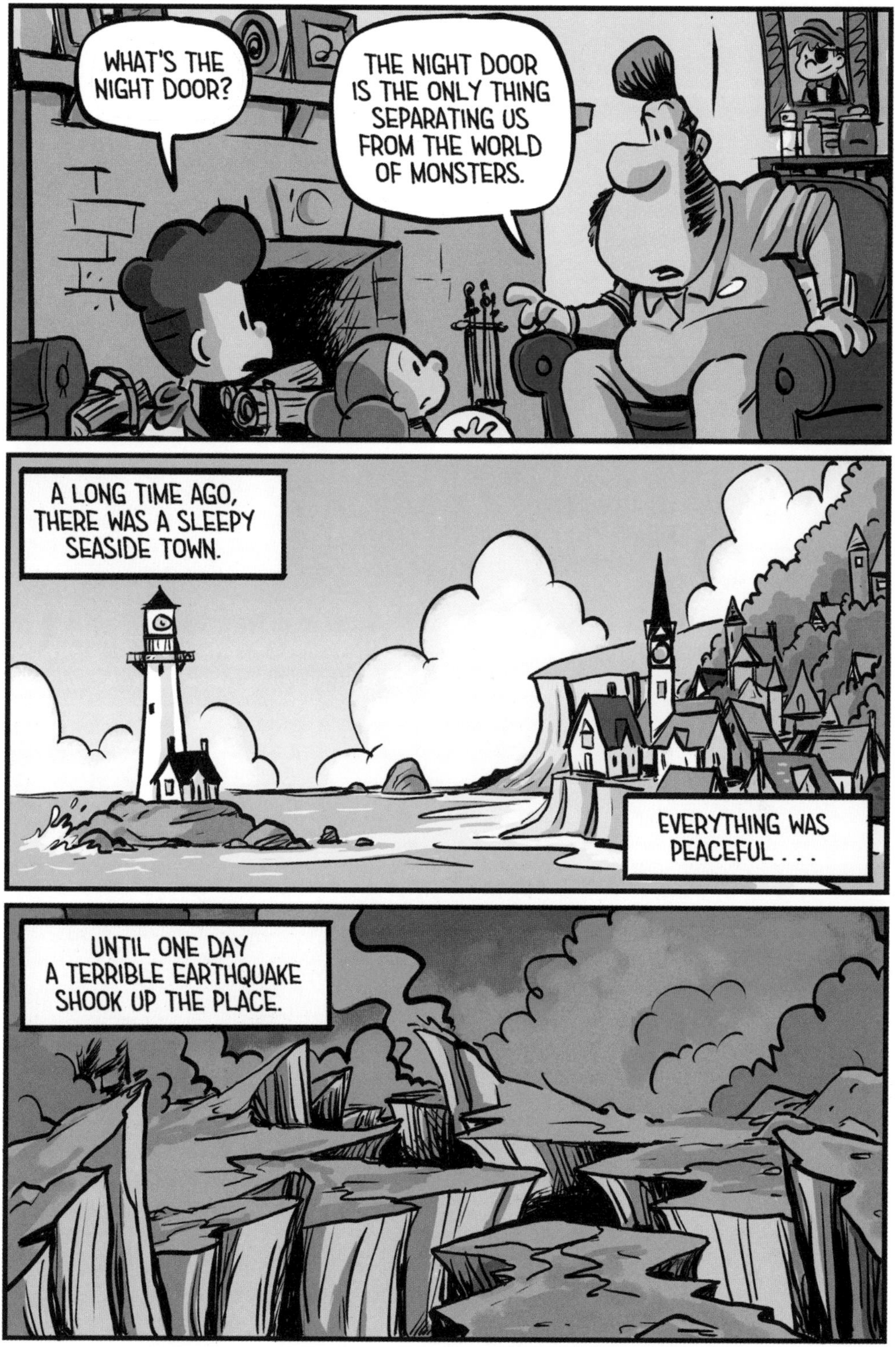

WHAT'S THE NIGHT DOOR?
THE NIGHT DOOR IS THE ONLY THING SEPARATING US FROM THE WORLD OF MONSTERS.
A LONG TIME AGO, THERE WAS A SLEEPY SEASIDE TOWN.
EVERYTHING WAS PEACEFUL . . .
UNTIL ONE DAY A TERRIBLE EARTHQUAKE SHOOK UP THE PLACE.

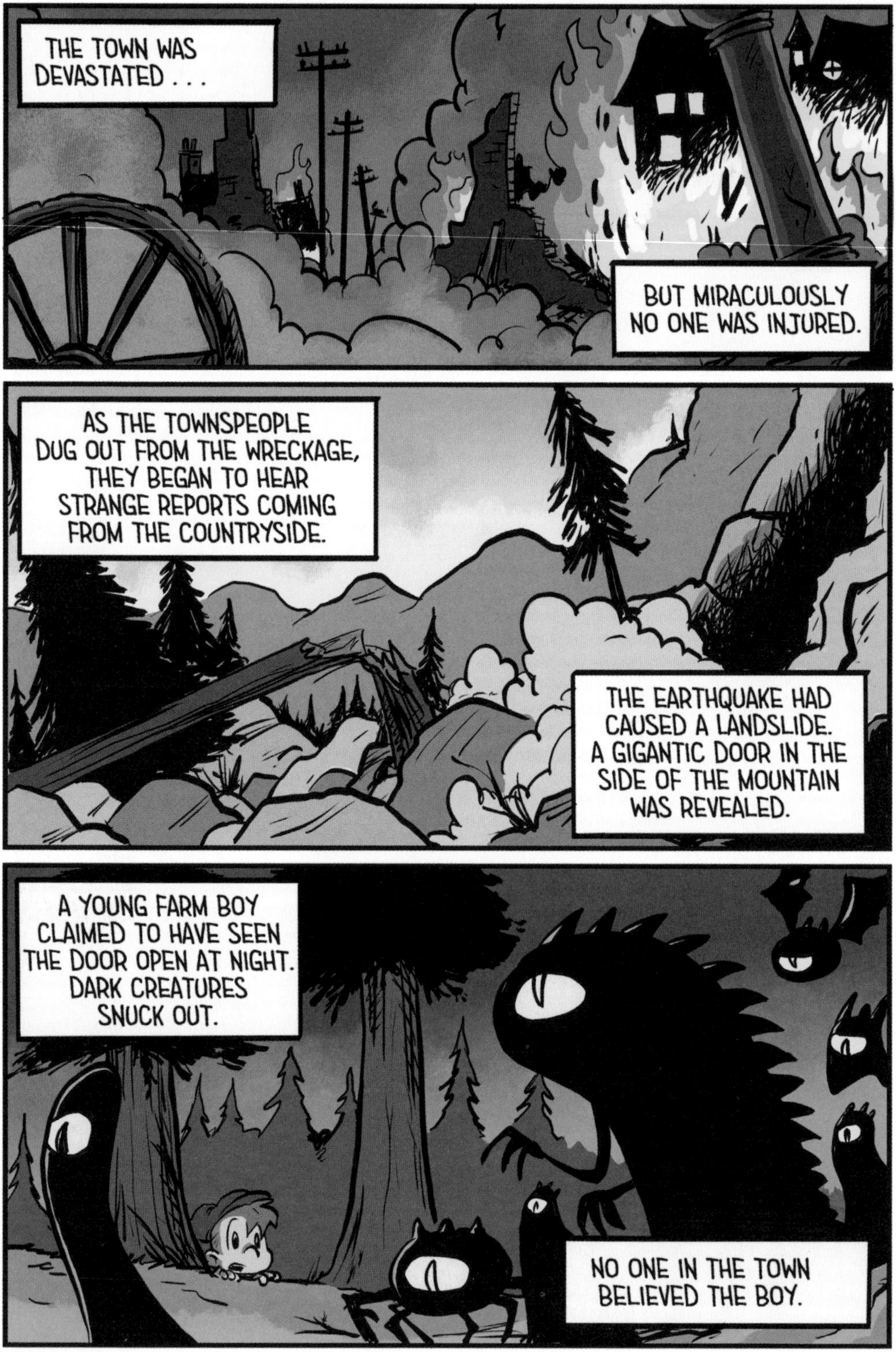
THE TOWN WAS DEVASTATED . . .
BUT MIRACULOUSLY NO ONE WAS INJURED.
AS THE TOWNSPEOPLE DUG OUT FROM THE WRECKAGE, THEY BEGAN TO HEAR STRANGE REPORTS COMING FROM THE COUNTRYSIDE.
THE EARTHQUAKE HAD CAUSED A LANDSLIDE. A GIGANTIC DOOR IN THE SIDE OF THE MOUNTAIN WAS REVEALED.
A YOUNG FARM BOY CLAIMED TO HAVE SEEN THE DOOR OPEN AT NIGHT. DARK CREATURES SNUCK OUT.
NO ONE IN THE TOWN BELIEVED THE BOY.

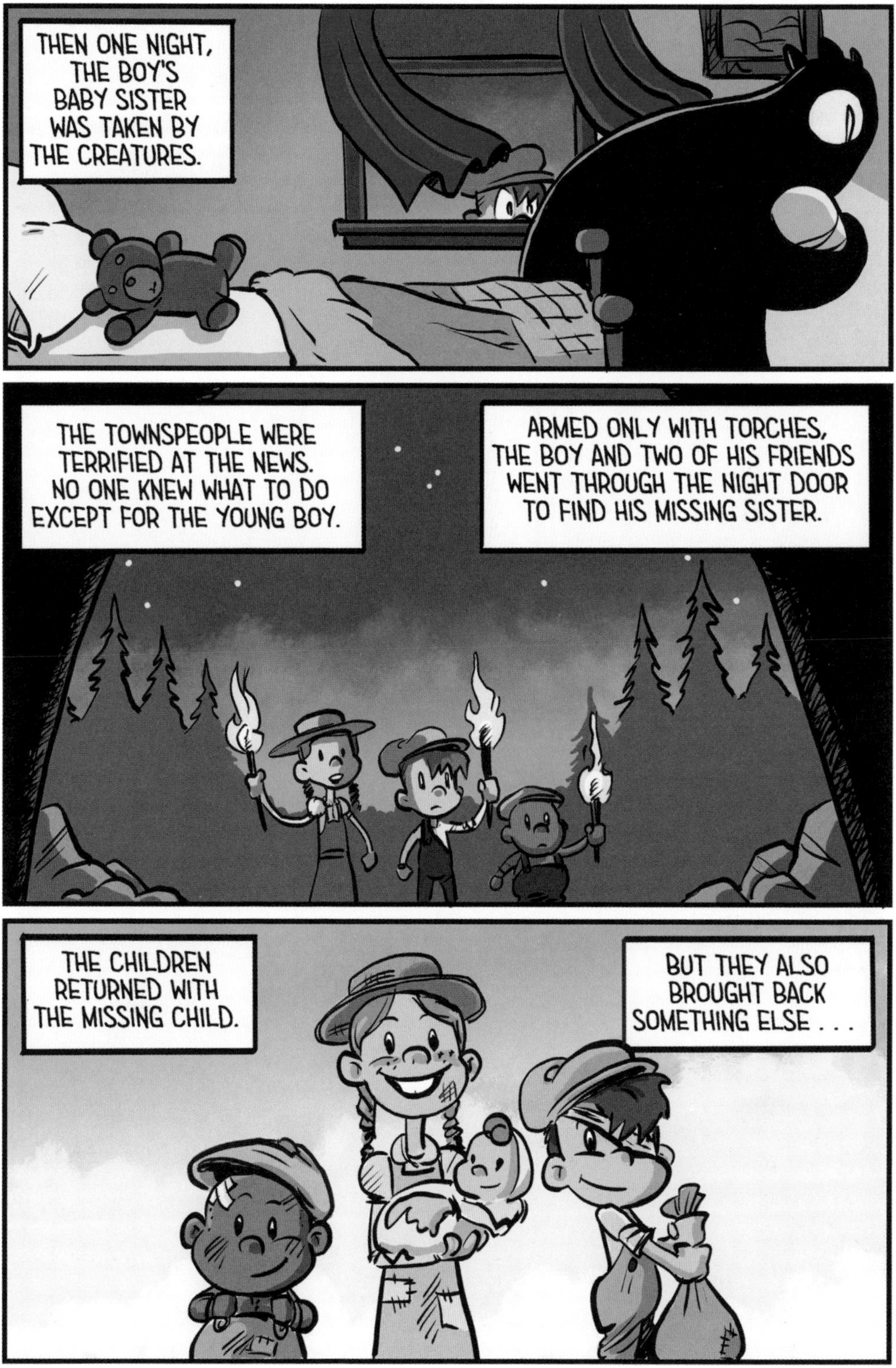
THEN ONE NIGHT, THE BOY'S BABY SISTER WAS TAKEN BY THE CREATURES.
THE TOWNSPEOPLE WERE TERRIFIED AT THE NEWS. NO ONE KNEW WHAT TO DO EXCEPT FOR THE YOUNG BOY.
ARMED ONLY WITH TORCHES, THE BOY AND TWO OF HIS FRIENDS WENT THROUGH THE NIGHT DOOR TO FIND HIS MISSING SISTER.
THE CHILDREN RETURNED WITH THE MISSING CHILD.
BUT THEY ALSO BROUGHT BACK SOMETHING ELSE . . .

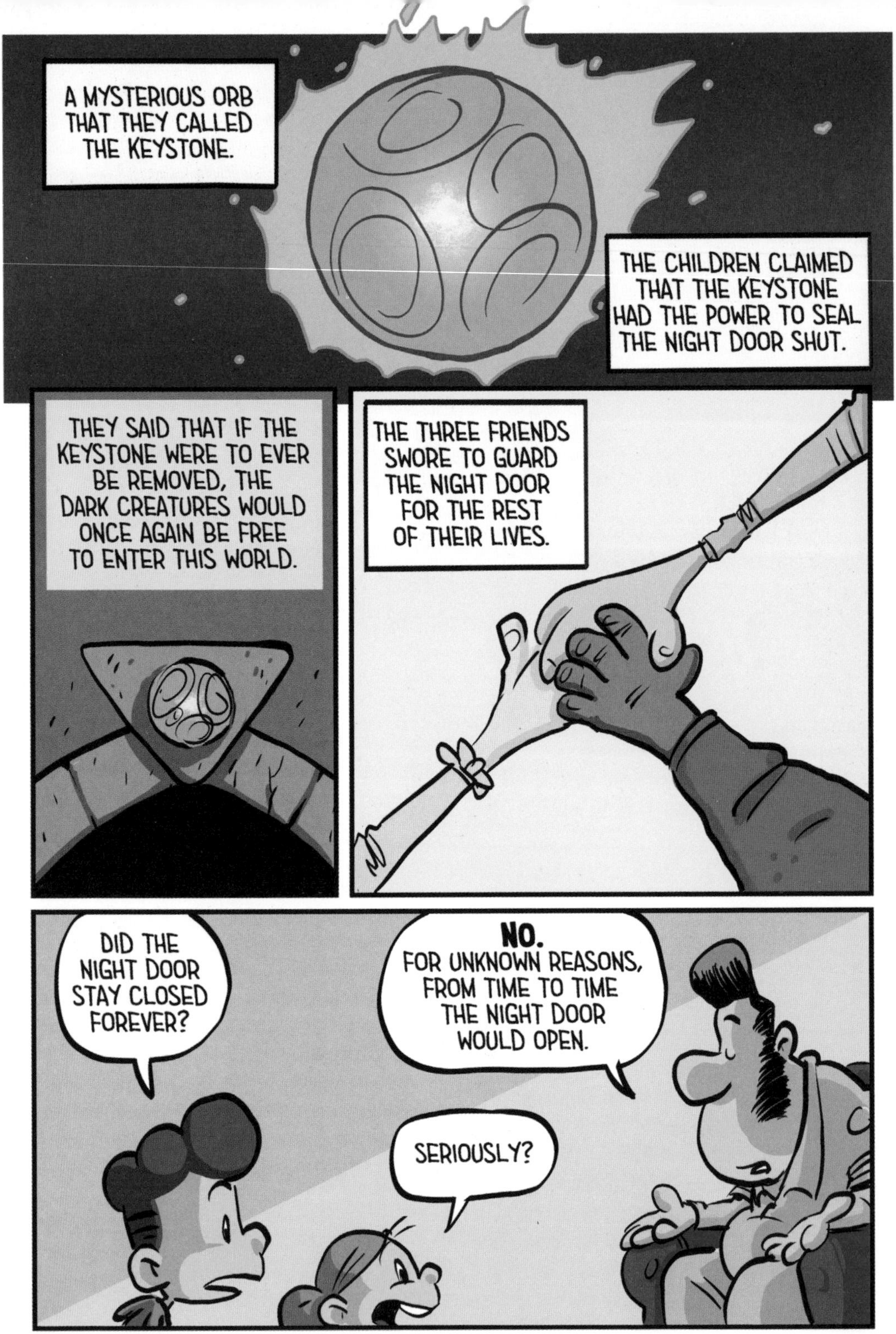
A MYSTERIOUS ORB THAT THEY CALLED THE KEYSTONE.
THE CHILDREN CLAIMED THAT THE KEYSTONE HAD THE POWER TO SEAL THE NIGHT DOOR SHUT.
THEY SAID THAT IF THE KEYSTONE WERE TO EVER BE REMOVED, THE DARK CREATURES WOULD ONCE AGAIN BE FREE TO ENTER THIS WORLD.
THE THREE FRIENDS SWORE TO GUARD THE NIGHT DOOR FOR THE REST OF THEIR LIVES.
DID THE NIGHT DOOR STAY CLOSED FOREVER?
NO. FOR UNKNOWN REASONS, FROM TIME TO TIME THE NIGHT DOOR WOULD OPEN.
SERIOUSLY?

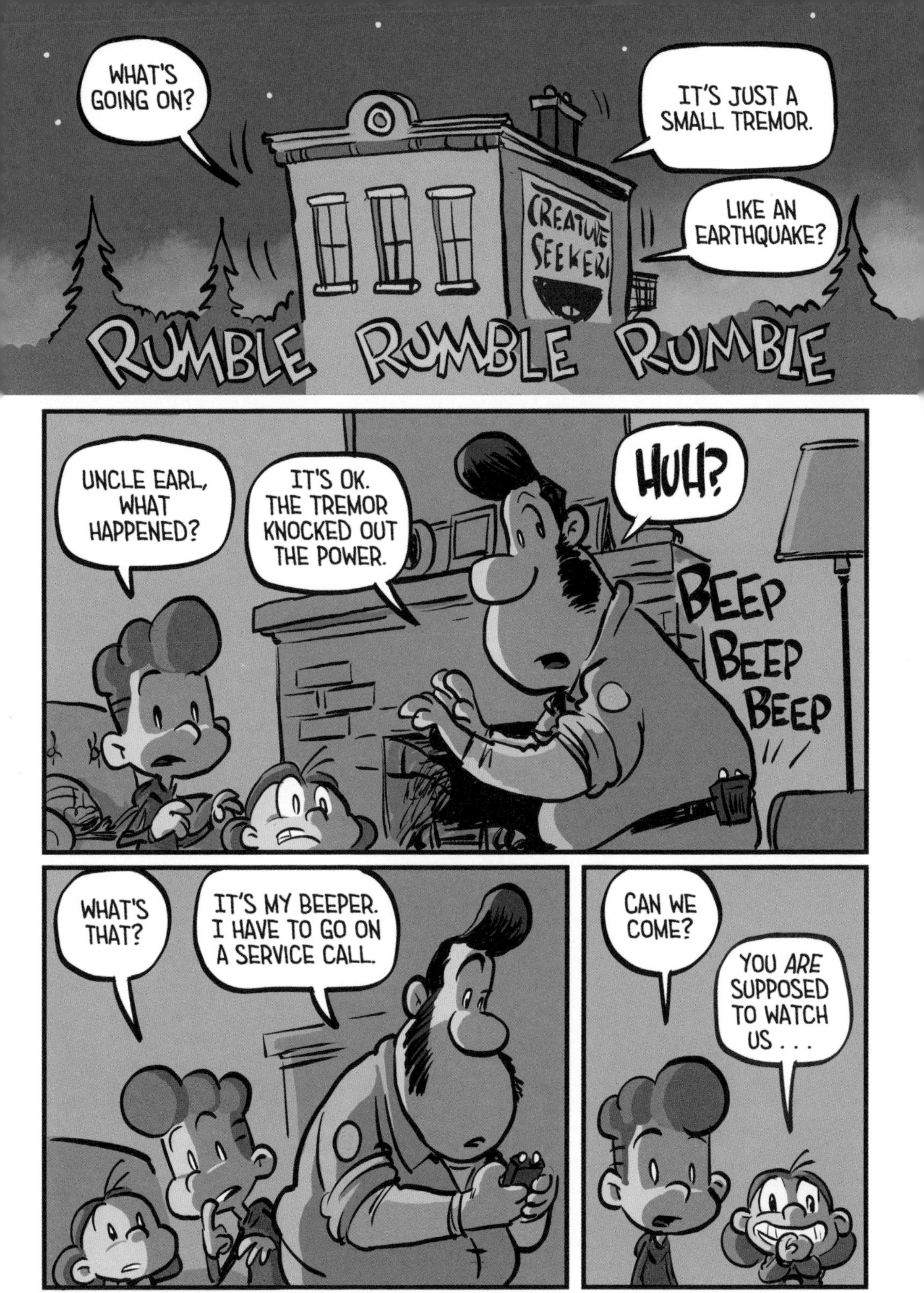
WHAT'S GOING ON?
IT'S JUST A SMALL TREMOR.
LIKE AN EARTHQUAKE?
CREATURE SEEKER
RUMBLE RUMBLE RUMBLE
UNCLE EARL, WHAT HAPPENED?
IT'S OK. THE TREMOR KNOCKED OUT THE POWER.
HUH?
BEEP BEEP BEEP
WHAT'S THAT?
IT'S MY BEEPER. I HAVE TO GO ON A SERVICE CALL.
CAN WE COME?
YOU *ARE* SUPPOSED TO WATCH US . . .

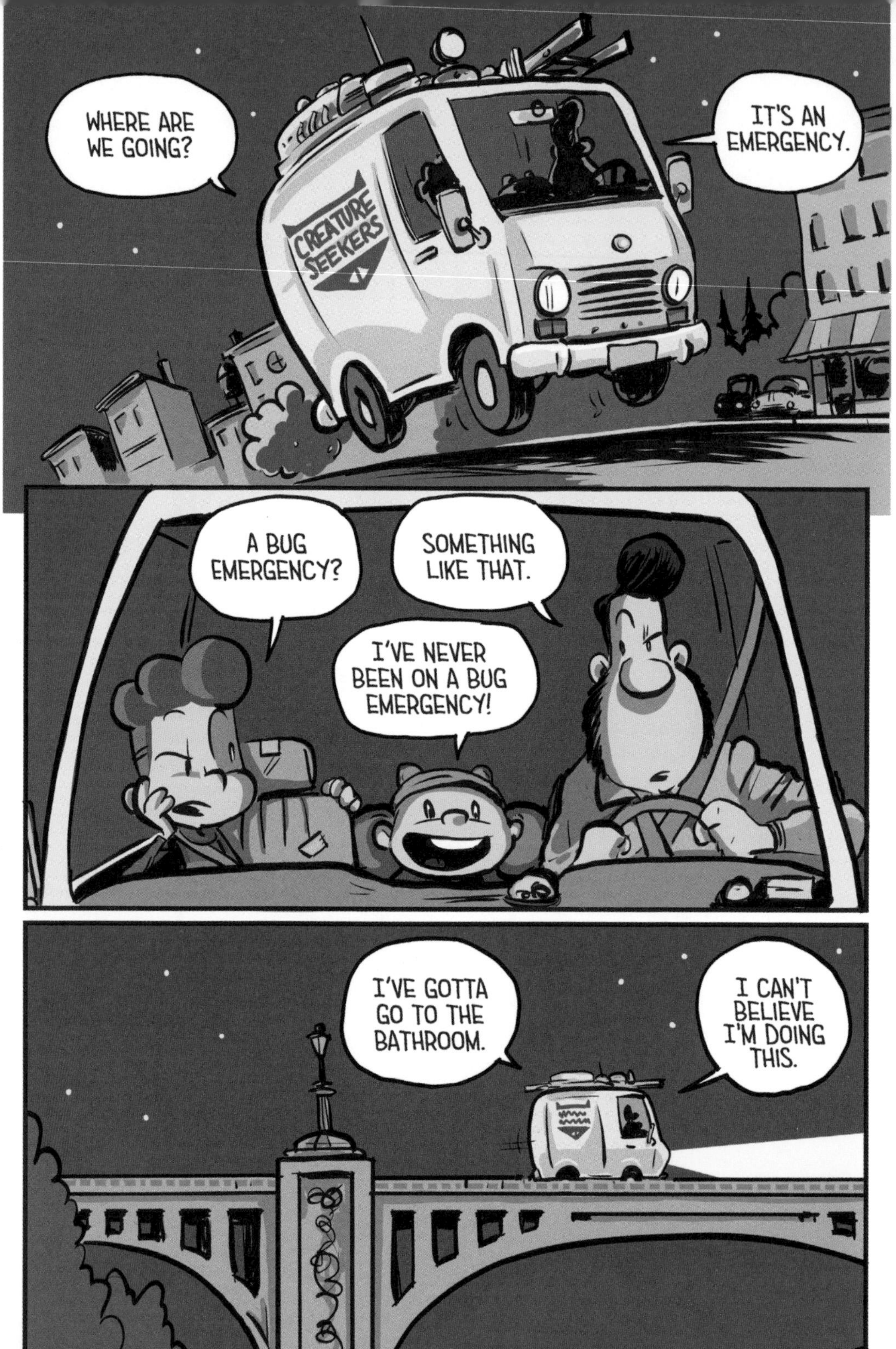
WHERE ARE WE GOING?
IT'S AN EMERGENCY.
CREATURE SEEKERS
A BUG EMERGENCY?
SOMETHING LIKE THAT.
I'VE NEVER BEEN ON A BUG EMERGENCY!
I'VE GOTTA GO TO THE BATHROOM.
I CAN'T BELIEVE I'M DOING THIS.

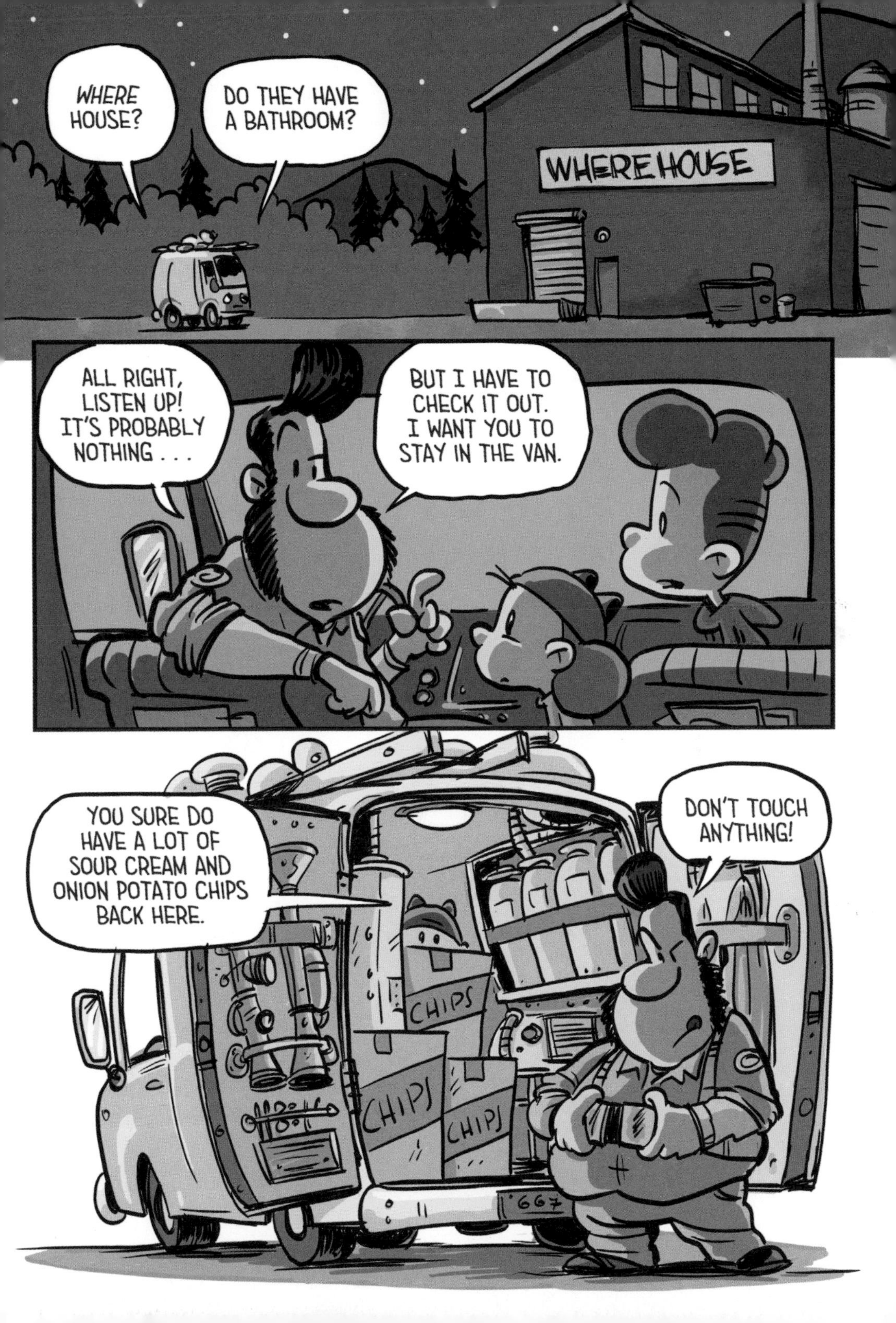
WHERE HOUSE?
DO THEY HAVE A BATHROOM?
WHEREHOUSE
ALL RIGHT, LISTEN UP! IT'S PROBABLY NOTHING . . .
BUT I HAVE TO CHECK IT OUT. I WANT YOU TO STAY IN THE VAN.
YOU SURE DO HAVE A LOT OF SOUR CREAM AND ONION POTATO CHIPS BACK HERE.
DON'T TOUCH ANYTHING!
CHIPS
CHIPS
CHIPS
667

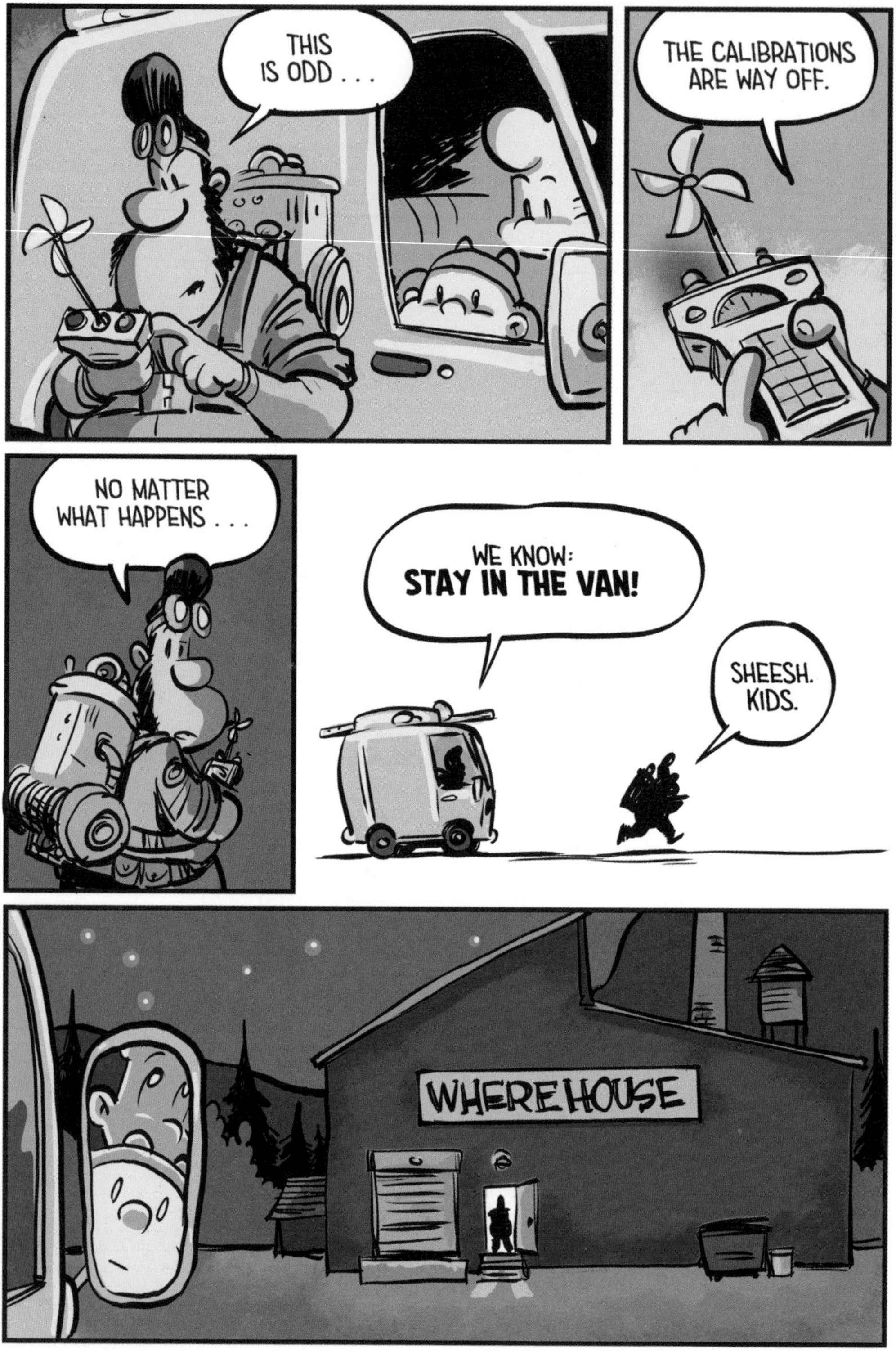
THIS IS ODD . . .
THE CALIBRATIONS ARE WAY OFF.
NO MATTER WHAT HAPPENS . . .
WE KNOW: **STAY IN THE VAN!**
SHEESH. KIDS.
WHEREHOUSE

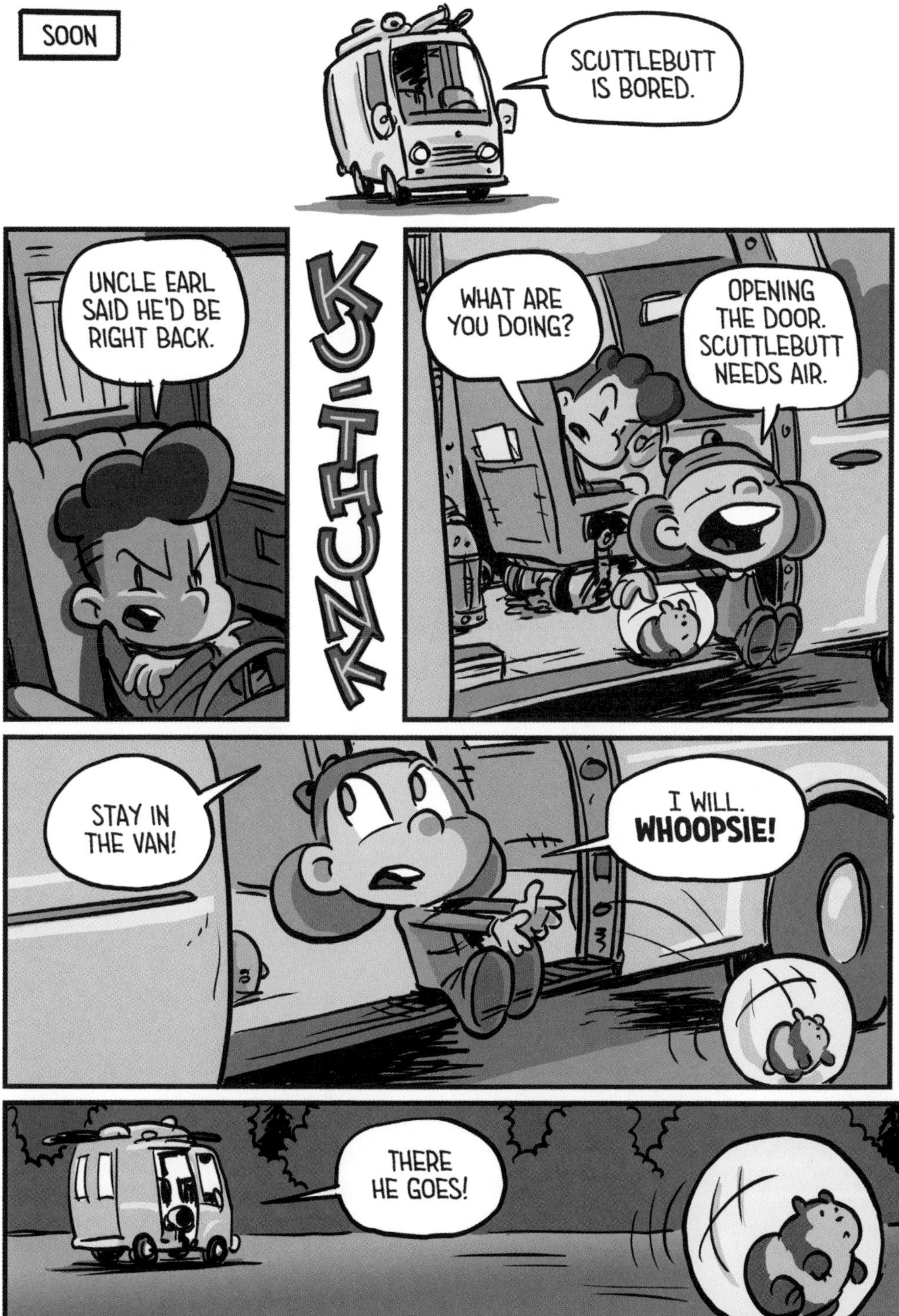
SOON
SCUTTLEBUTT IS BORED.
UNCLE EARL SAID HE'D BE RIGHT BACK.
KA-THUNK
WHAT ARE YOU DOING?
OPENING THE DOOR. SCUTTLEBUTT NEEDS AIR.
STAY IN THE VAN!
I WILL. **WHOOPSIE!**
THERE HE GOES!

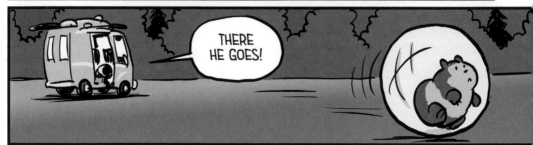

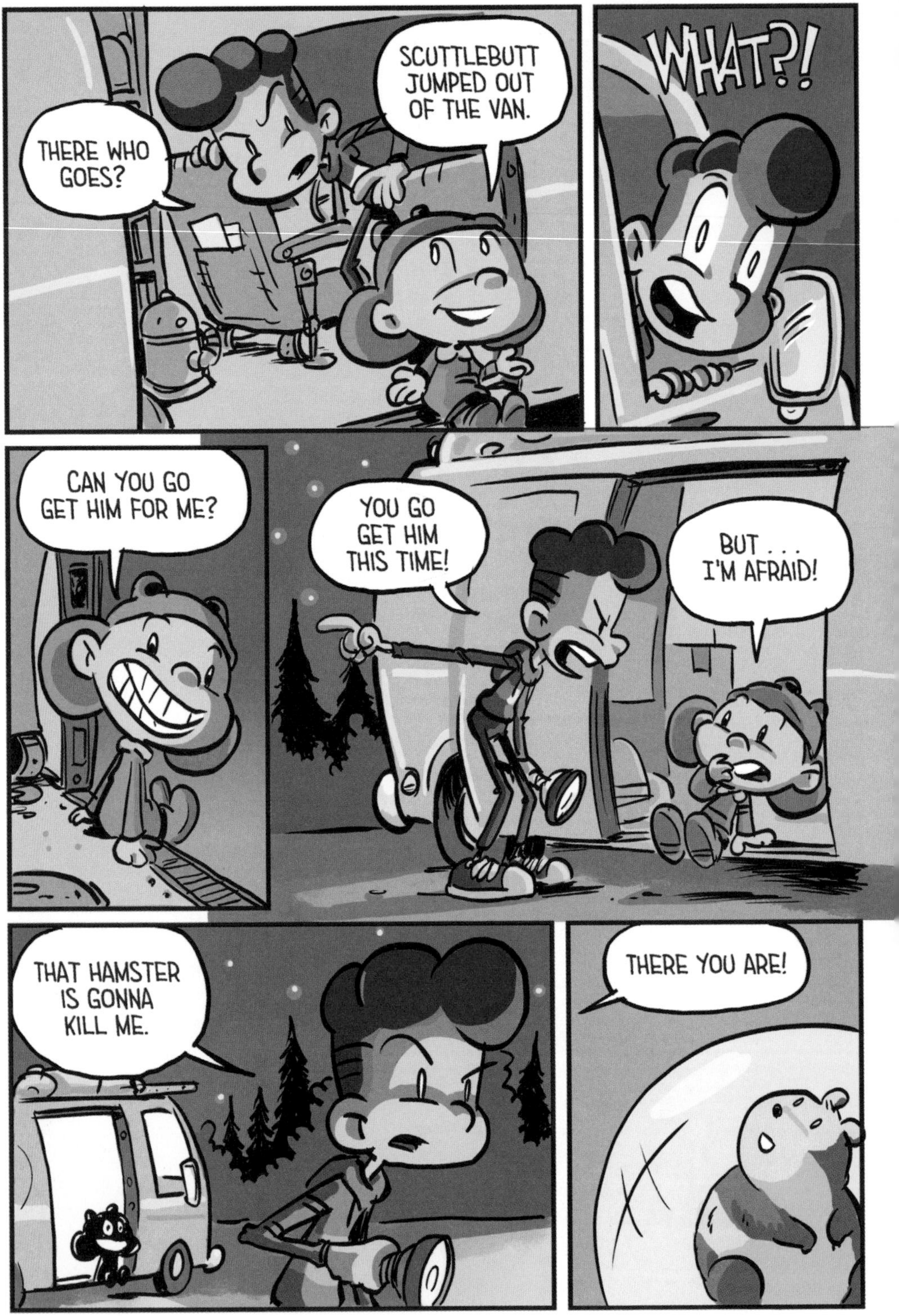
THERE WHO GOES?
SCUTTLEBUTT JUMPED OUT OF THE VAN.
WHAT?!
CAN YOU GO GET HIM FOR ME?
YOU GO GET HIM THIS TIME!
BUT . . . I'M AFRAID!
THAT HAMSTER IS GONNA KILL ME.
THERE YOU ARE!

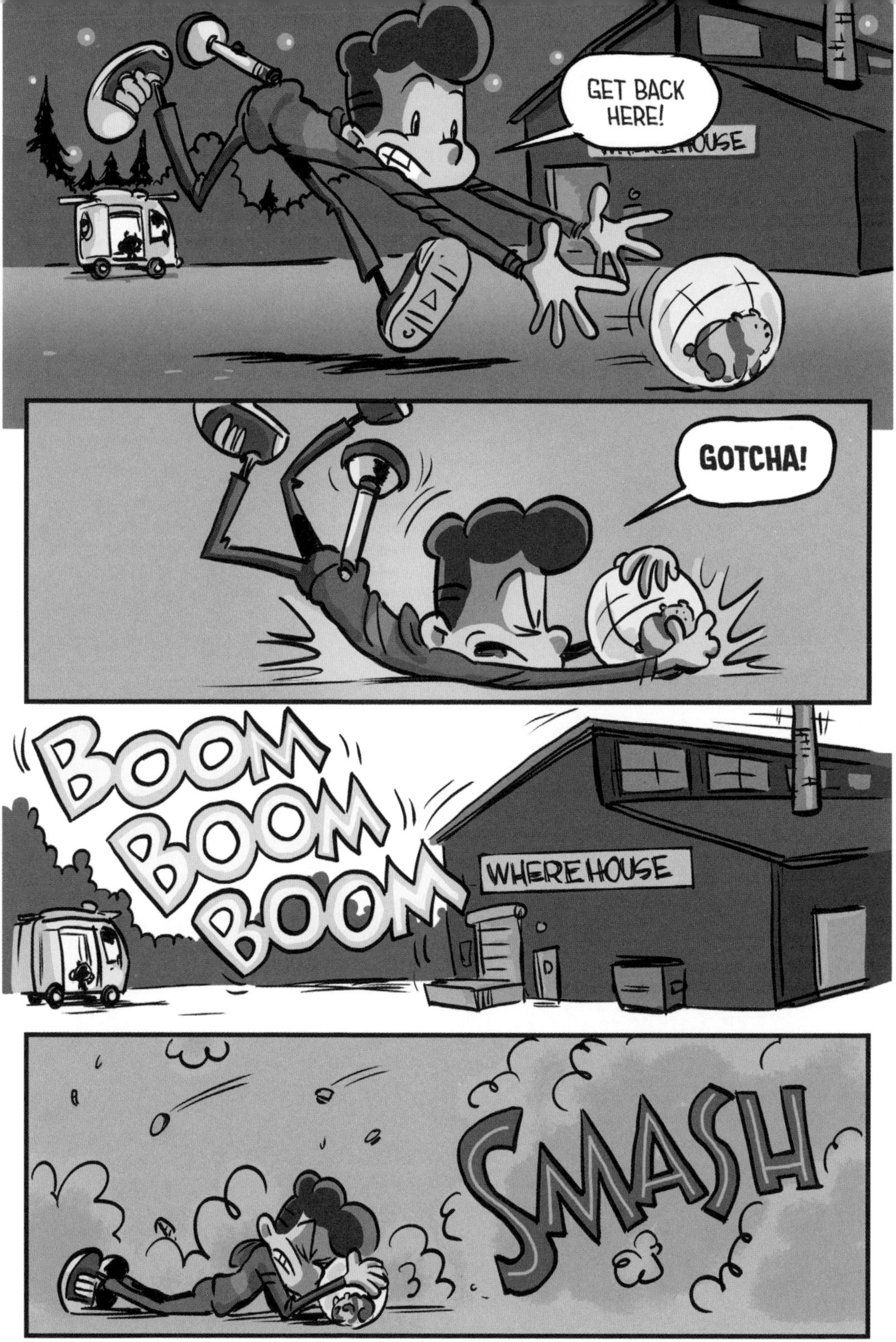
GET BACK HERE!
WHEREHOUSE
GOTCHA!
BOOM BOOM BOOM
WHEREHOUSE
SMASH

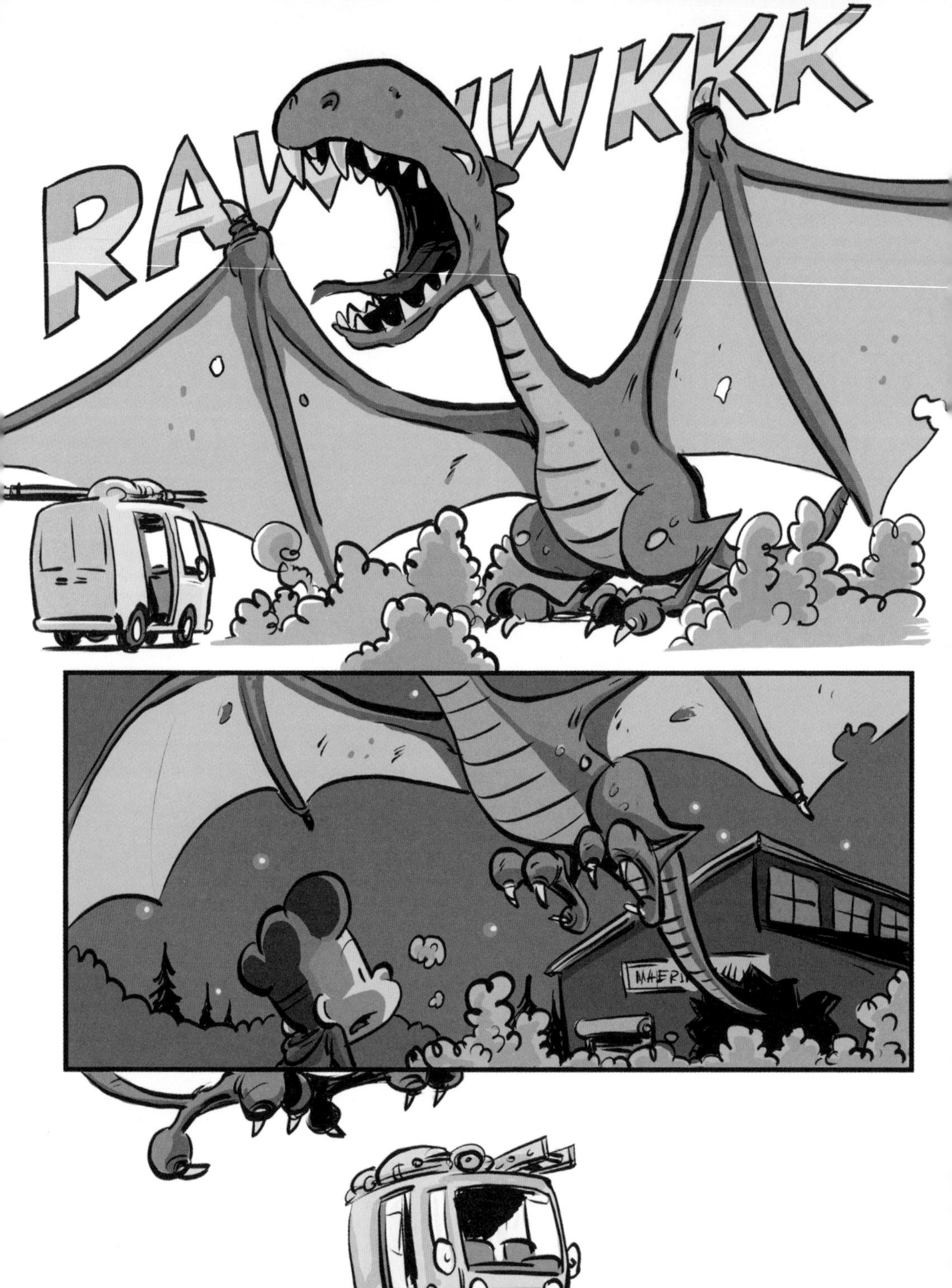
RA
WKKK

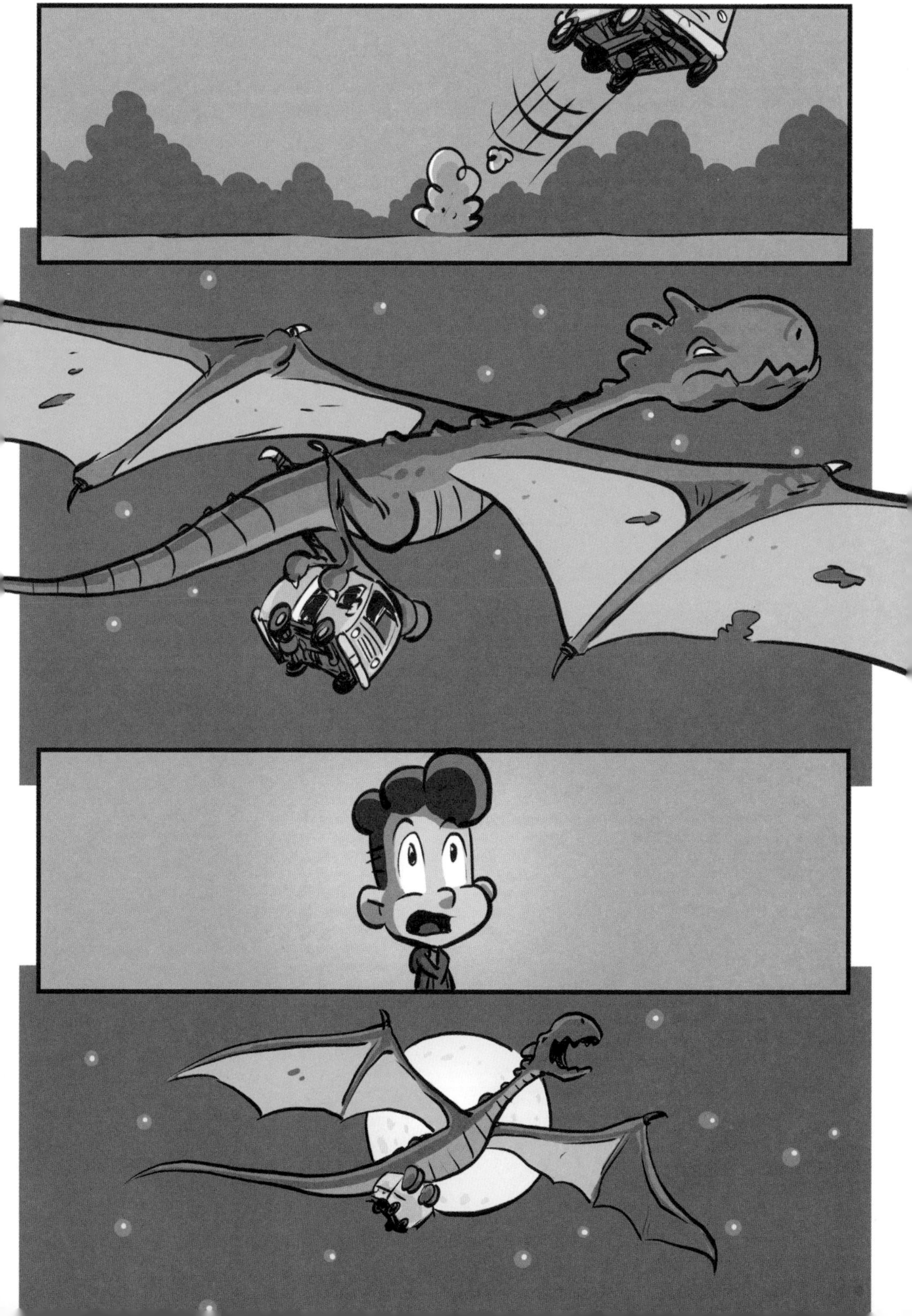

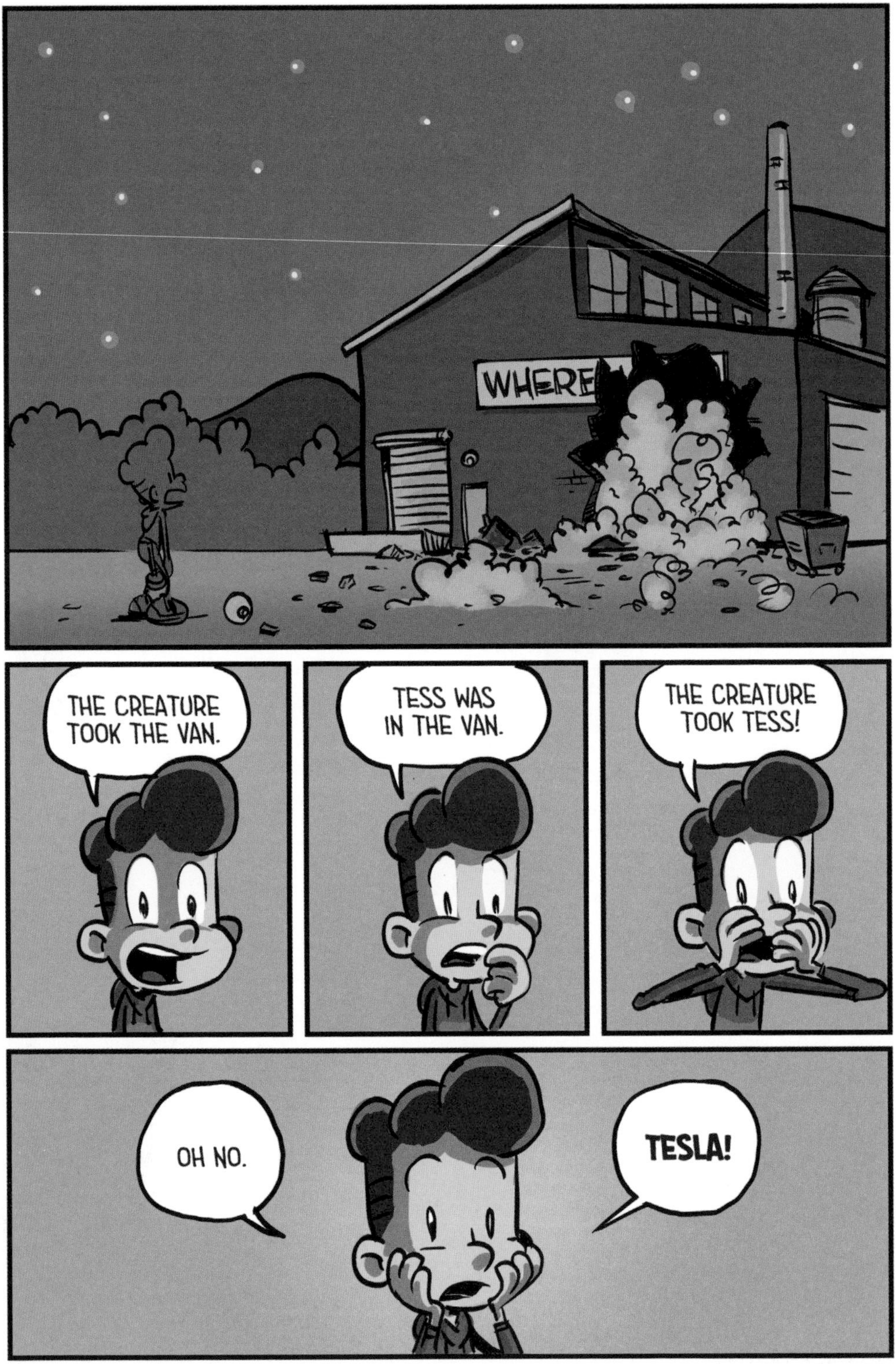
WHERE
THE CREATURE TOOK THE VAN.
TESS WAS IN THE VAN.
THE CREATURE TOOK TESS!
OH NO.
TESLA!

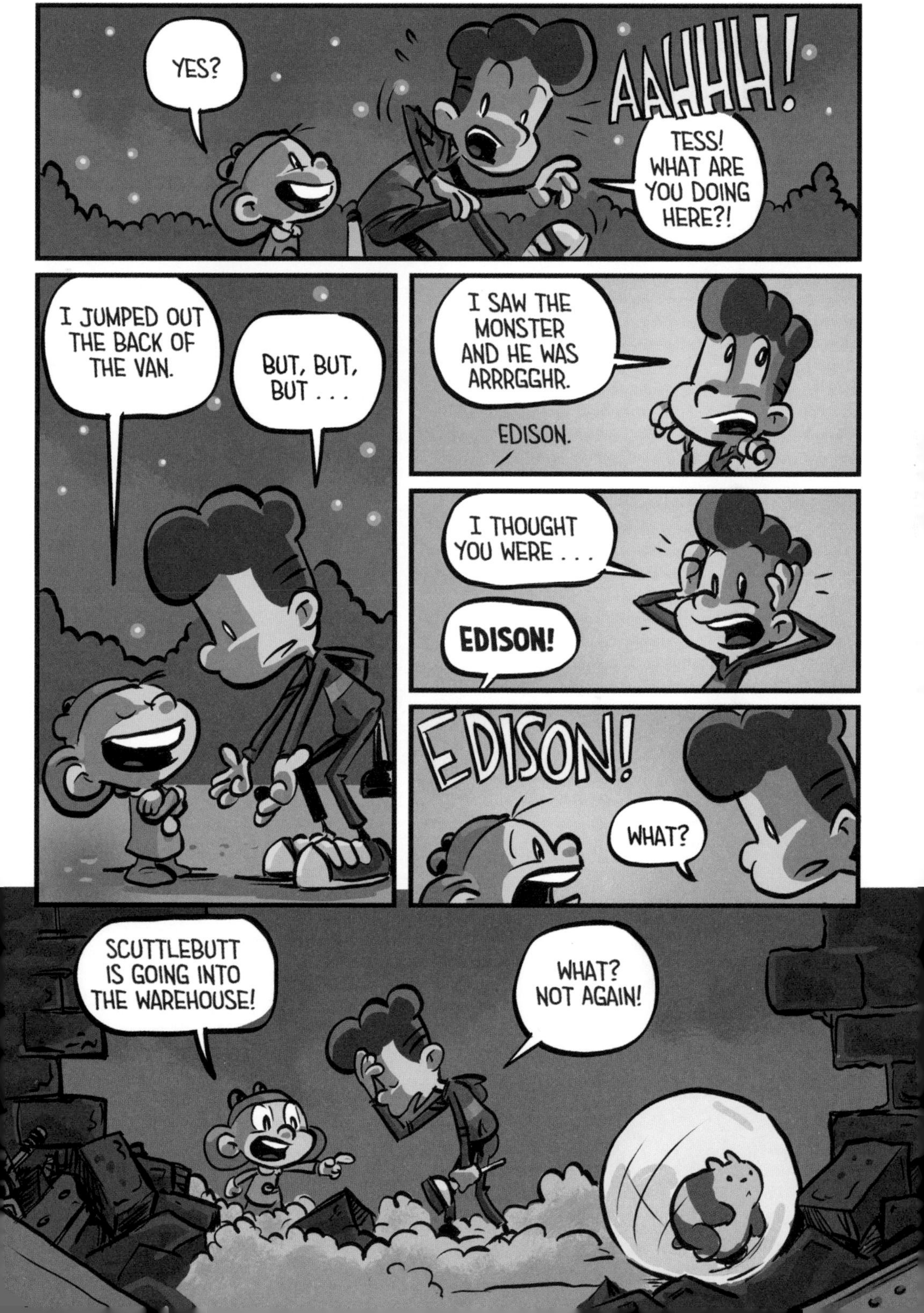
YES?
AAHHH!
TESS! WHAT ARE YOU DOING HERE?!
I JUMPED OUT THE BACK OF THE VAN.
BUT, BUT, BUT . . .
I SAW THE MONSTER AND HE WAS ARRRGGHR.
EDISON.
I THOUGHT YOU WERE . . .
EDISON!
EDISON!
WHAT?
SCUTTLEBUTT IS GOING INTO THE WAREHOUSE!
WHAT? NOT AGAIN!

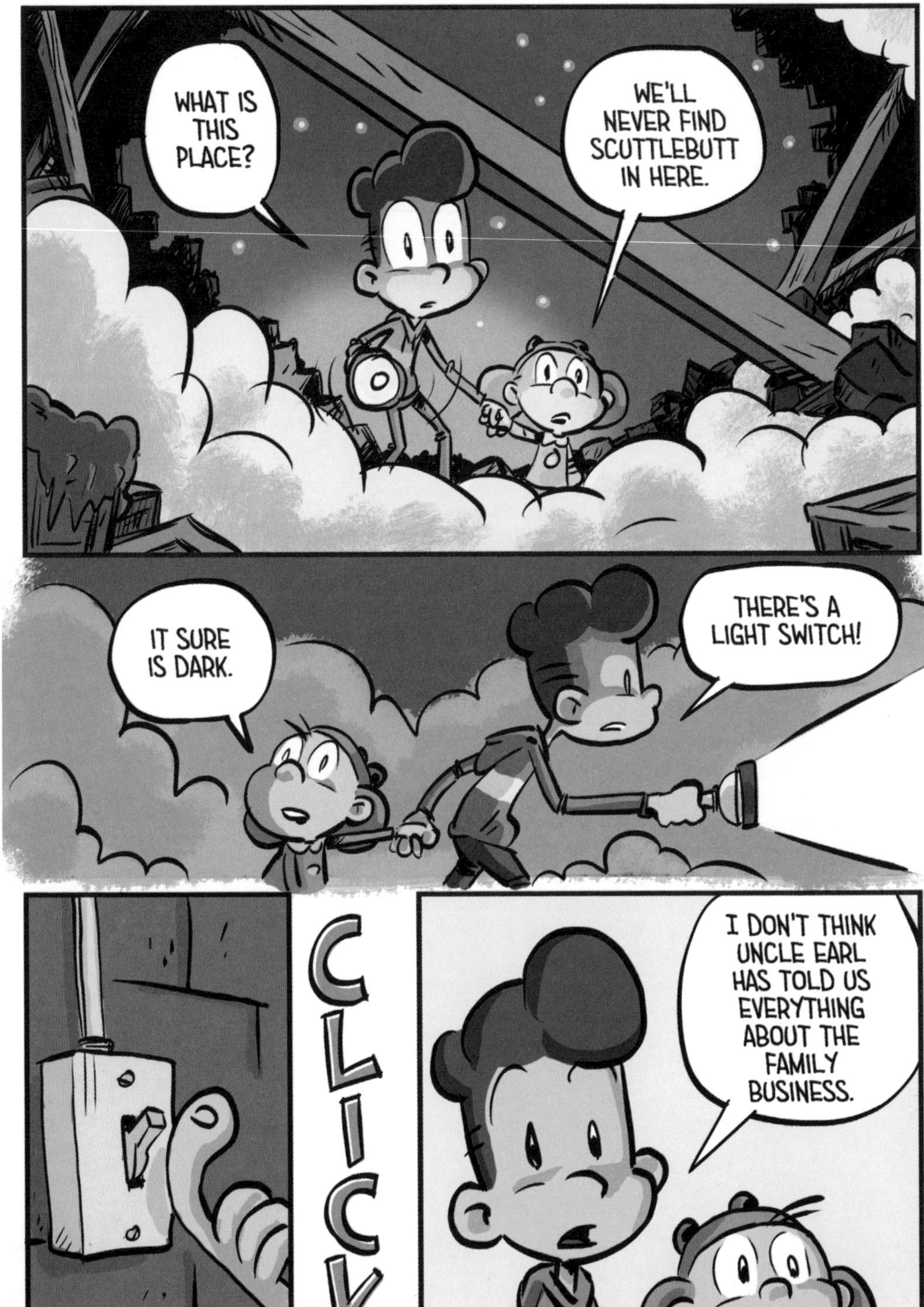
WHAT IS THIS PLACE?
WE'LL NEVER FIND SCUTTLEBUTT IN HERE.
IT SURE IS DARK.
THERE'S A LIGHT SWITCH!
CLICK
I DON'T THINK UNCLE EARL HAS TOLD US EVERYTHING ABOUT THE FAMILY BUSINESS.

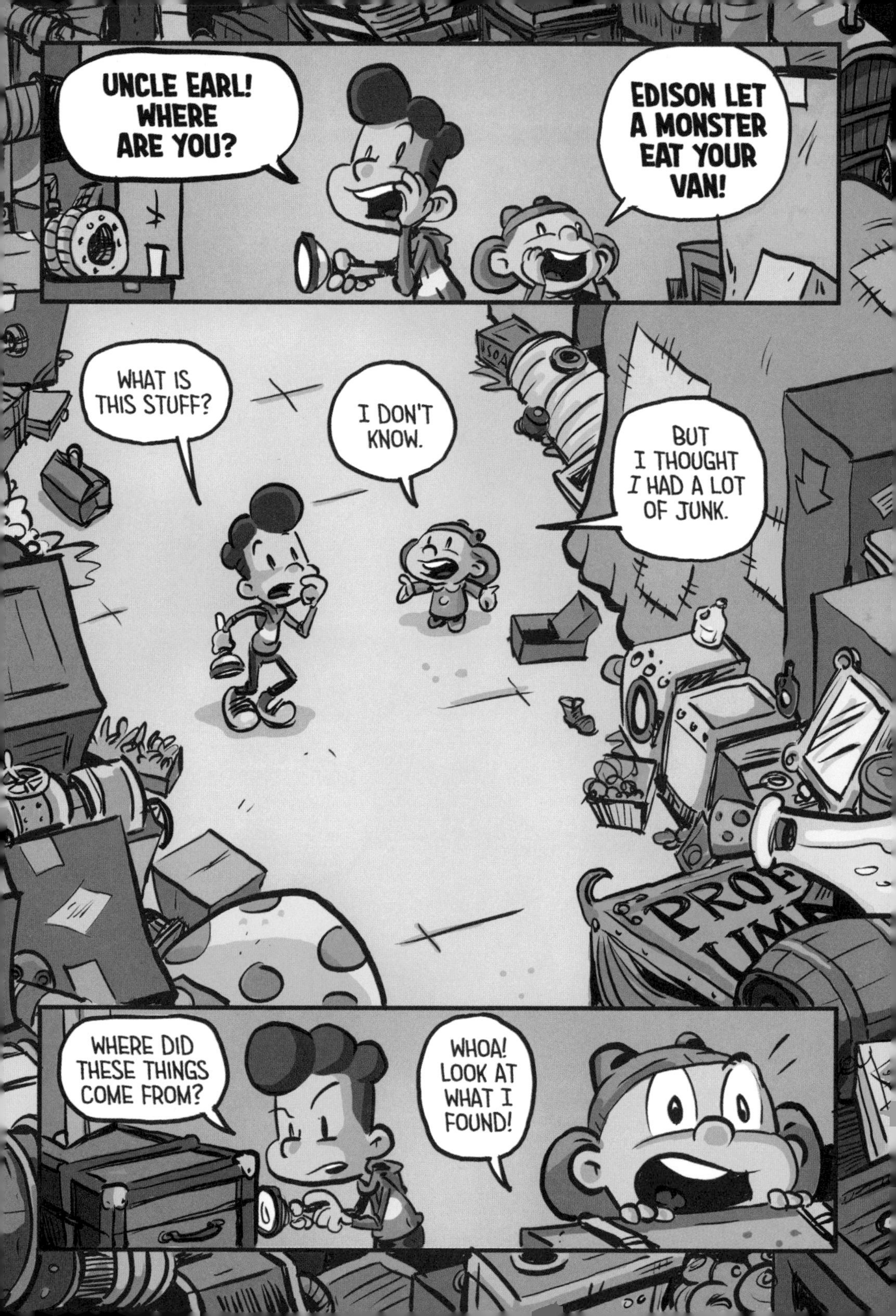

UNCLE EARL! WHERE ARE YOU?
EDISON LET A MONSTER EAT YOUR VAN!
WHAT IS THIS STUFF?
I DON'T KNOW.
BUT I THOUGHT *I* HAD A LOT OF JUNK.
PROF
WHERE DID THESE THINGS COME FROM?
WHOA! LOOK AT WHAT I FOUND!

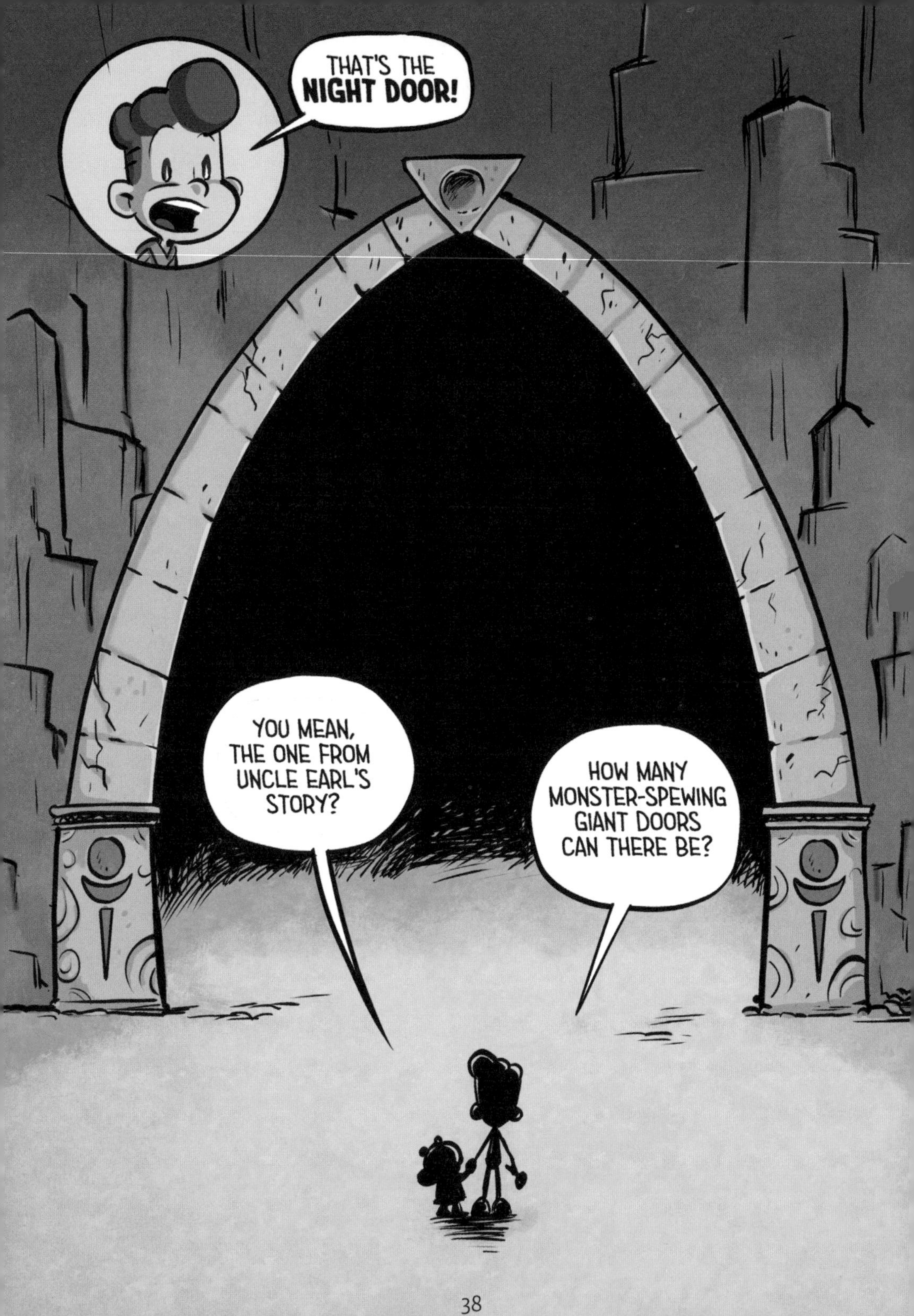
THAT'S THE **NIGHT DOOR!**
YOU MEAN, THE ONE FROM UNCLE EARL'S STORY?
HOW MANY MONSTER-SPEWING GIANT DOORS CAN THERE BE?

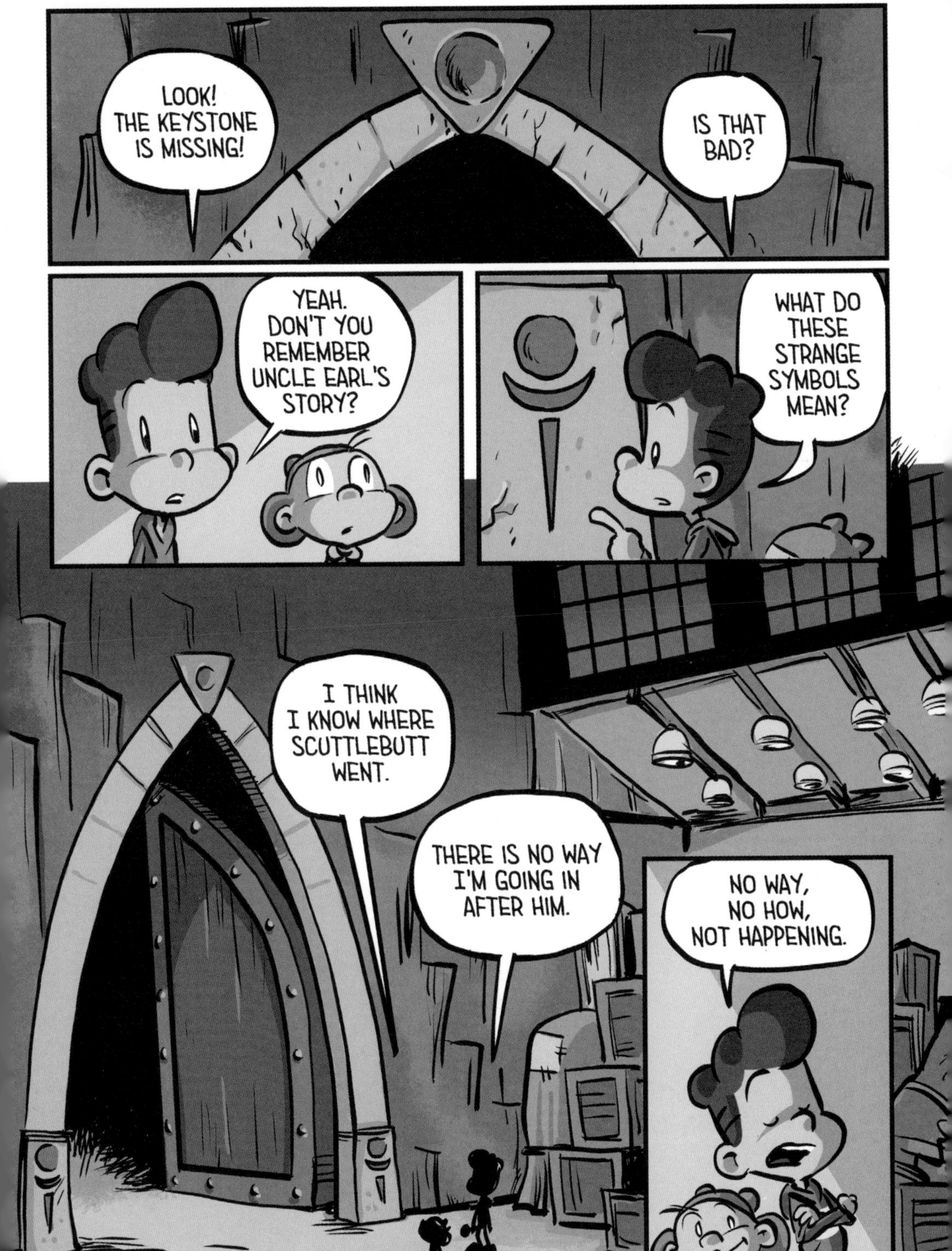
LOOK!
THE KEYSTONE
IS MISSING!
IS THAT
BAD?
YEAH.
DON'T YOU
REMEMBER
UNCLE EARL'S
STORY?
WHAT DO
THESE
STRANGE
SYMBOLS
MEAN?
I THINK
I KNOW WHERE
SCUTTLEBUTT
WENT.
THERE IS NO WAY
I'M GOING IN
AFTER HIM.
NO WAY,
NO HOW,
NOT HAPPENING.

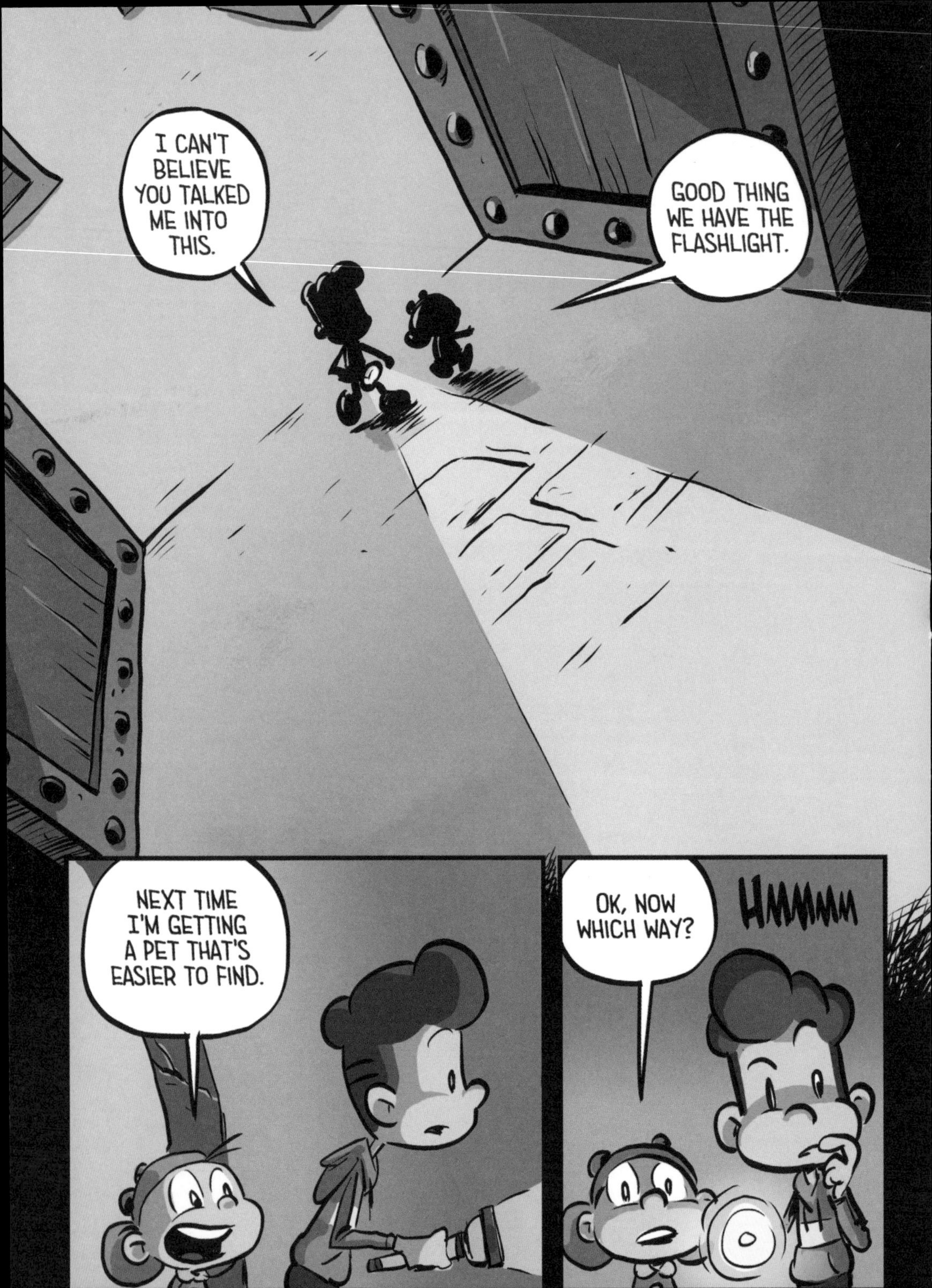
I CAN'T BELIEVE YOU TALKED ME INTO THIS.
GOOD THING WE HAVE THE FLASHLIGHT.
NEXT TIME I'M GETTING A PET THAT'S EASIER TO FIND.
OK, NOW WHICH WAY?
HMMMM

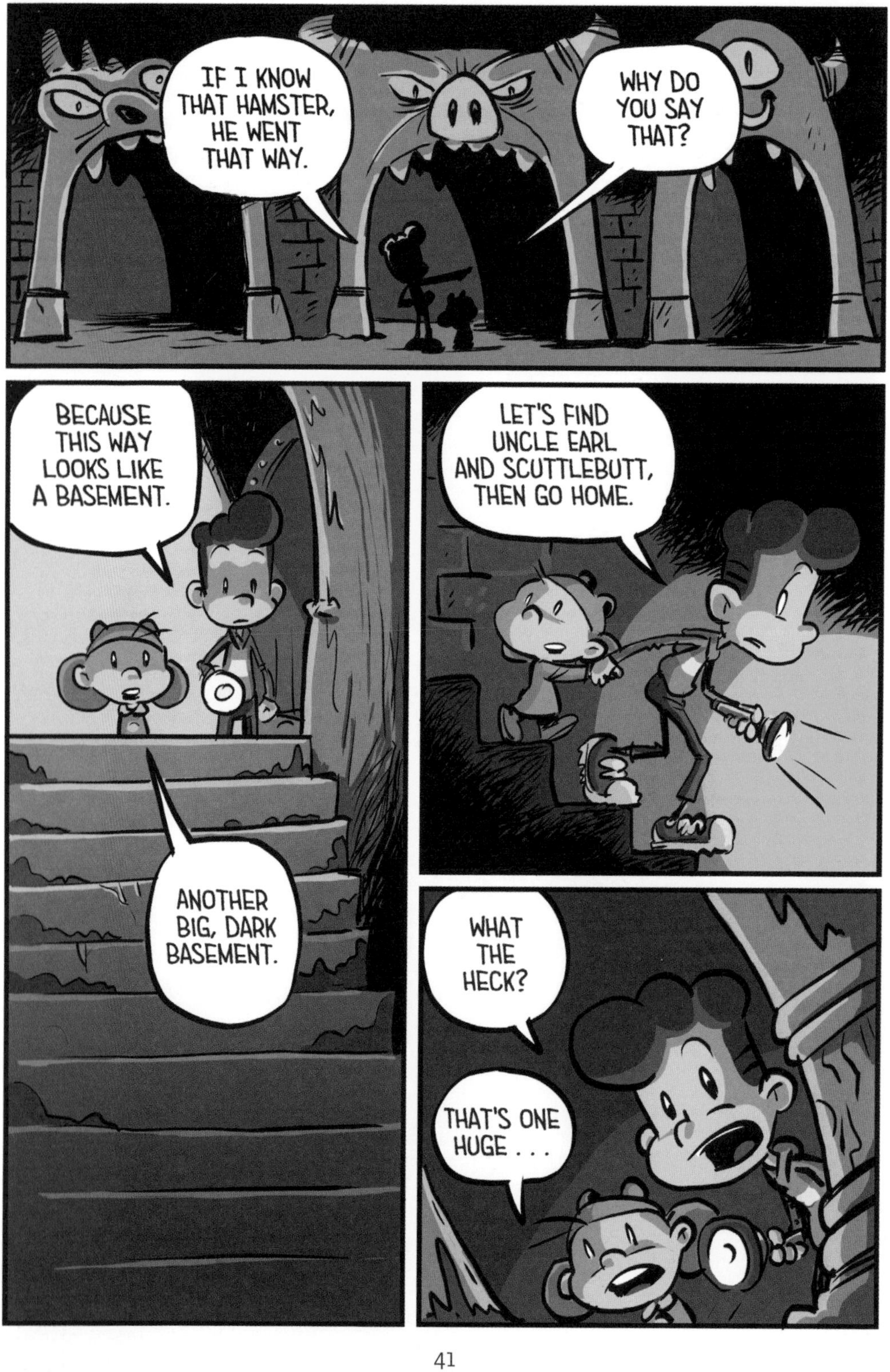
IF I KNOW THAT HAMSTER, HE WENT THAT WAY.
WHY DO YOU SAY THAT?
BECAUSE THIS WAY LOOKS LIKE A BASEMENT.
ANOTHER BIG, DARK BASEMENT.
LET'S FIND UNCLE EARL AND SCUTTLEBUTT, THEN GO HOME.
WHAT THE HECK?
THAT'S ONE HUGE . . .

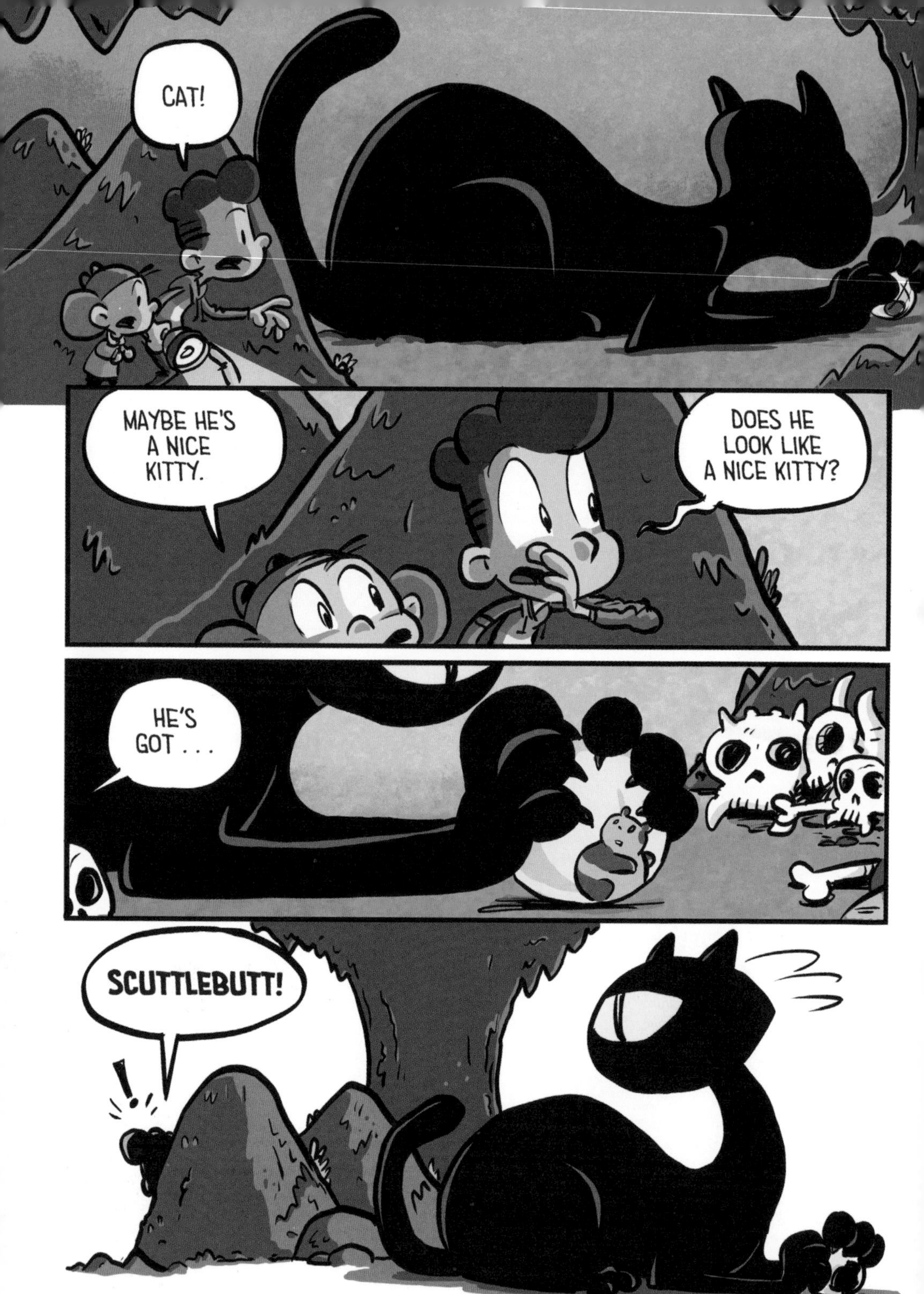
CAT!
MAYBE HE'S A NICE KITTY.
DOES HE LOOK LIKE A NICE KITTY?
HE'S GOT . . .
SCUTTLEBUTT!

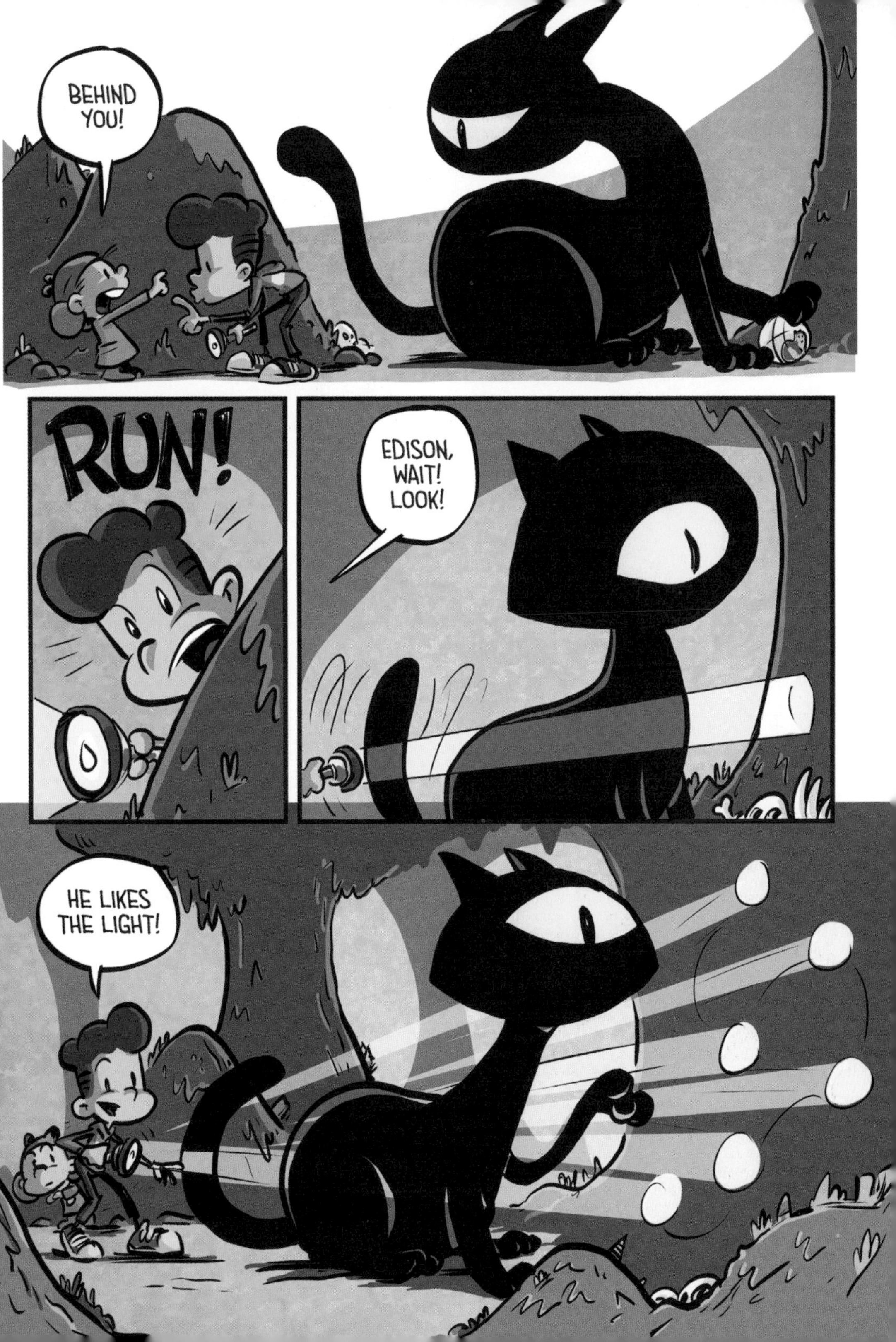
BEHIND YOU!
RUN!
EDISON, WAIT! LOOK!
HE LIKES THE LIGHT!

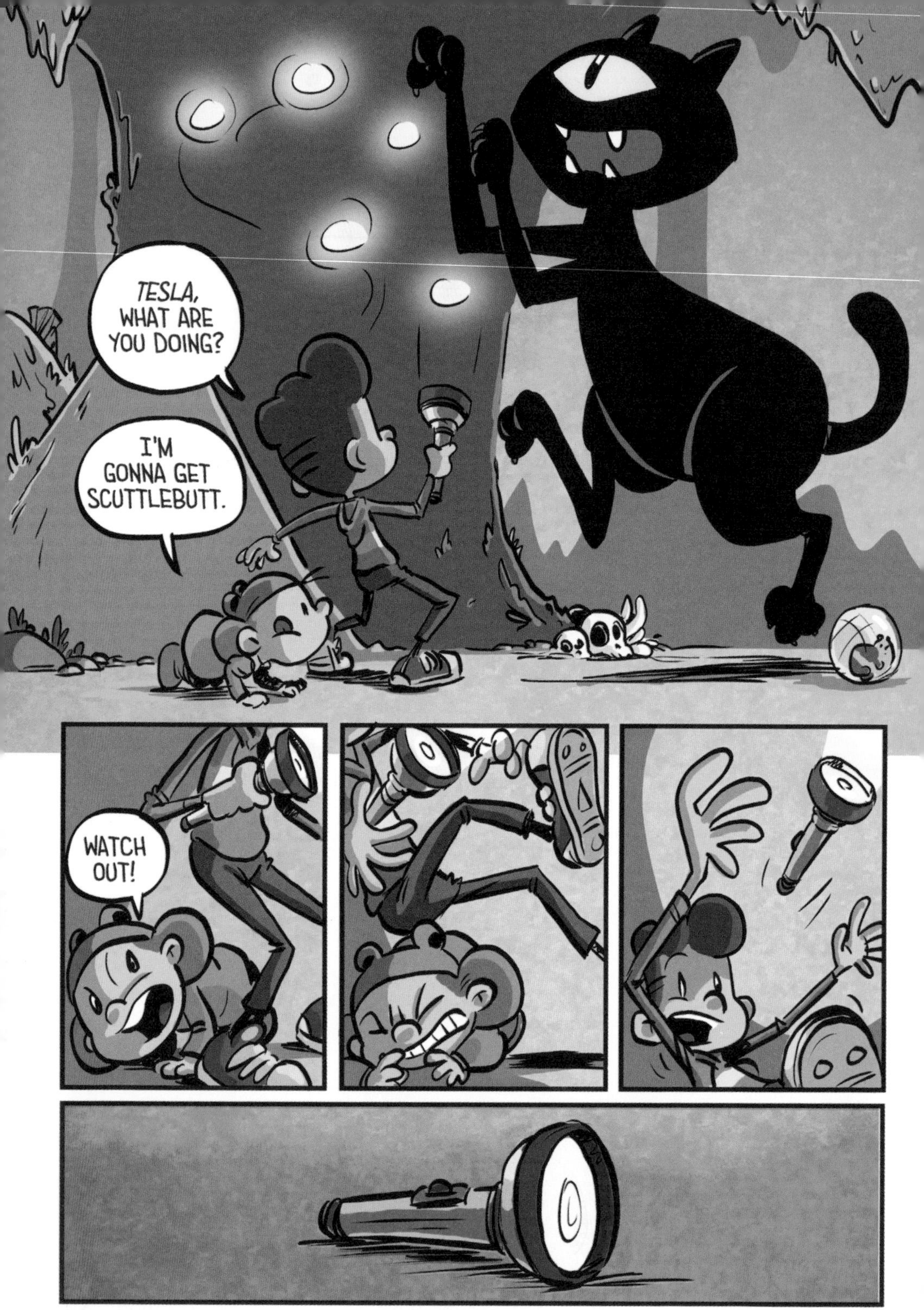
TESLA, WHAT ARE YOU DOING?
I'M GONNA GET SCUTTLEBUTT.
WATCH OUT!

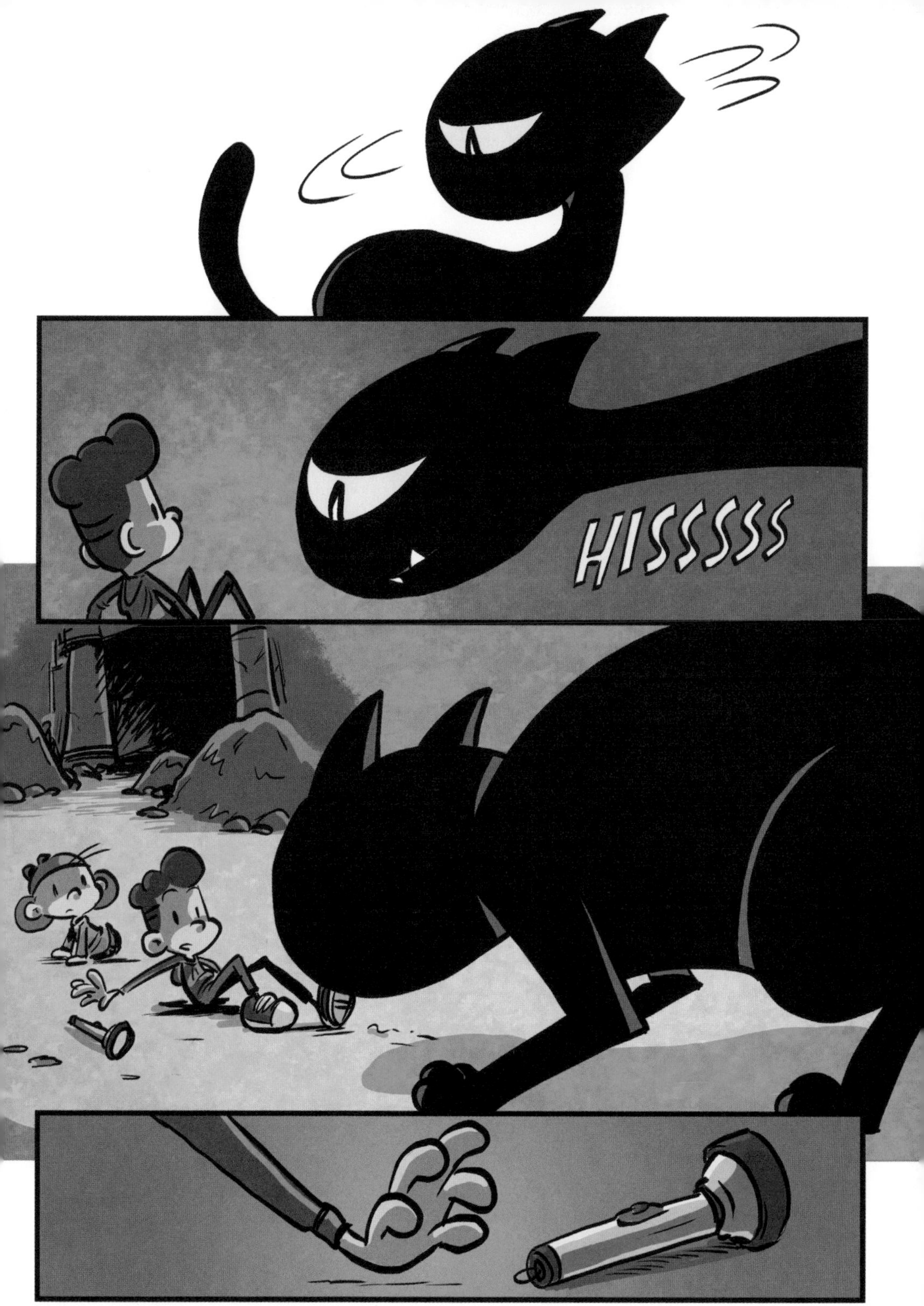
HISSSSS

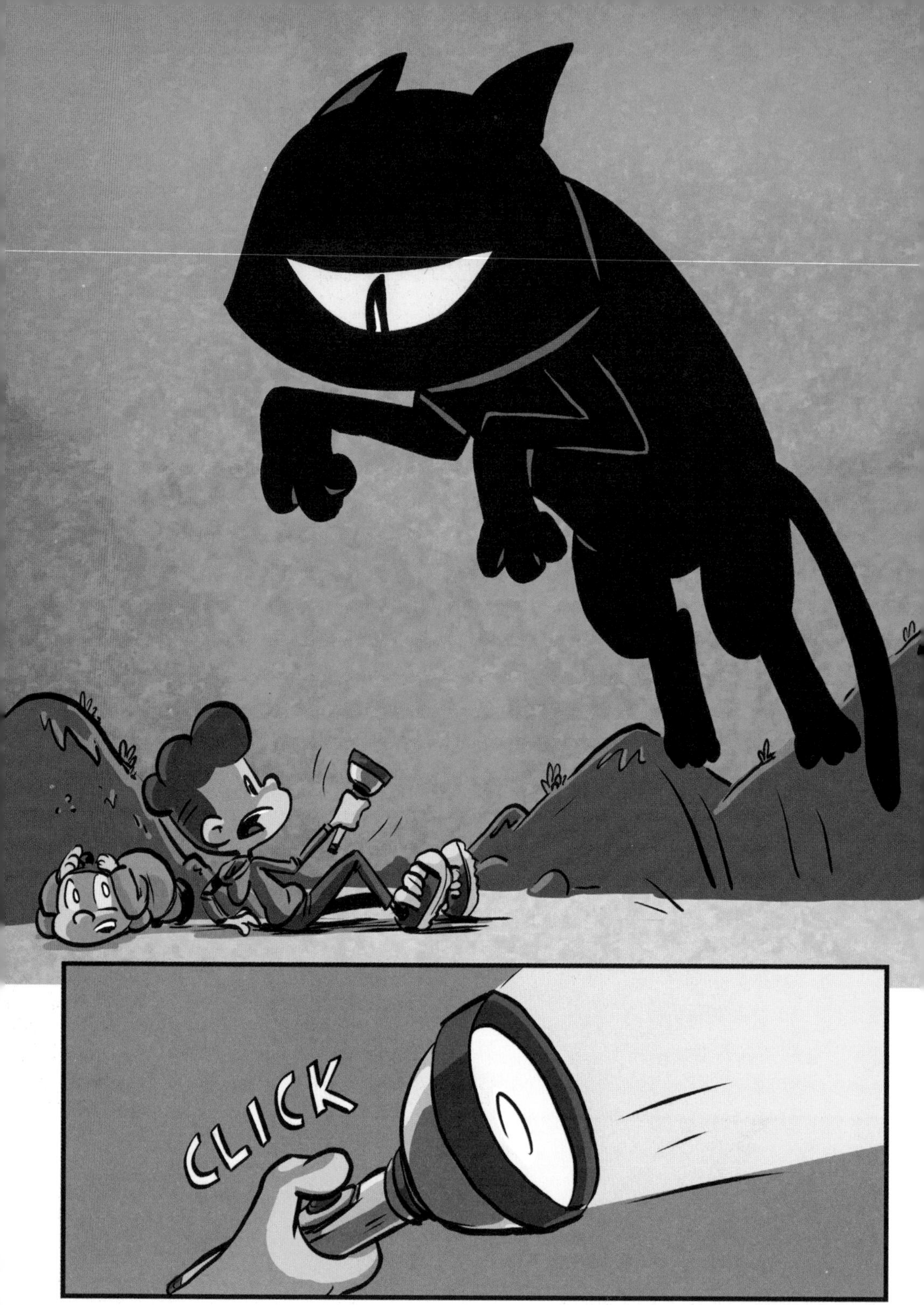
CLICK

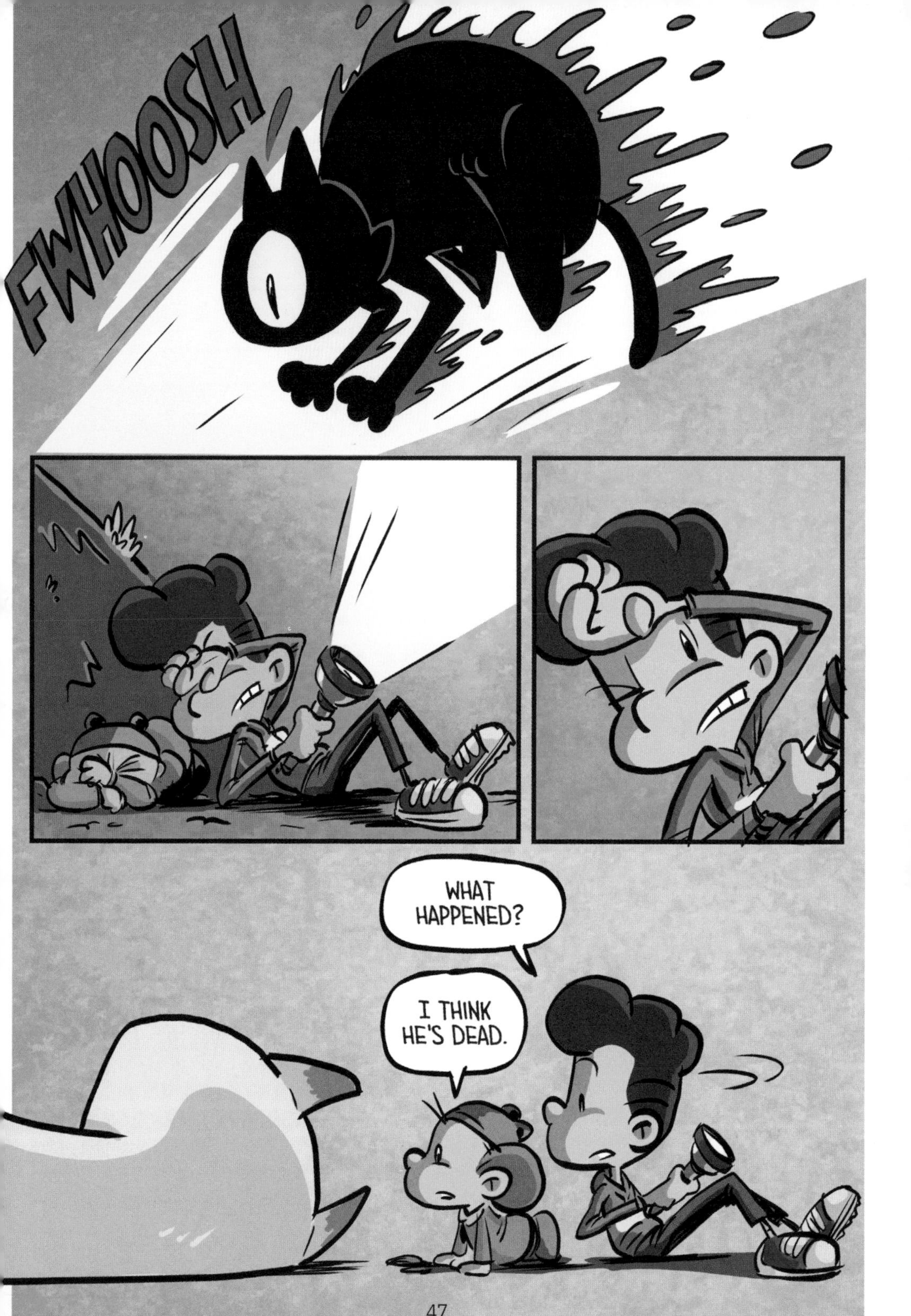
FWHOOSH
WHAT HAPPENED?
I THINK HE'S DEAD.

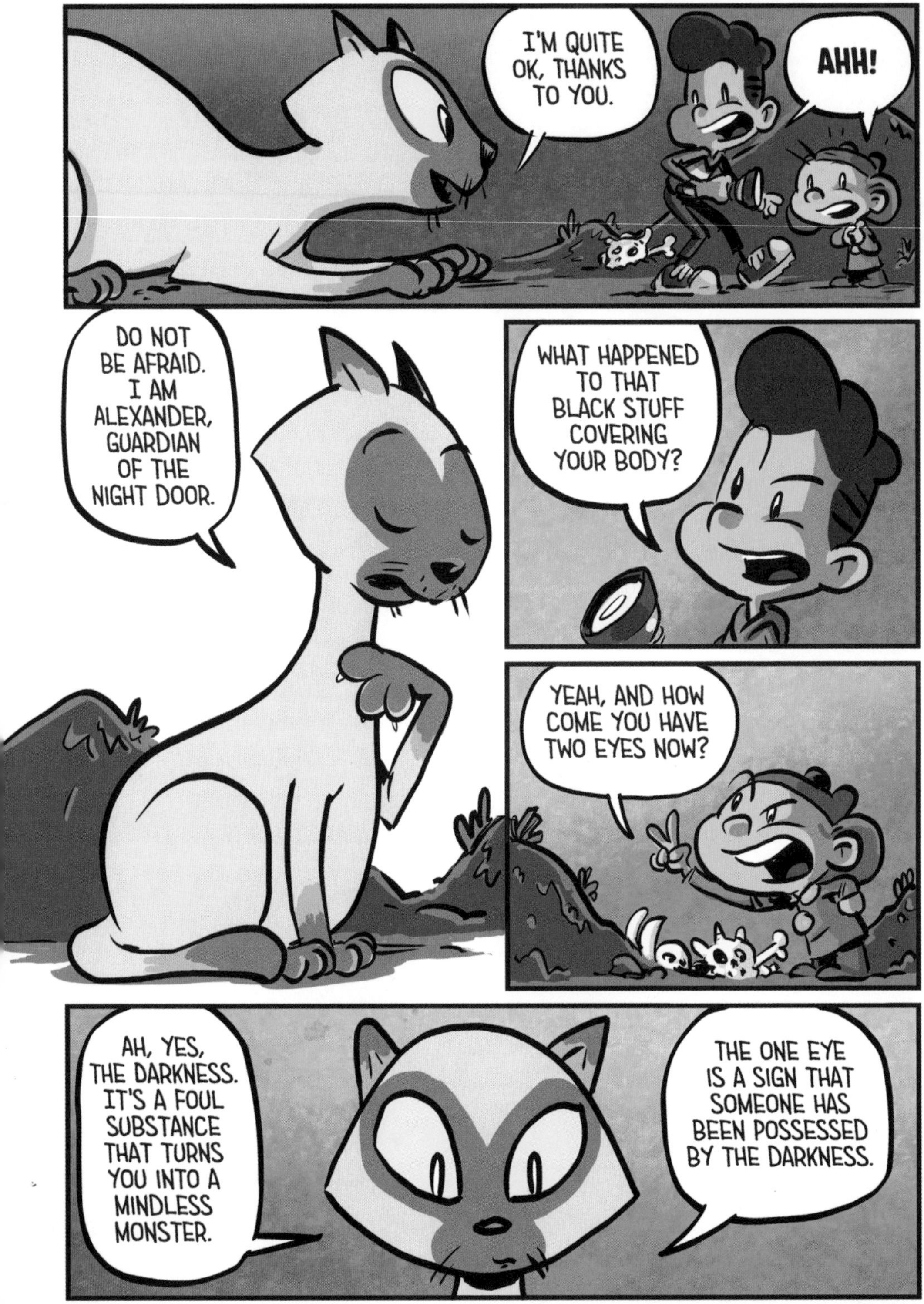

I'M QUITE OK, THANKS TO YOU.
AHH!
DO NOT BE AFRAID. I AM ALEXANDER, GUARDIAN OF THE NIGHT DOOR.
WHAT HAPPENED TO THAT BLACK STUFF COVERING YOUR BODY?
YEAH, AND HOW COME YOU HAVE TWO EYES NOW?
AH, YES, THE DARKNESS. IT'S A FOUL SUBSTANCE THAT TURNS YOU INTO A MINDLESS MONSTER.
THE ONE EYE IS A SIGN THAT SOMEONE HAS BEEN POSSESSED BY THE DARKNESS.

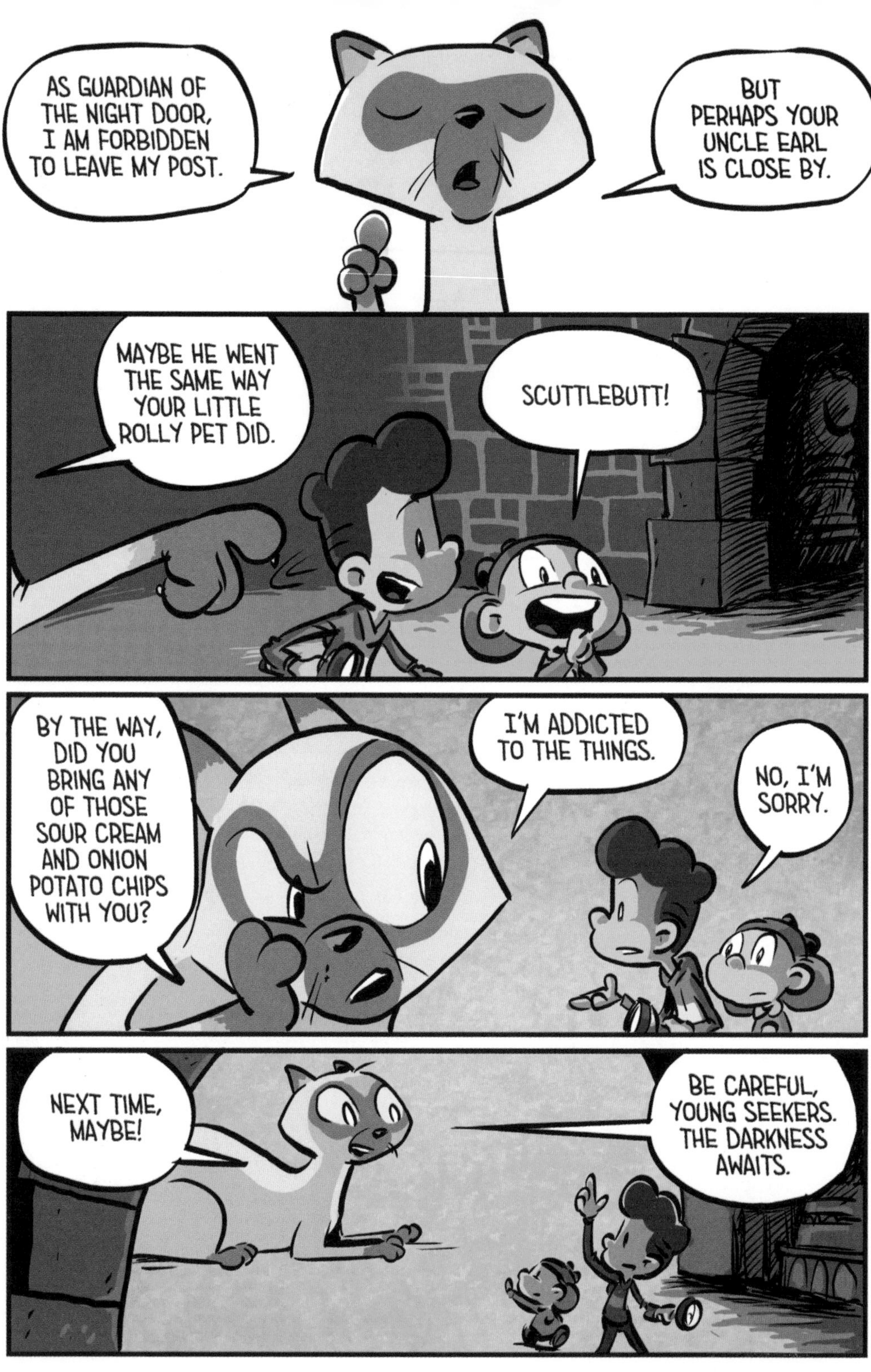
AS GUARDIAN OF THE NIGHT DOOR, I AM FORBIDDEN TO LEAVE MY POST.
BUT PERHAPS YOUR UNCLE EARL IS CLOSE BY.
MAYBE HE WENT THE SAME WAY YOUR LITTLE ROLLY PET DID.
SCUTTLEBUTT!
BY THE WAY, DID YOU BRING ANY OF THOSE SOUR CREAM AND ONION POTATO CHIPS WITH YOU?
I'M ADDICTED TO THE THINGS.
NO, I'M SORRY.
NEXT TIME, MAYBE!
BE CAREFUL, YOUNG SEEKERS. THE DARKNESS AWAITS.

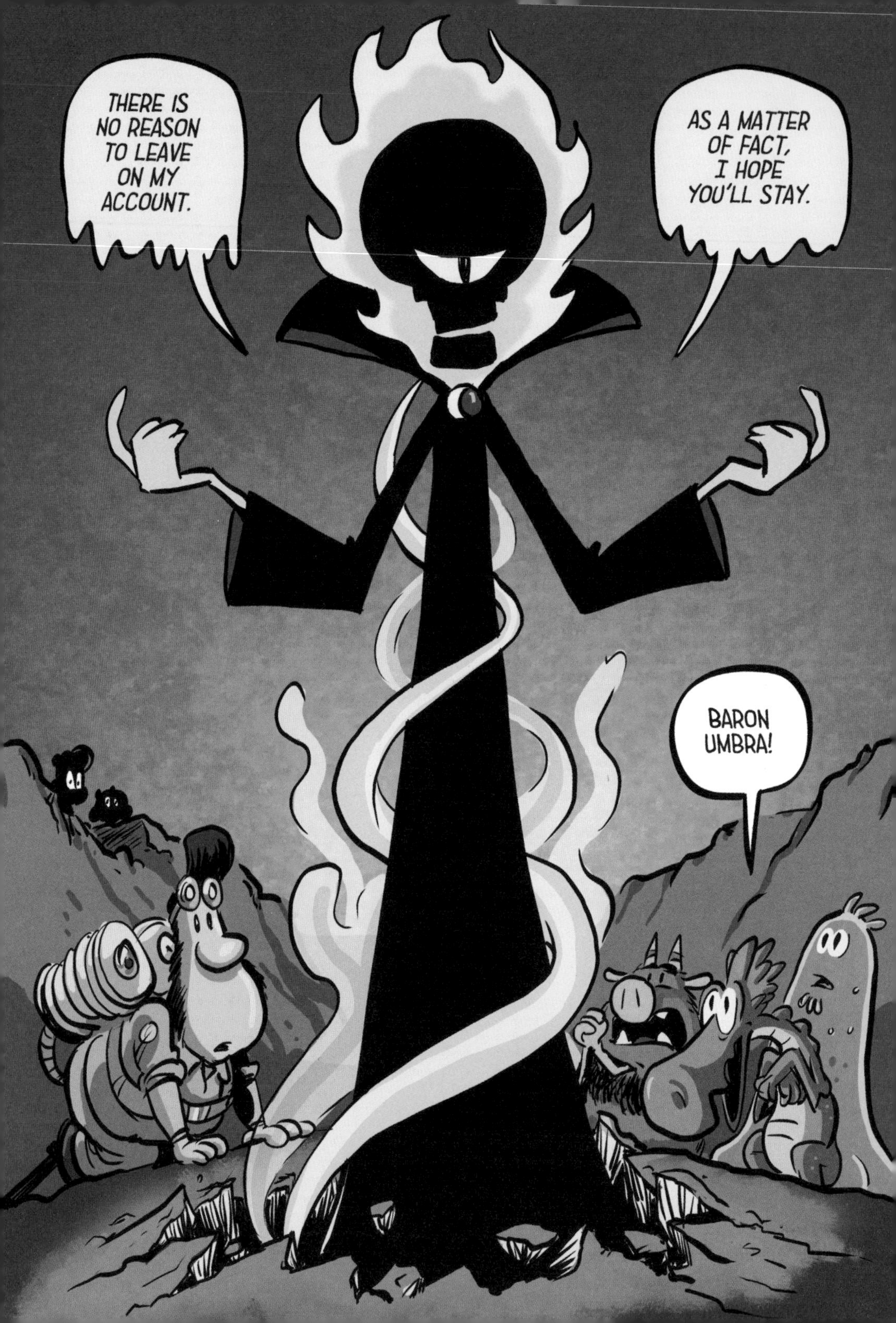
THERE IS NO REASON TO LEAVE ON MY ACCOUNT.
AS A MATTER OF FACT, I HOPE YOU'LL STAY.
BARON UMBRA!

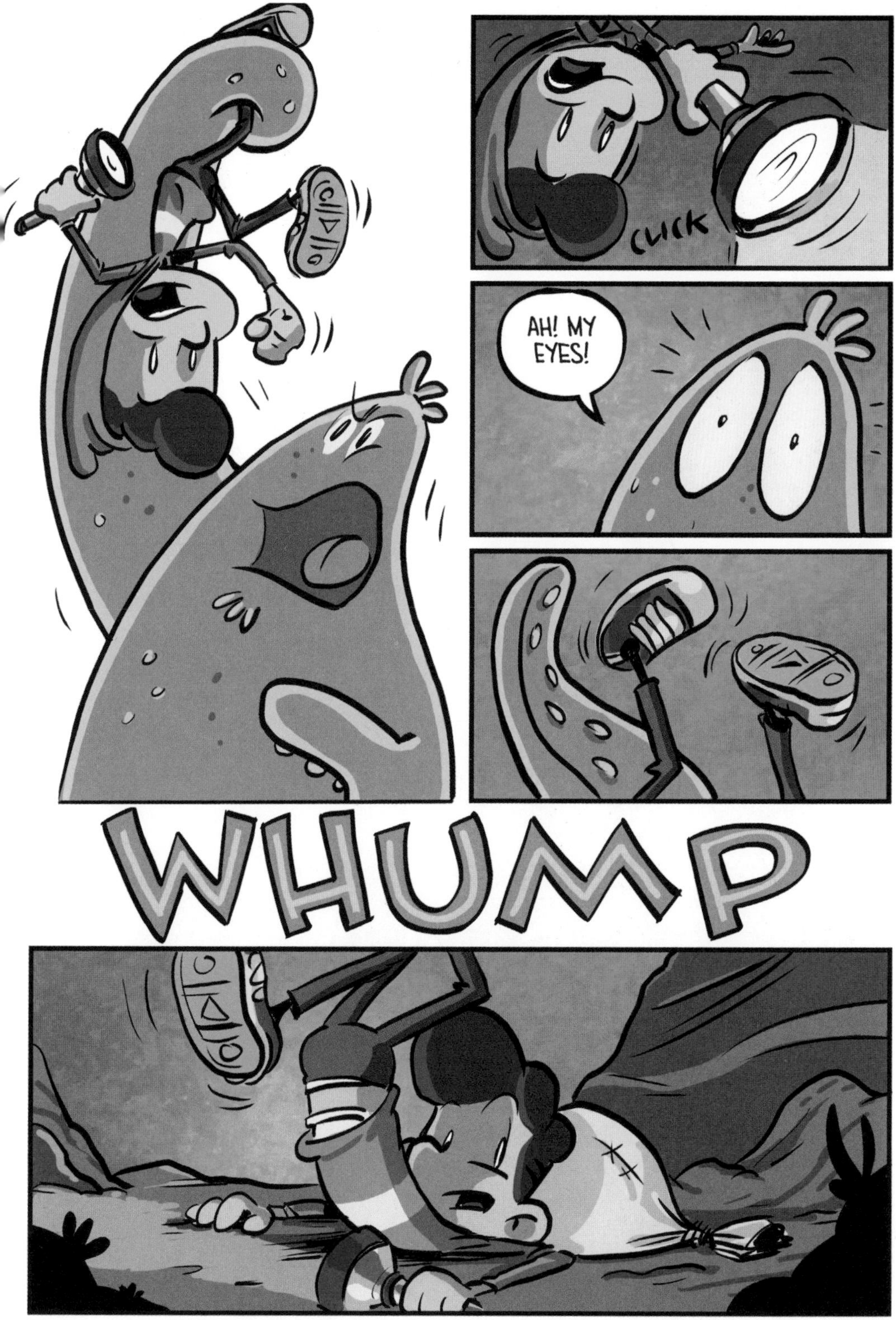
CLICK
AH! MY EYES!
WHUMP

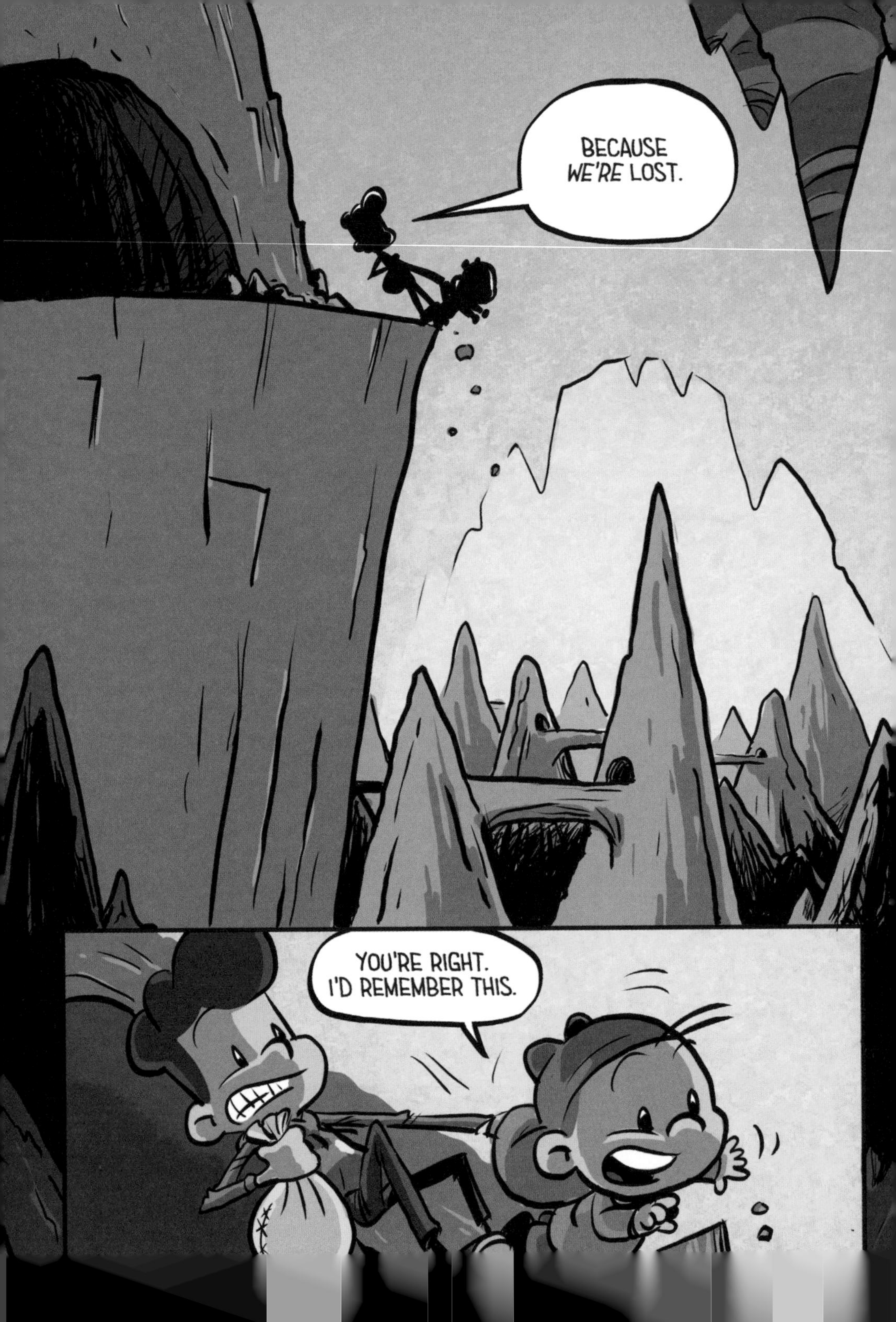
BECAUSE *WE'RE* LOST.
YOU'RE RIGHT. I'D REMEMBER THIS.

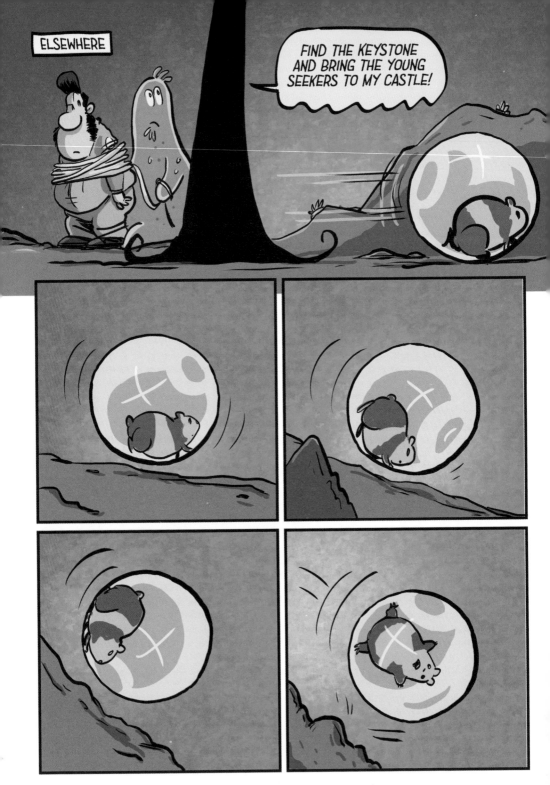

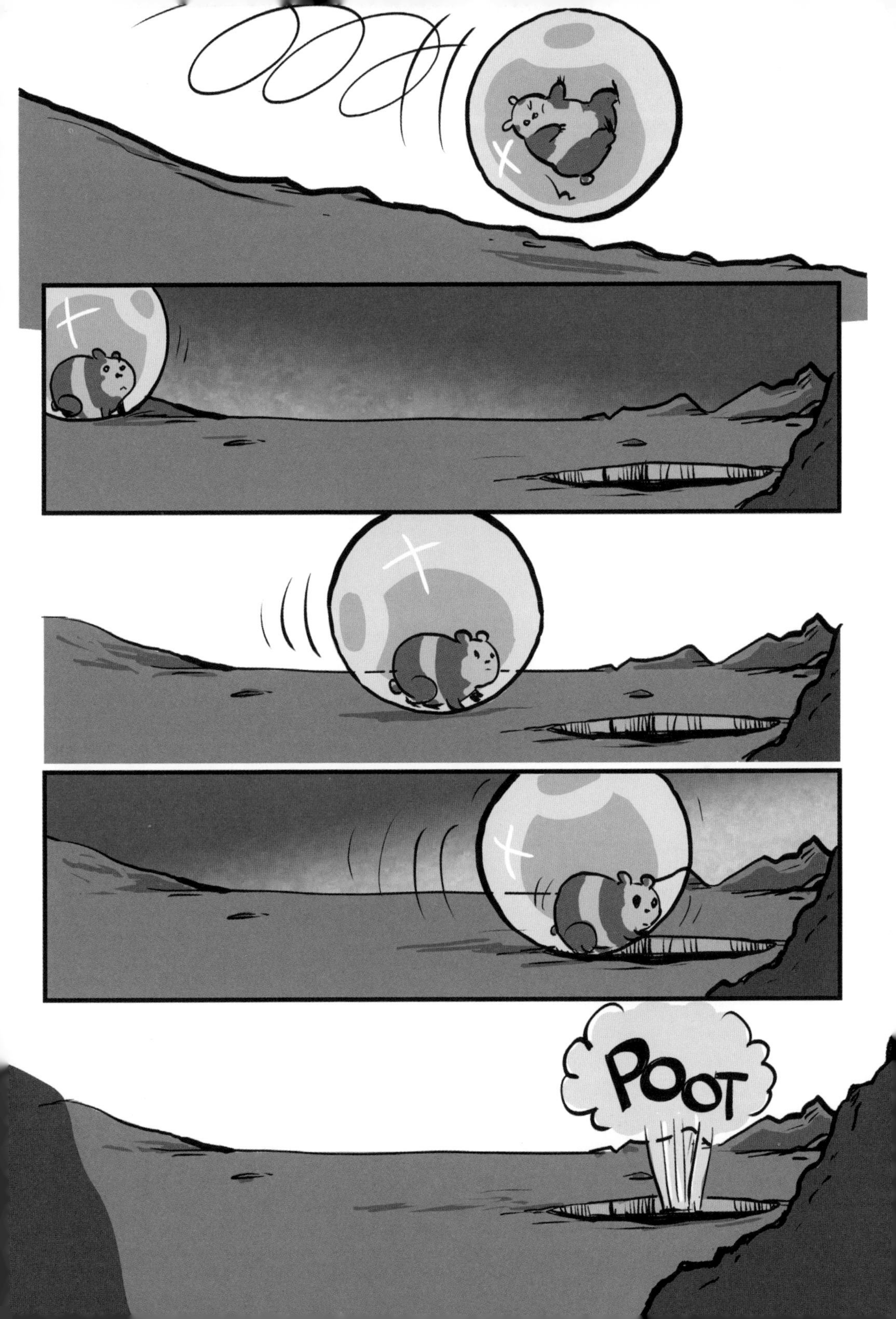
POOT

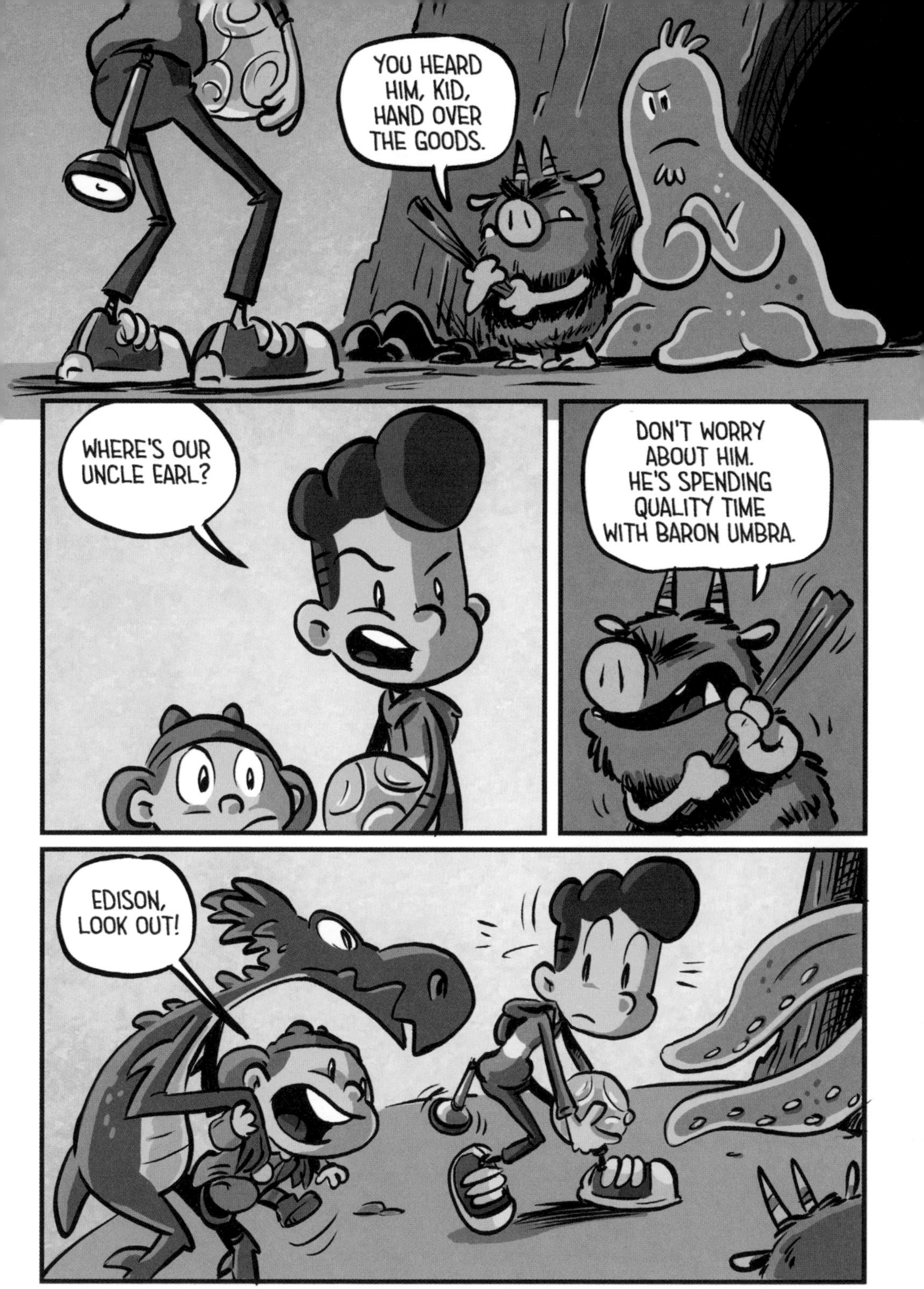
YOU HEARD HIM, KID, HAND OVER THE GOODS.
WHERE'S OUR UNCLE EARL?
DON'T WORRY ABOUT HIM. HE'S SPENDING QUALITY TIME WITH BARON UMBRA.
EDISON, LOOK OUT!

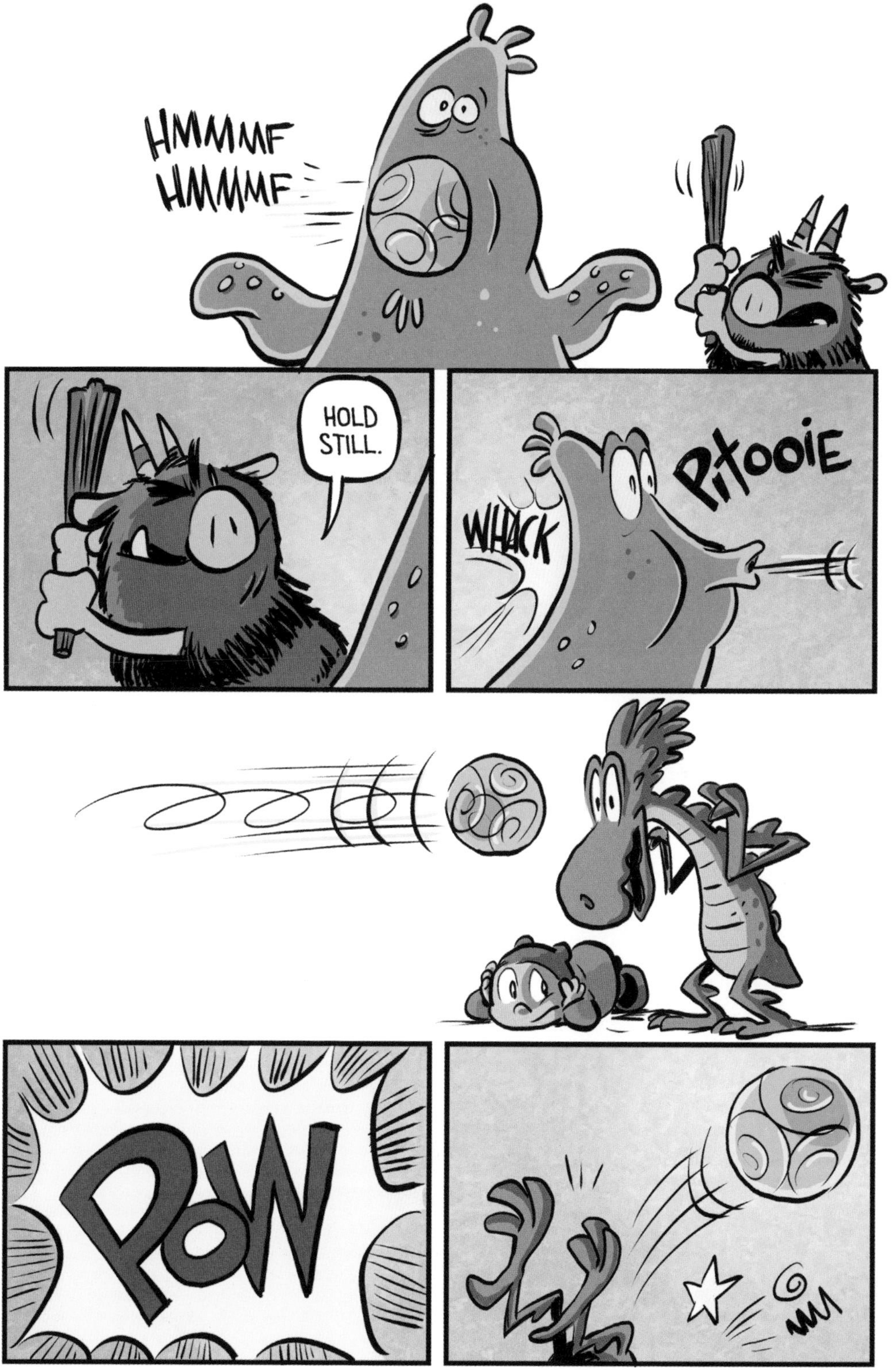
HMMMF
HMMMF
HOLD STILL.
WHACK
PITOOIE
POW

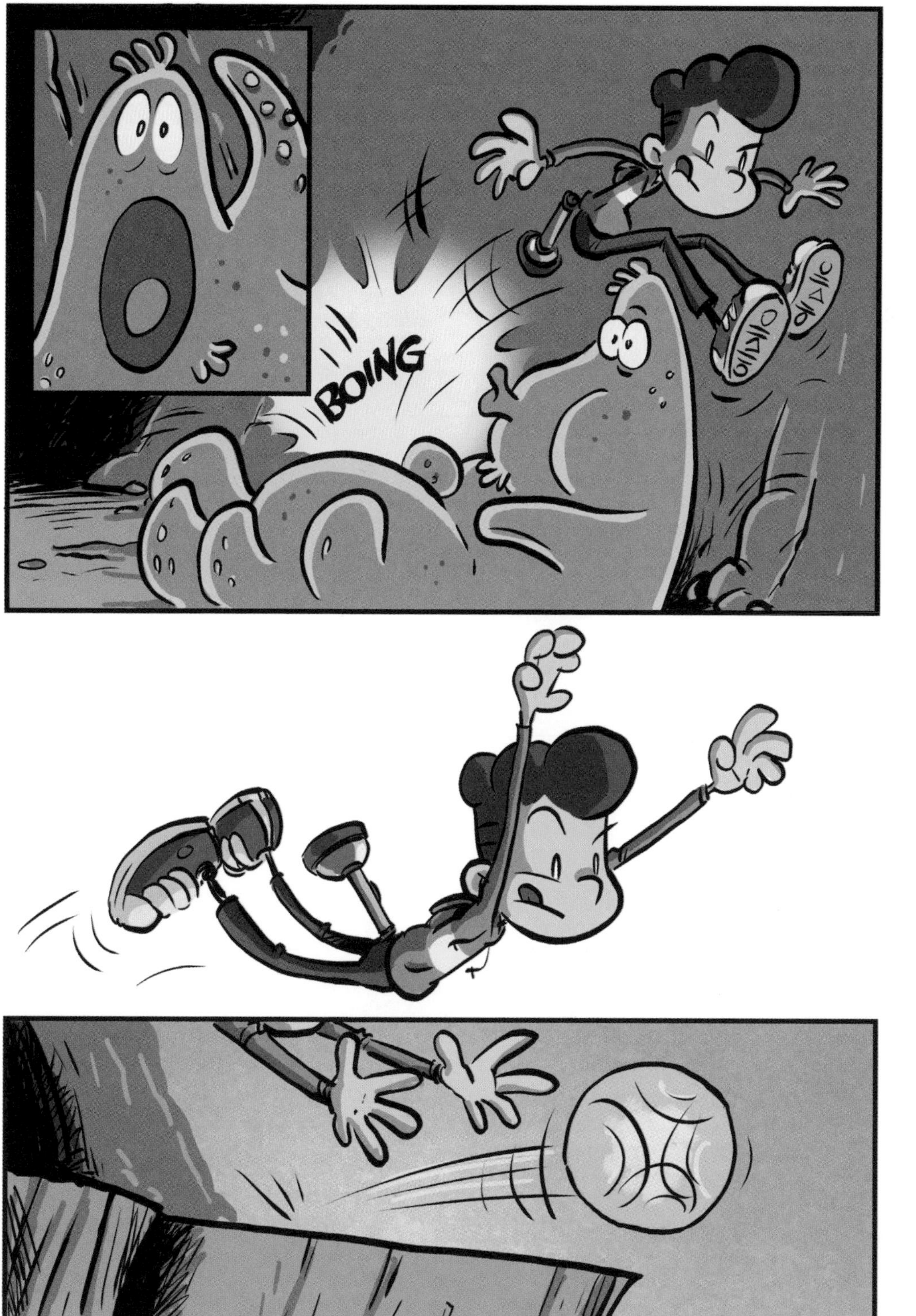
BOING

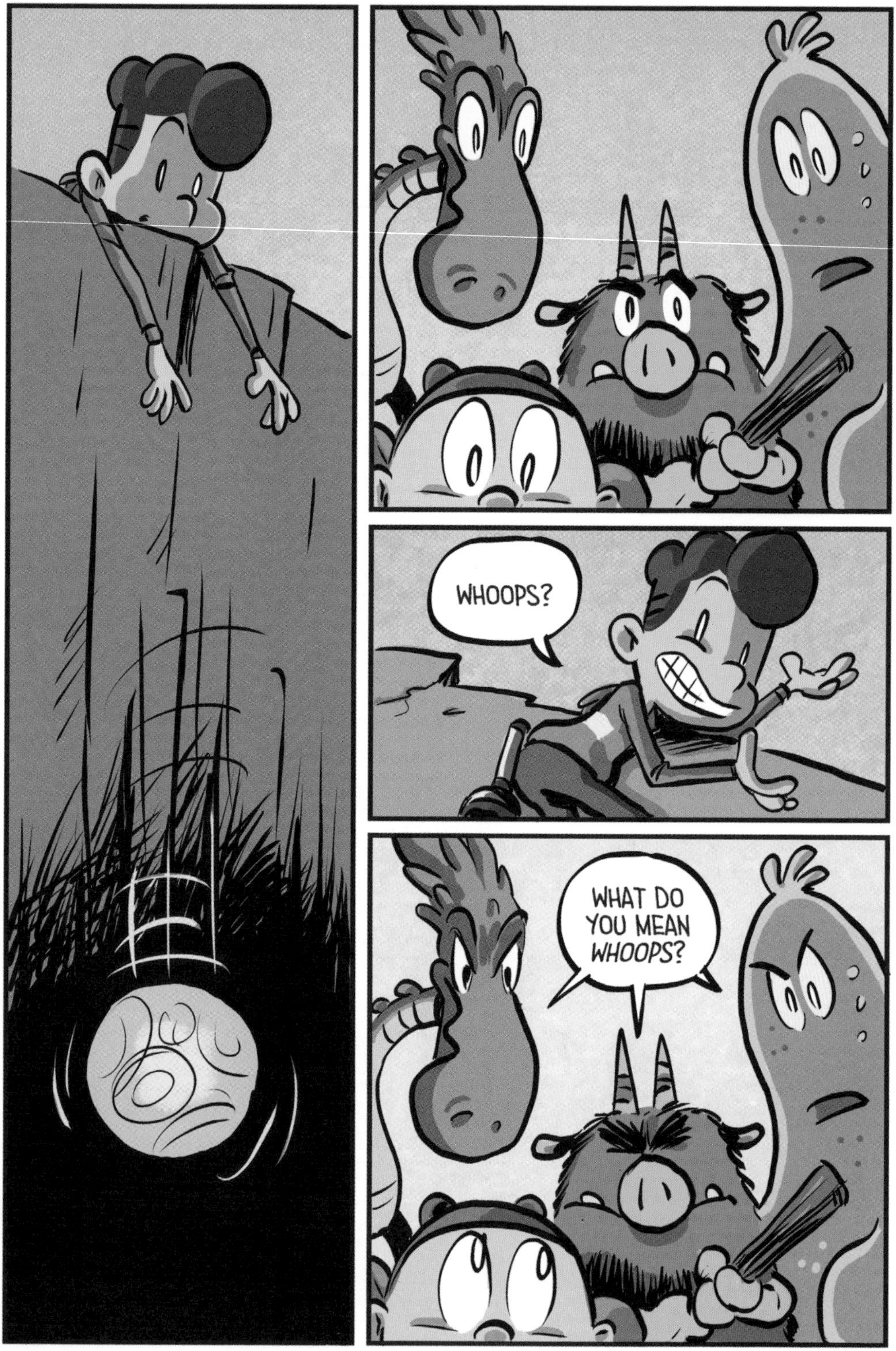
WHOOPS?
WHAT DO YOU MEAN *WHOOPS*?

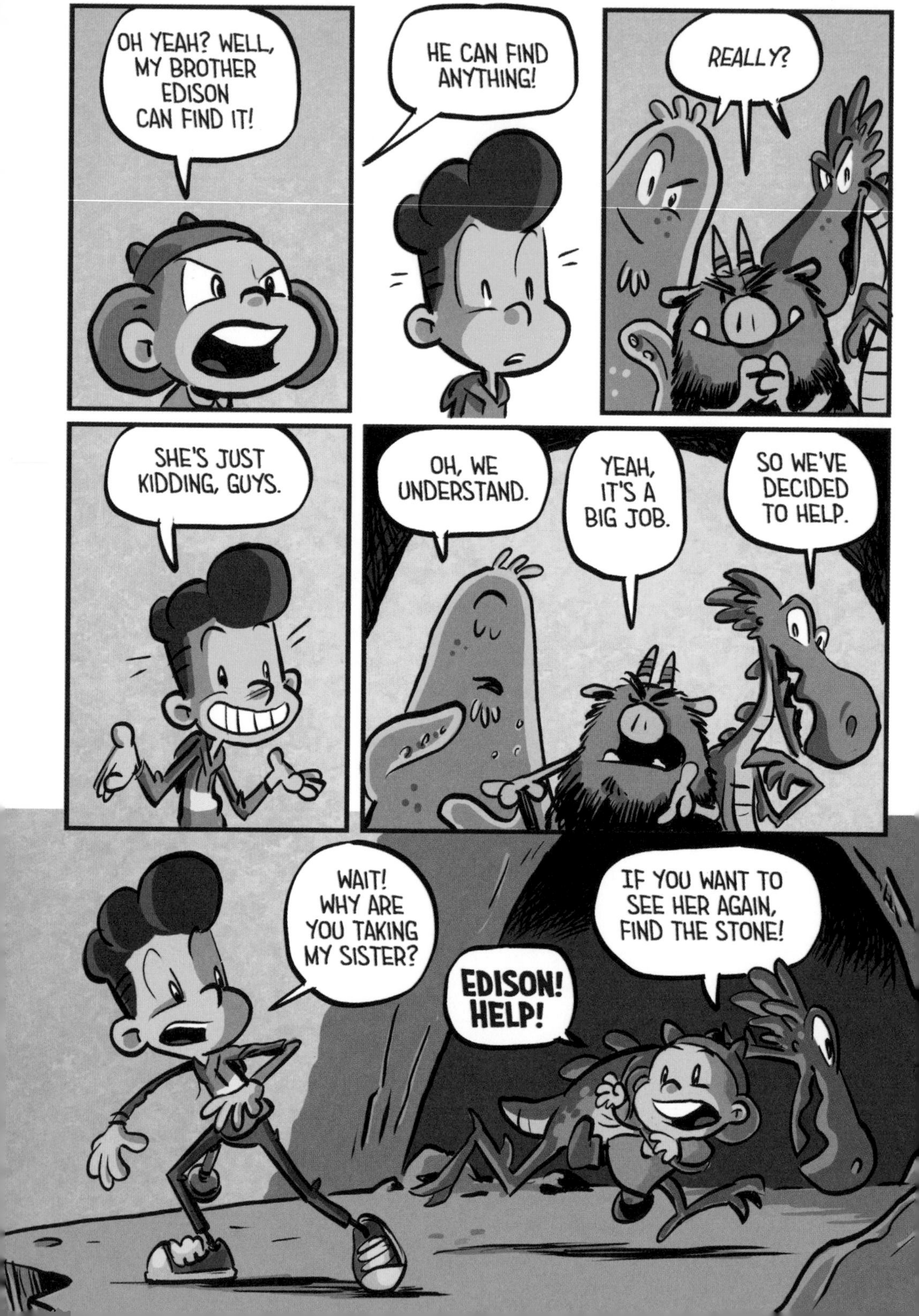
OH YEAH? WELL, MY BROTHER EDISON CAN FIND IT!
HE CAN FIND ANYTHING!
REALLY?
SHE'S JUST KIDDING, GUYS.
OH, WE UNDERSTAND.
YEAH, IT'S A BIG JOB.
SO WE'VE DECIDED TO HELP.
WAIT! WHY ARE YOU TAKING MY SISTER?
EDISON! HELP!
IF YOU WANT TO SEE HER AGAIN, FIND THE STONE!

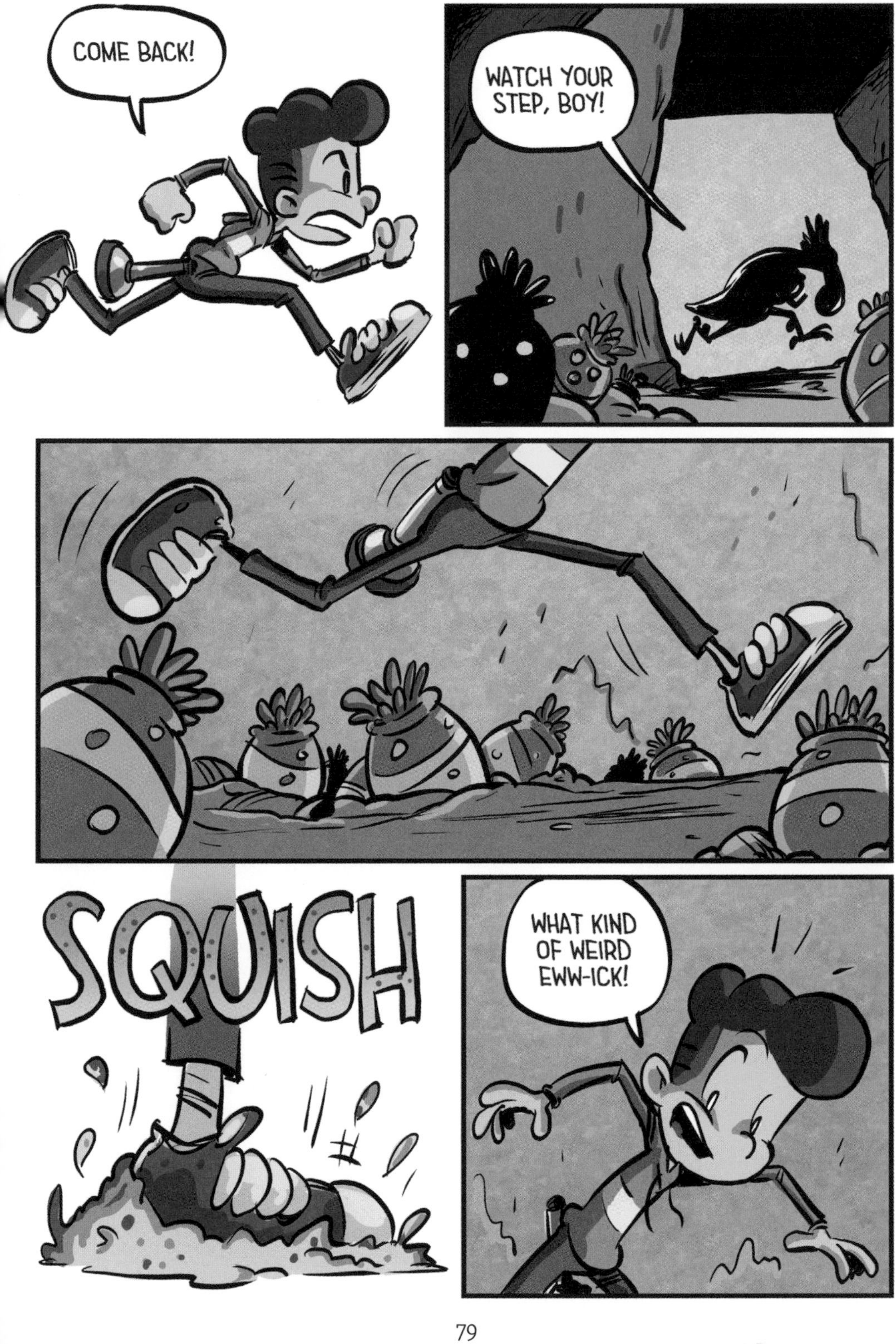
COME BACK!
WATCH YOUR STEP, BOY!
SQUISH
WHAT KIND OF WEIRD EWW-ICK!

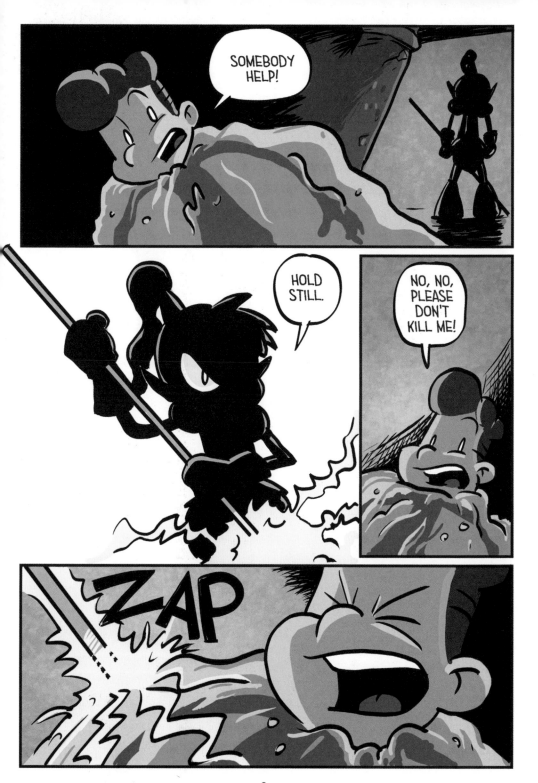

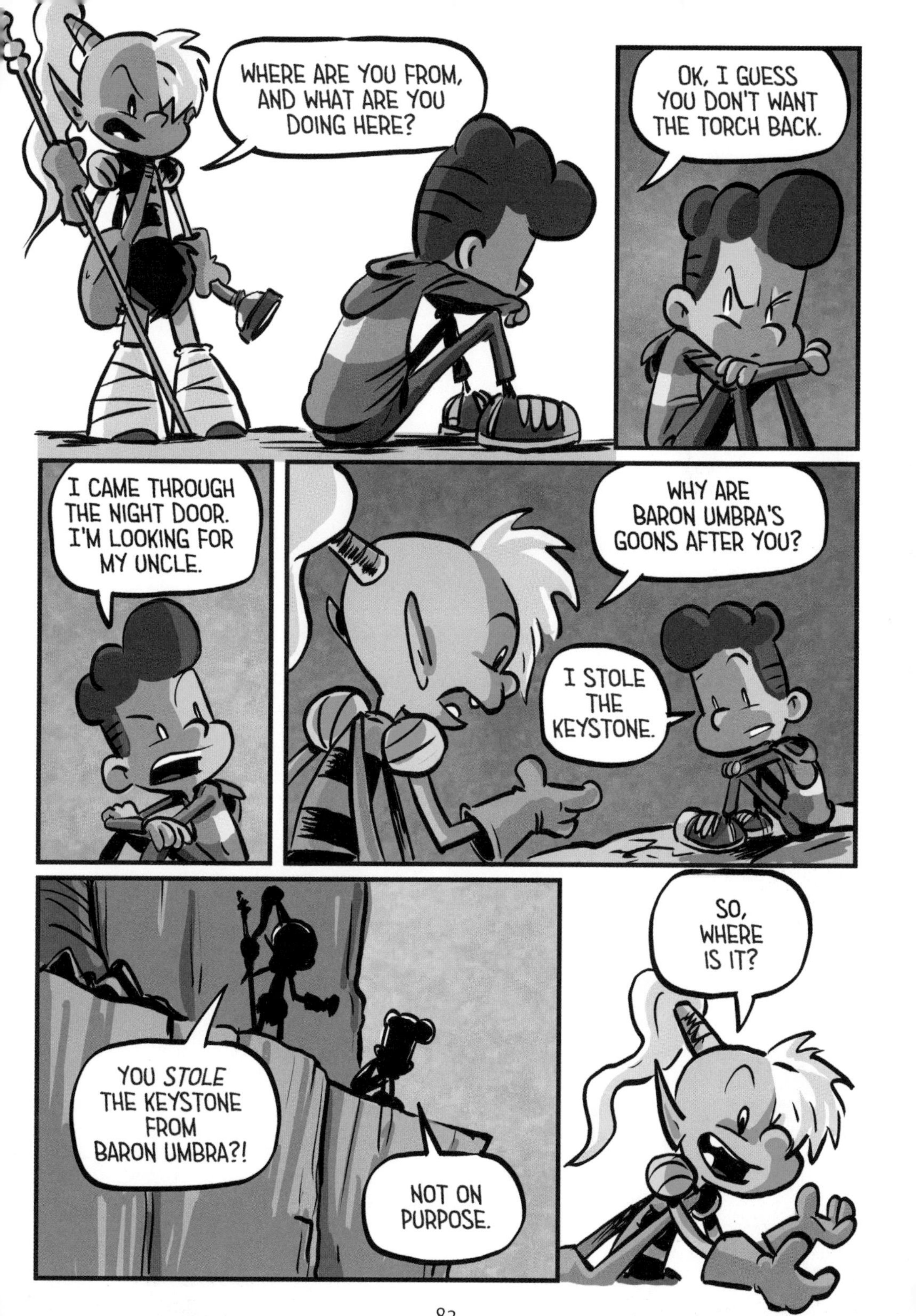
WHERE ARE YOU FROM, AND WHAT ARE YOU DOING HERE?
OK, I GUESS YOU DON'T WANT THE TORCH BACK.
I CAME THROUGH THE NIGHT DOOR. I'M LOOKING FOR MY UNCLE.
WHY ARE BARON UMBRA'S GOONS AFTER YOU?
I STOLE THE KEYSTONE.
YOU *STOLE* THE KEYSTONE FROM BARON UMBRA?!
NOT ON PURPOSE.
SO, WHERE IS IT?

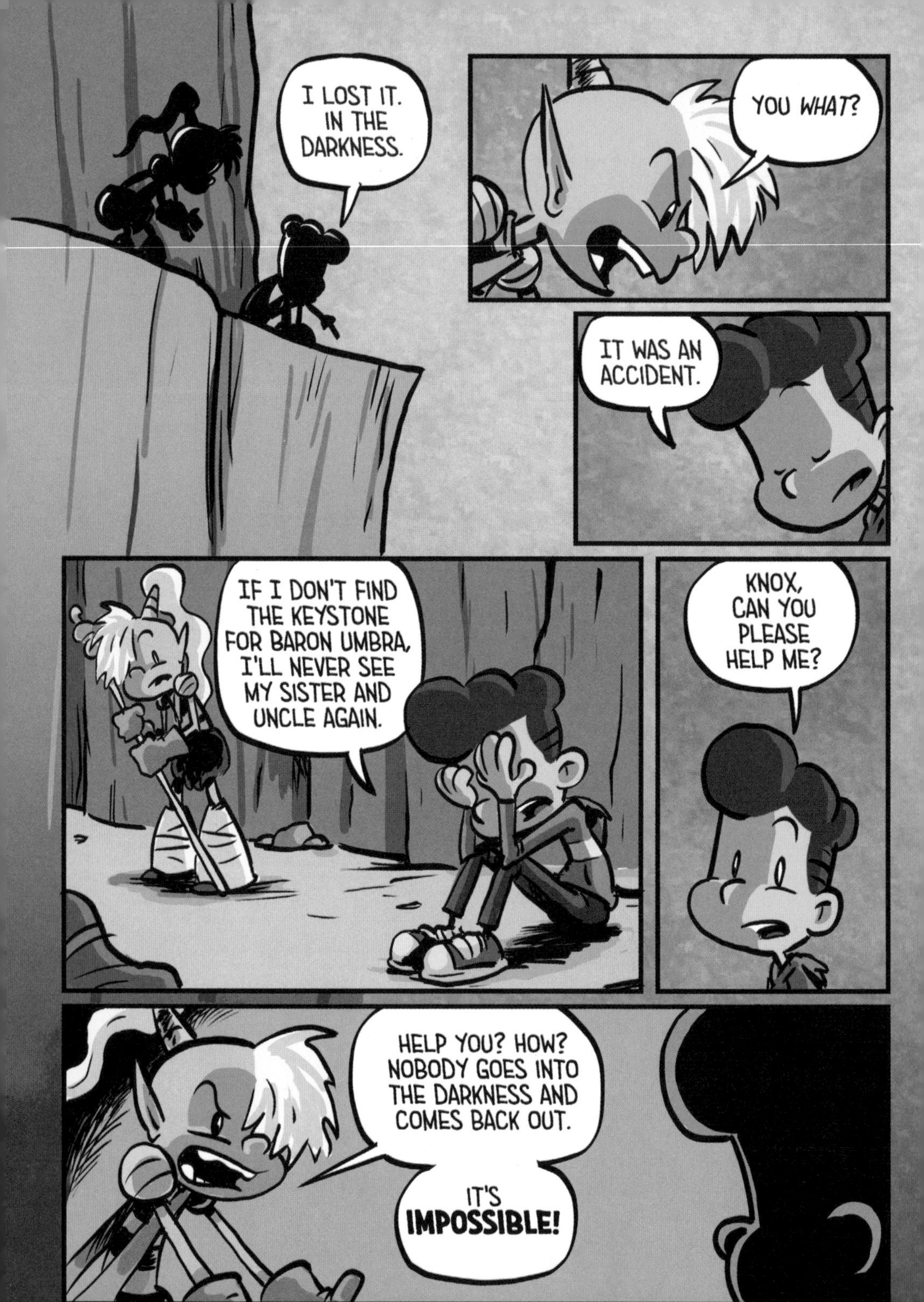
I LOST IT. IN THE DARKNESS.
YOU WHAT?
IT WAS AN ACCIDENT.
IF I DON'T FIND THE KEYSTONE FOR BARON UMBRA, I'LL NEVER SEE MY SISTER AND UNCLE AGAIN.
KNOX, CAN YOU PLEASE HELP ME?
HELP YOU? HOW? NOBODY GOES INTO THE DARKNESS AND COMES BACK OUT.
IT'S **IMPOSSIBLE!**

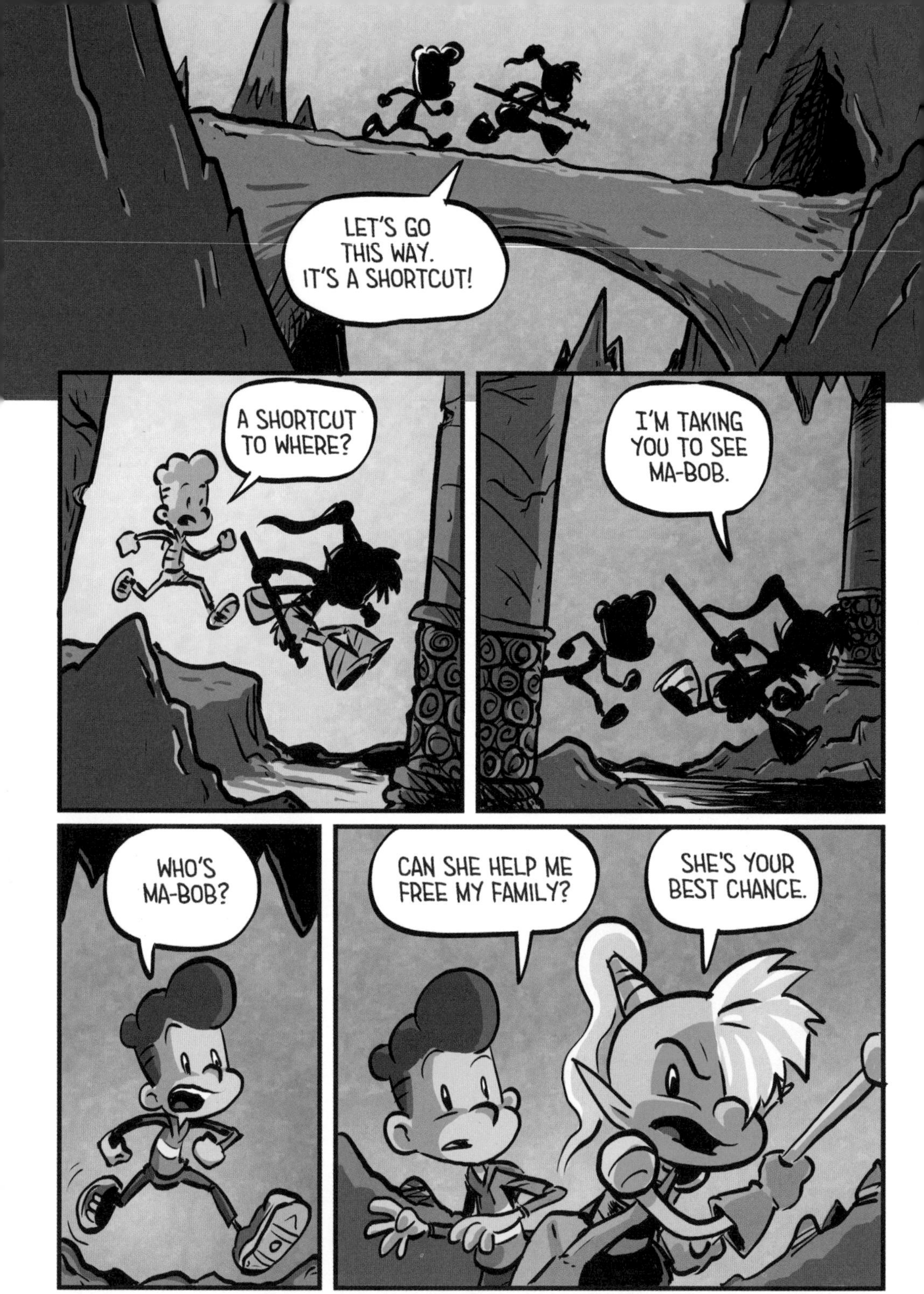
LET'S GO THIS WAY. IT'S A SHORTCUT!
A SHORTCUT TO WHERE?
I'M TAKING YOU TO SEE MA-BOB.
WHO'S MA-BOB?
CAN SHE HELP ME FREE MY FAMILY?
SHE'S YOUR BEST CHANCE.

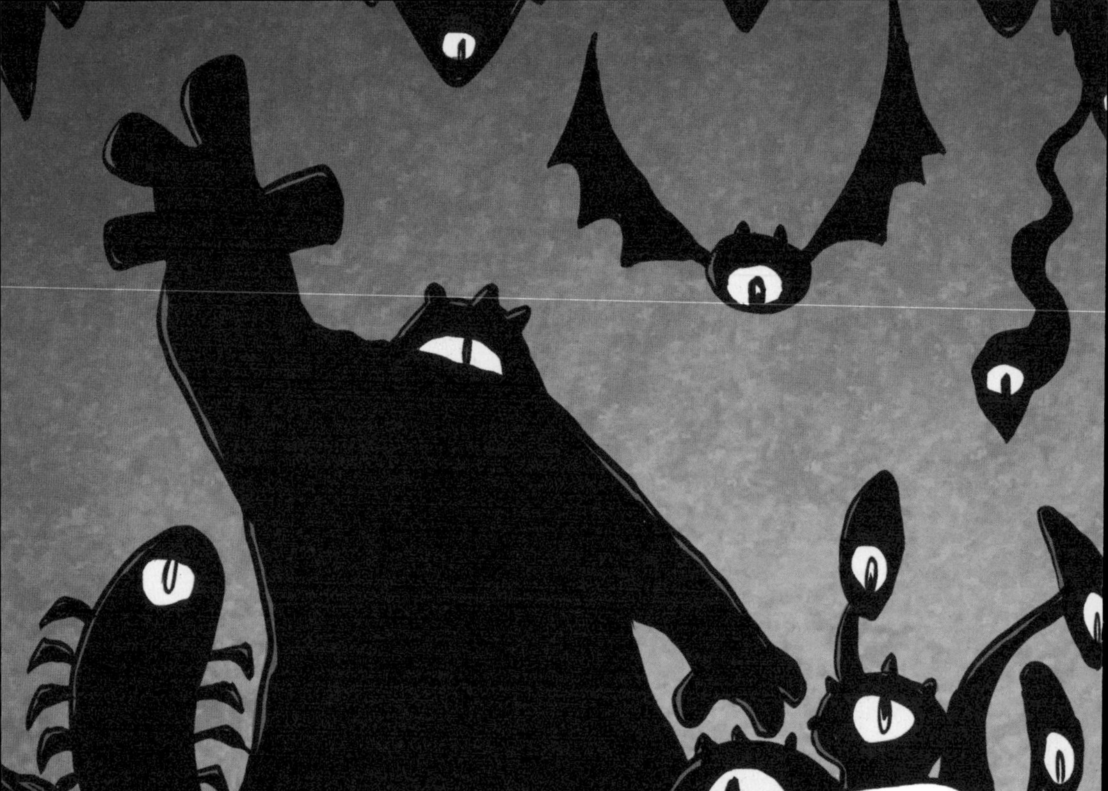
OH NO,
UNDERLINGS!
WE GOTTA RUN!!

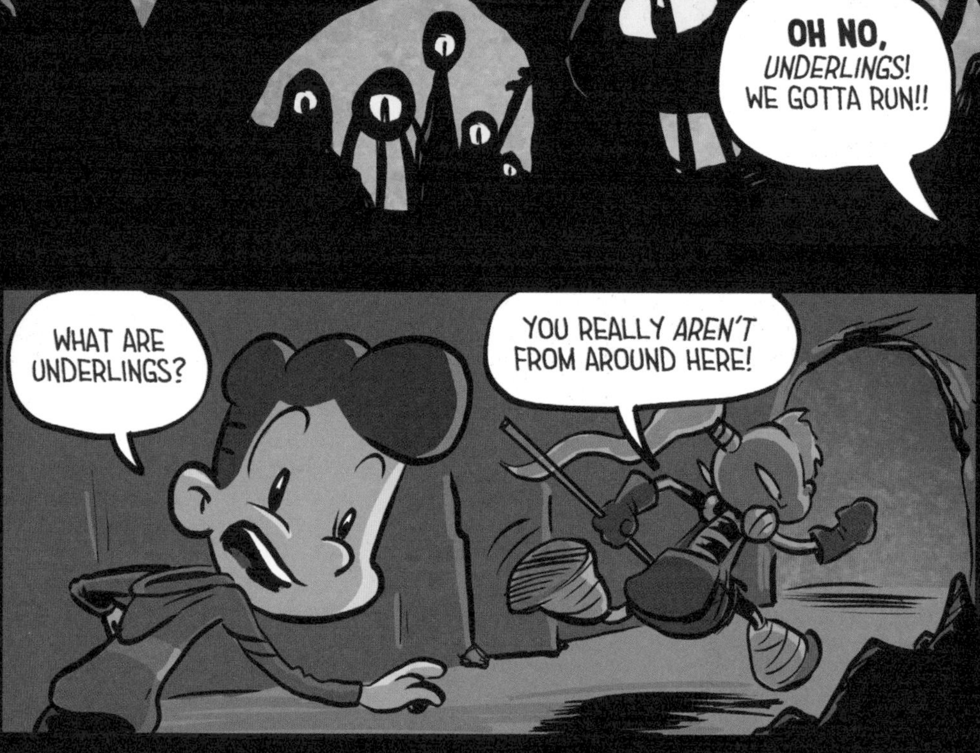
WHAT ARE UNDERLINGS?
YOU REALLY *AREN'T* FROM AROUND HERE!

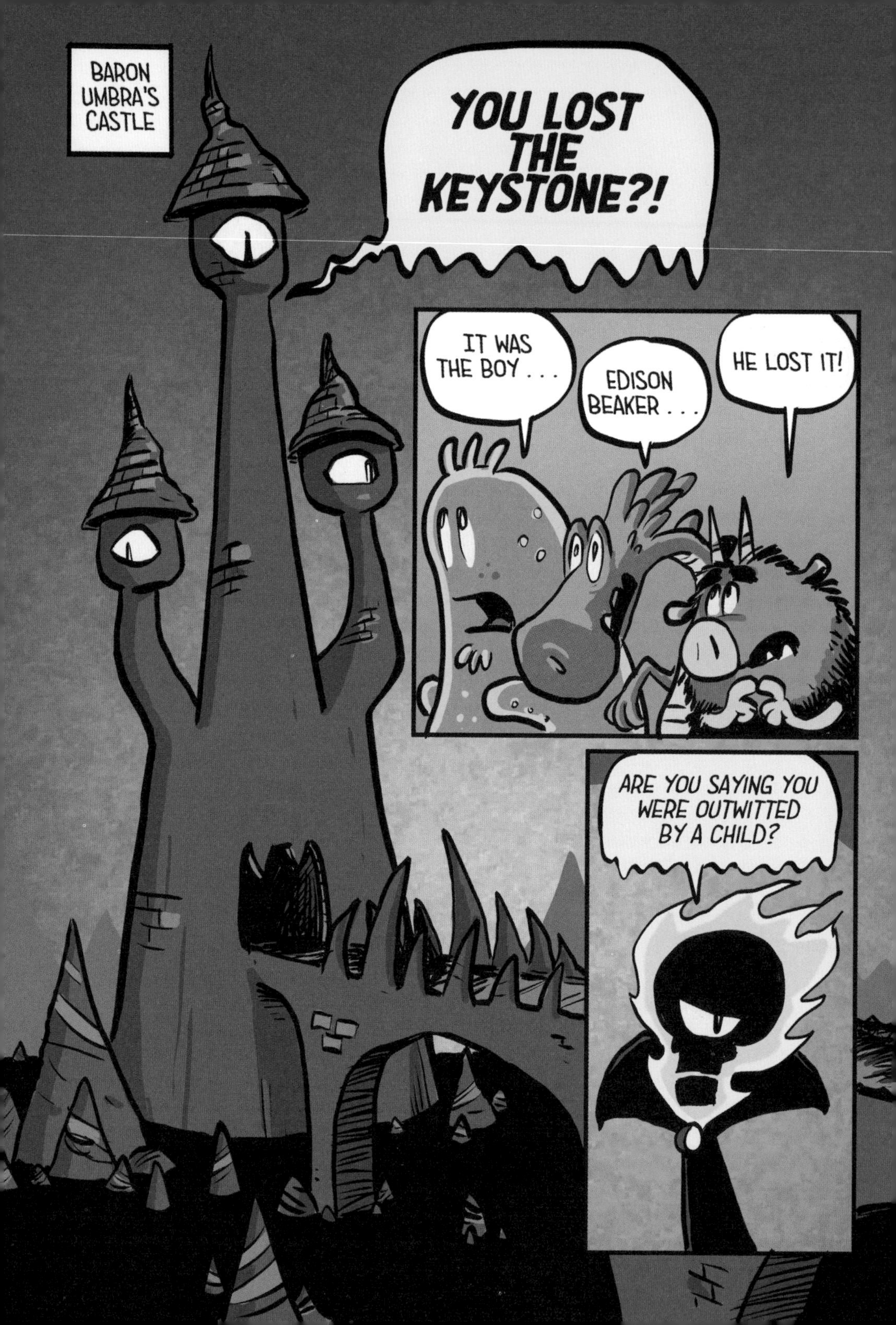
BARON UMBRA'S CASTLE
YOU LOST THE KEYSTONE?!
IT WAS THE BOY . . .
EDISON BEAKER . . .
HE LOST IT!
ARE YOU SAYING YOU WERE OUTWITTED BY A CHILD?

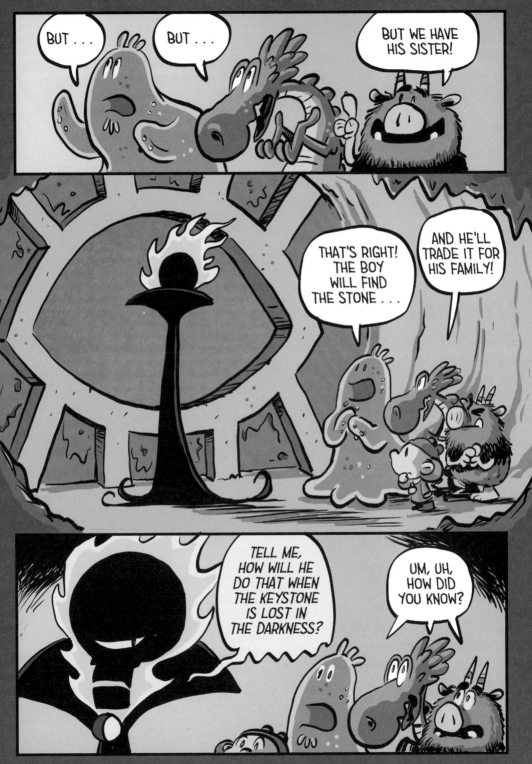

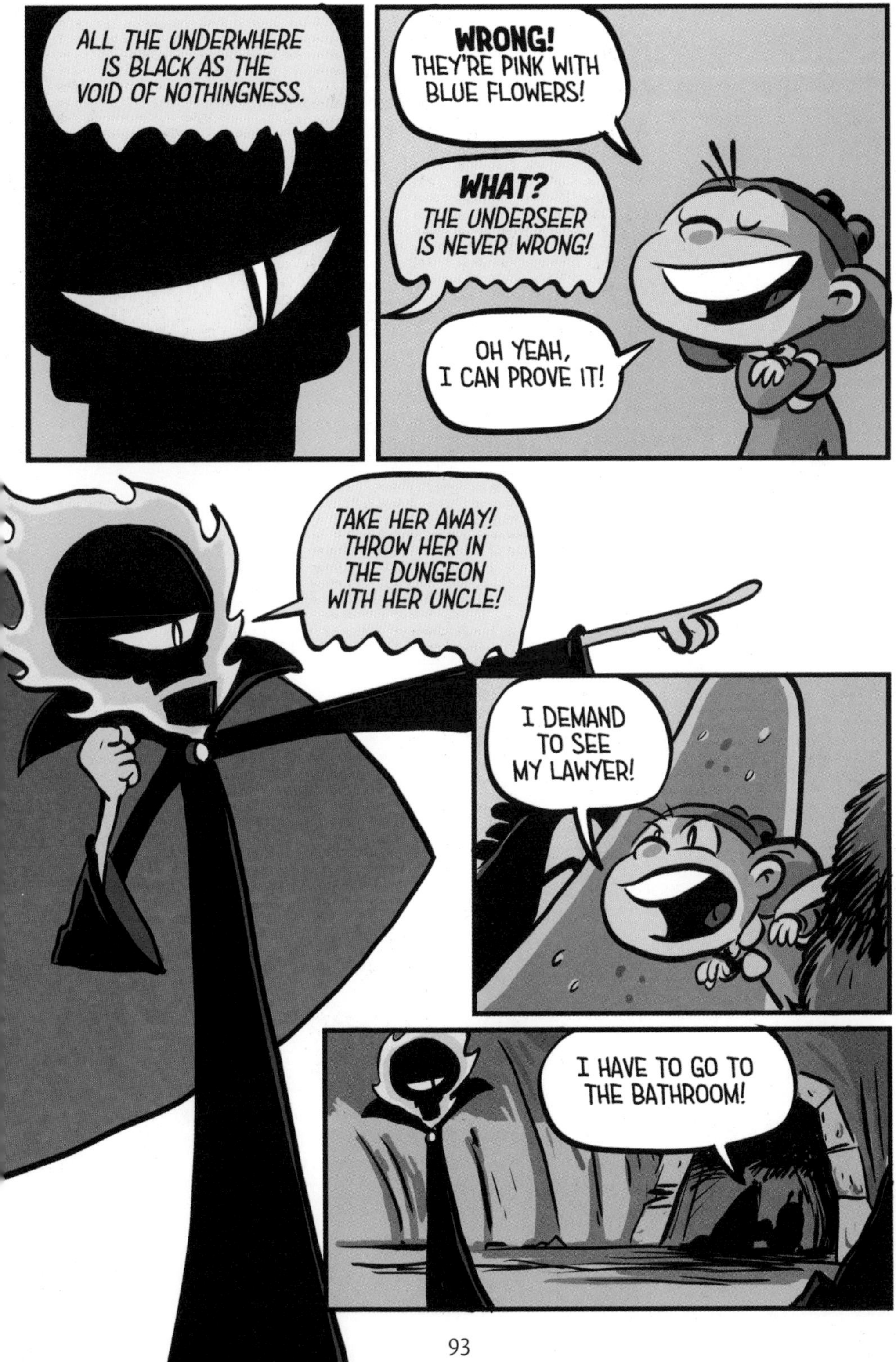
ALL THE UNDERWHERE IS BLACK AS THE VOID OF NOTHINGNESS.
WRONG! THEY'RE PINK WITH BLUE FLOWERS!
WHAT? THE UNDERSEER IS NEVER WRONG!
OH YEAH, I CAN PROVE IT!
TAKE HER AWAY! THROW HER IN THE DUNGEON WITH HER UNCLE!
I DEMAND TO SEE MY LAWYER!
I HAVE TO GO TO THE BATHROOM!

103

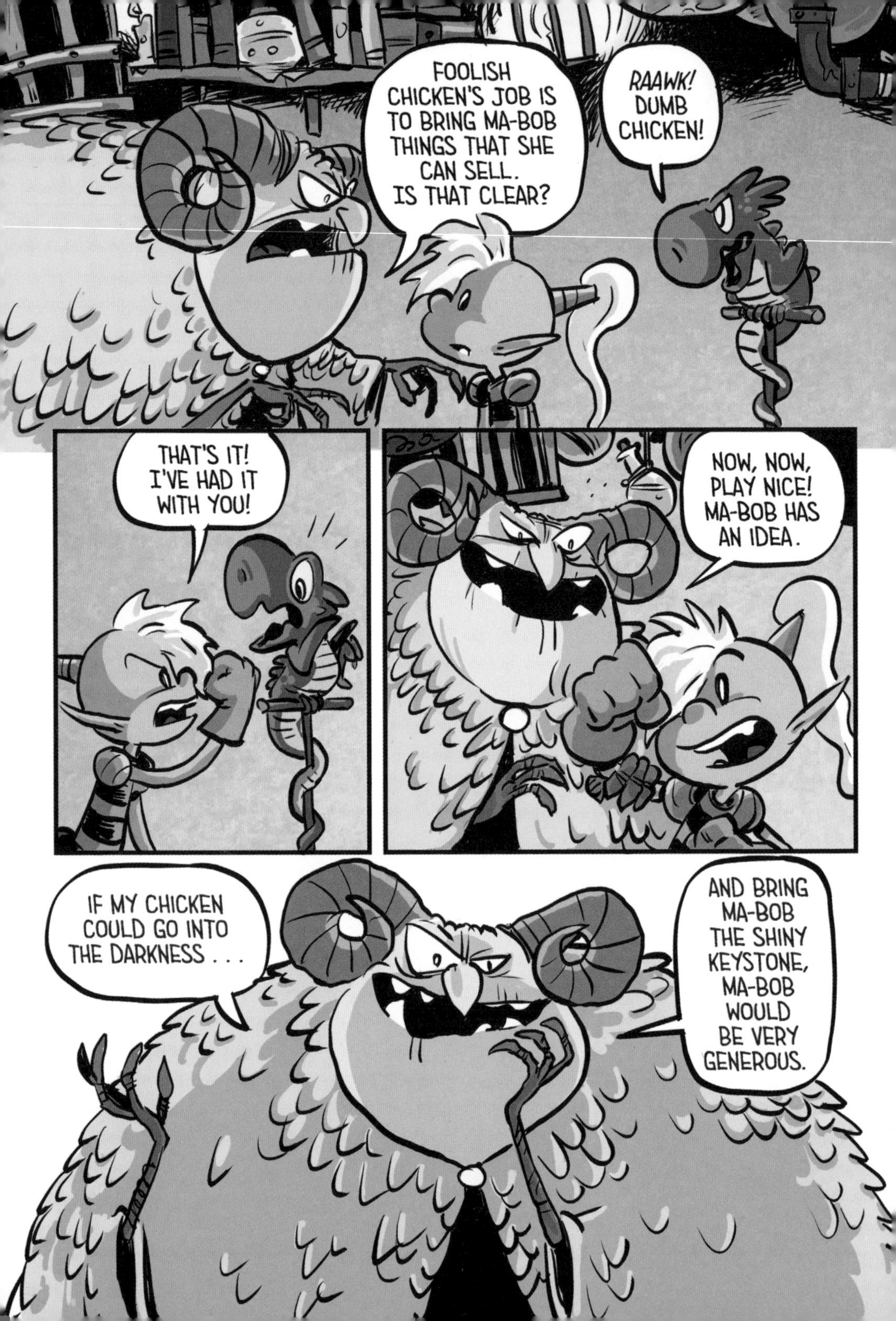
FOOLISH CHICKEN'S JOB IS TO BRING MA-BOB THINGS THAT SHE CAN SELL. IS THAT CLEAR?
RAAWK! DUMB CHICKEN!
THAT'S IT! I'VE HAD IT WITH YOU!
NOW, NOW, PLAY NICE! MA-BOB HAS AN IDEA.
IF MY CHICKEN COULD GO INTO THE DARKNESS . . .
AND BRING MA-BOB THE SHINY KEYSTONE, MA-BOB WOULD BE VERY GENEROUS.

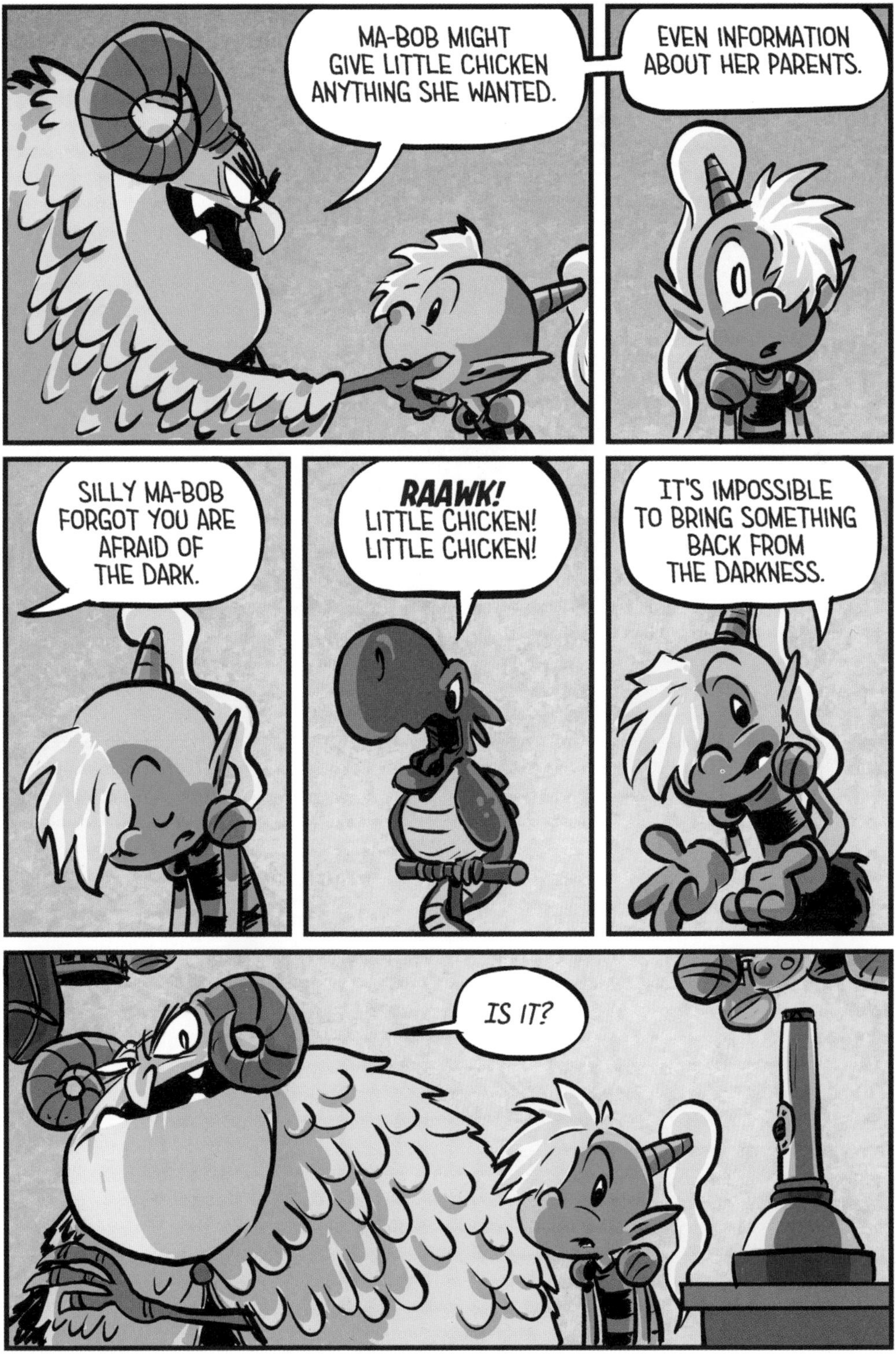
MA-BOB MIGHT GIVE LITTLE CHICKEN ANYTHING SHE WANTED.
EVEN INFORMATION ABOUT HER PARENTS.
SILLY MA-BOB FORGOT YOU ARE AFRAID OF THE DARK.
RAAWK! LITTLE CHICKEN! LITTLE CHICKEN!
IT'S IMPOSSIBLE TO BRING SOMETHING BACK FROM THE DARKNESS.
IS IT?

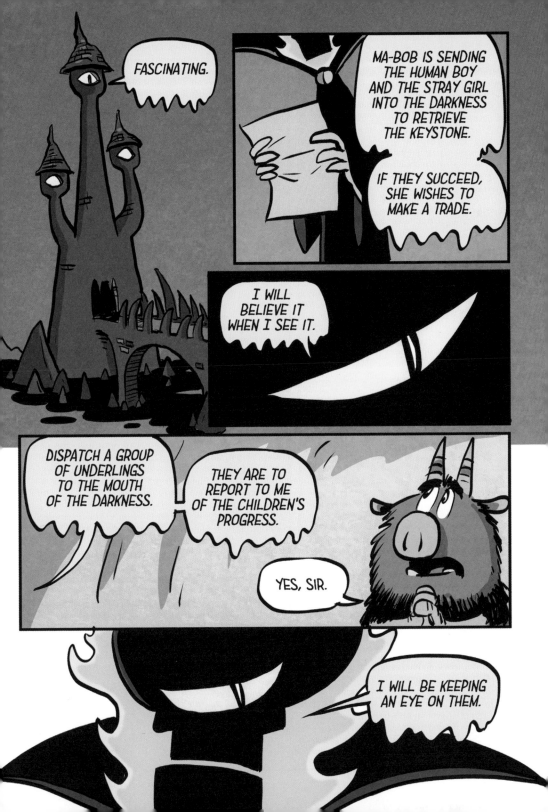

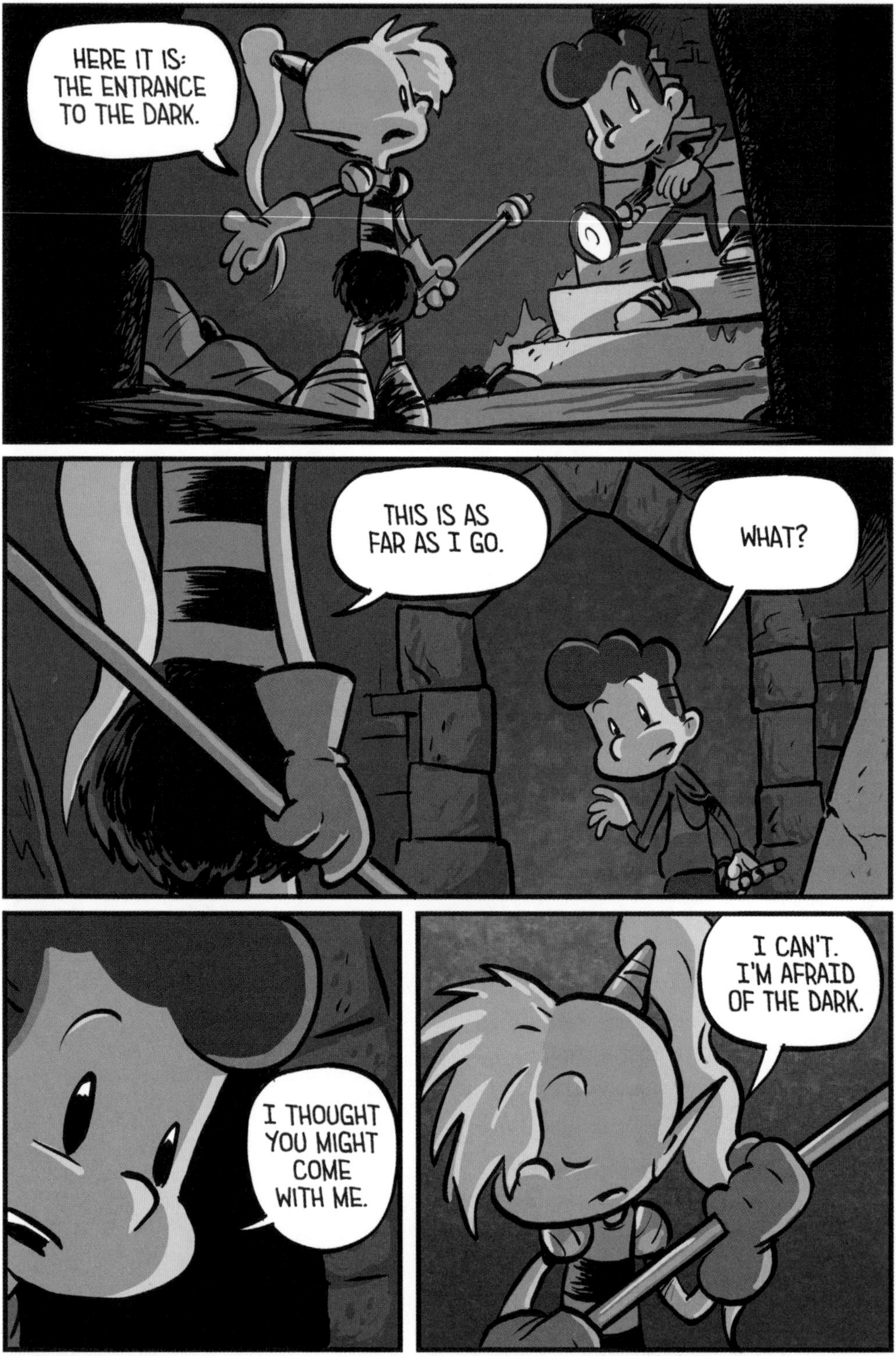
HERE IT IS: THE ENTRANCE TO THE DARK.
THIS IS AS FAR AS I GO.
WHAT?
I THOUGHT YOU MIGHT COME WITH ME.
I CAN'T. I'M AFRAID OF THE DARK.

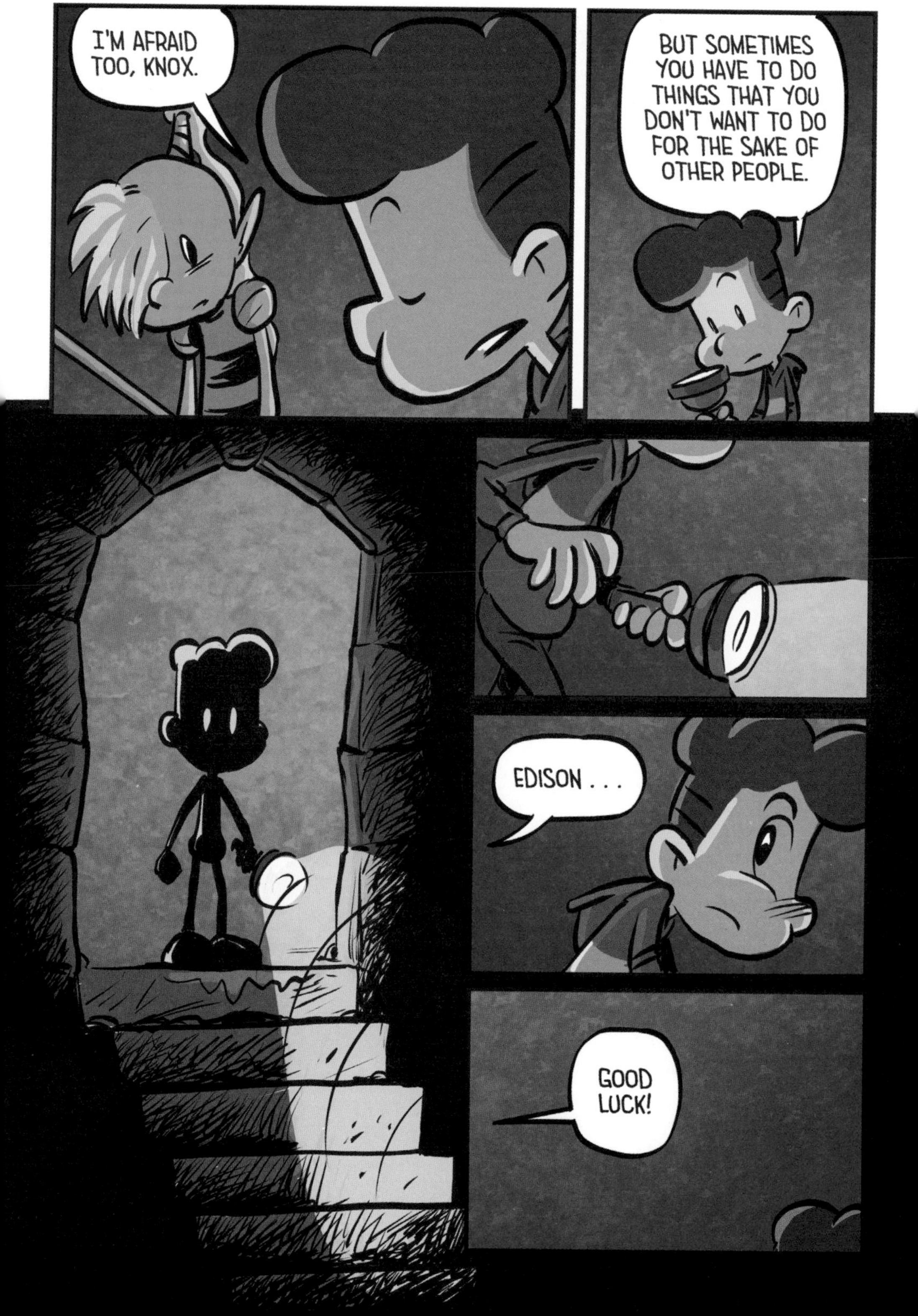
I'M AFRAID TOO, KNOX.
BUT SOMETIMES YOU HAVE TO DO THINGS THAT YOU DON'T WANT TO DO FOR THE SAKE OF OTHER PEOPLE.
EDISON . . .
GOOD LUCK!

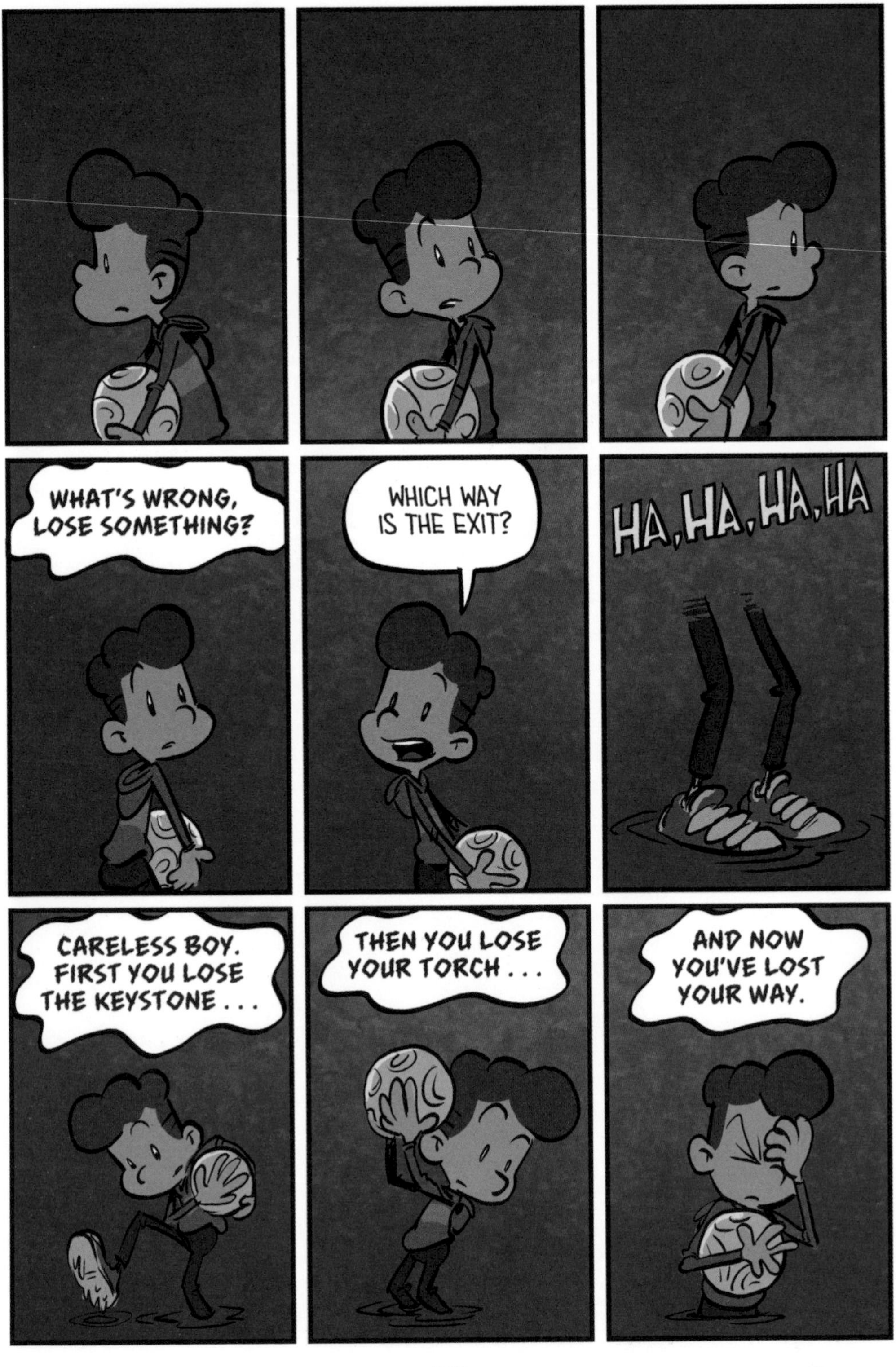
WHAT'S WRONG, LOSE SOMETHING?
WHICH WAY IS THE EXIT?
HA, HA, HA, HA
CARELESS BOY. FIRST YOU LOSE THE KEYSTONE . . .
THEN YOU LOSE YOUR TORCH . . .
AND NOW YOU'VE LOST YOUR WAY.

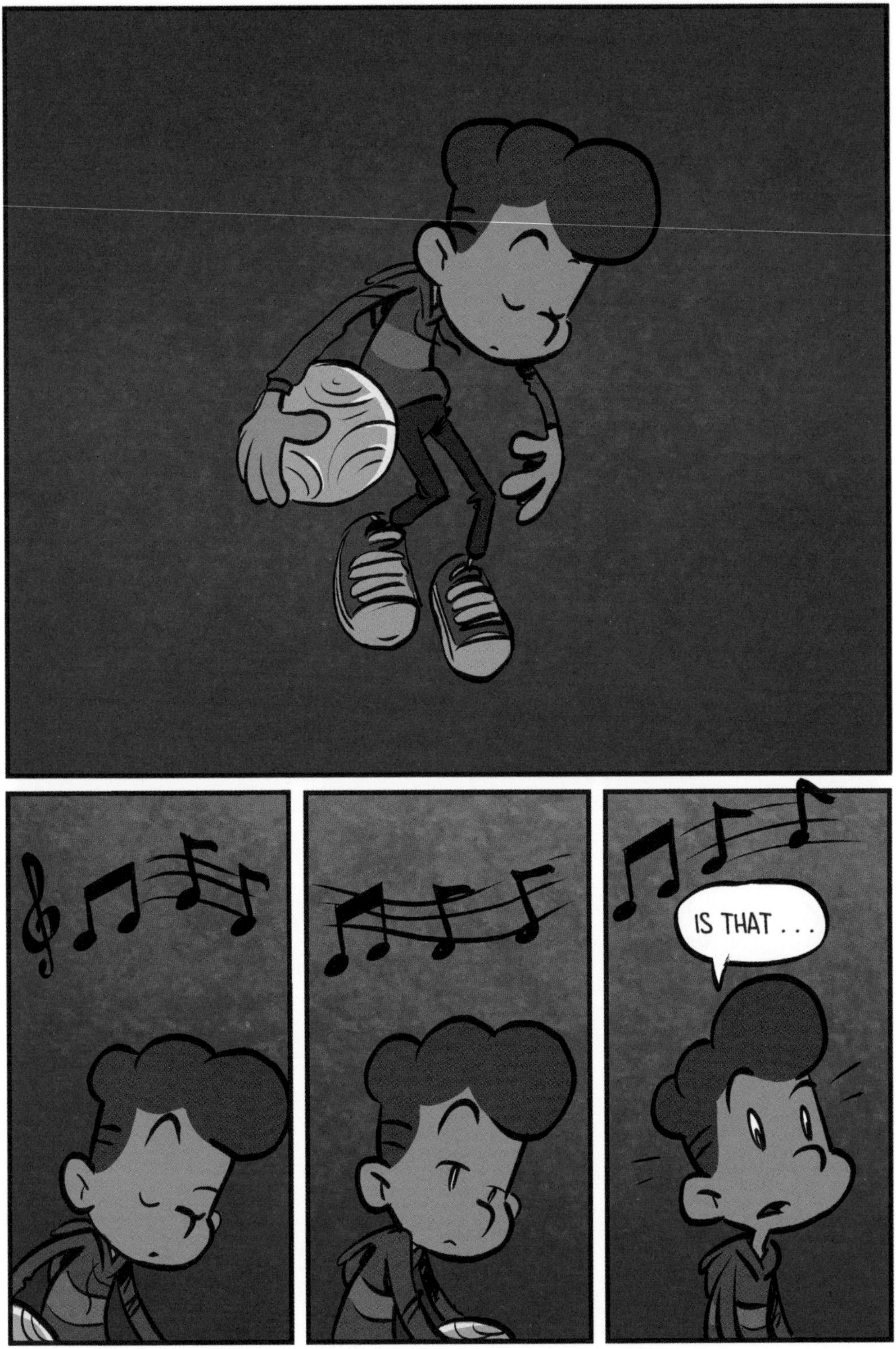
IS THAT . . .

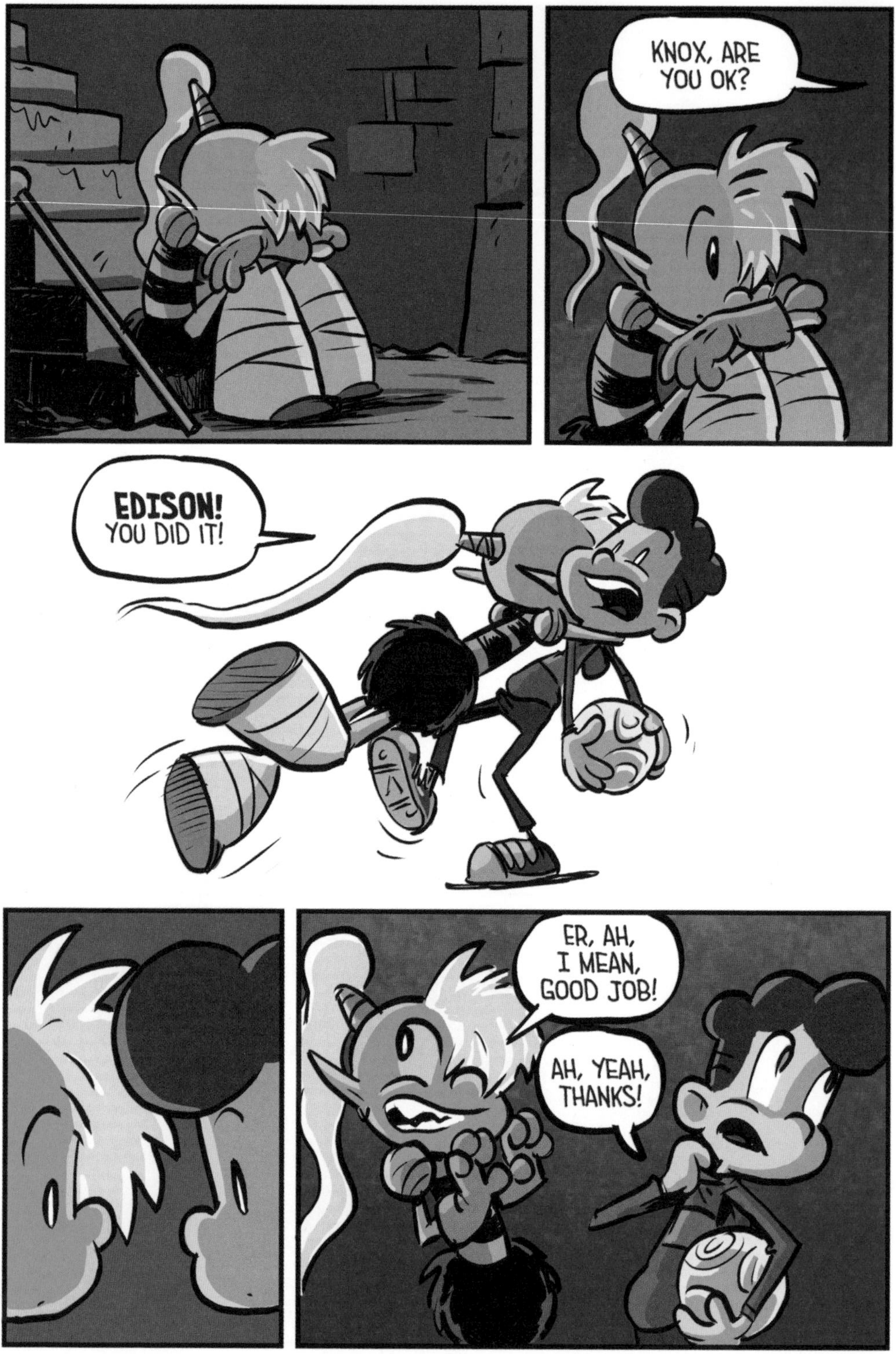
KNOX, ARE YOU OK?
EDISON! YOU DID IT!
ER, AH, I MEAN, GOOD JOB!
AH, YEAH, THANKS!

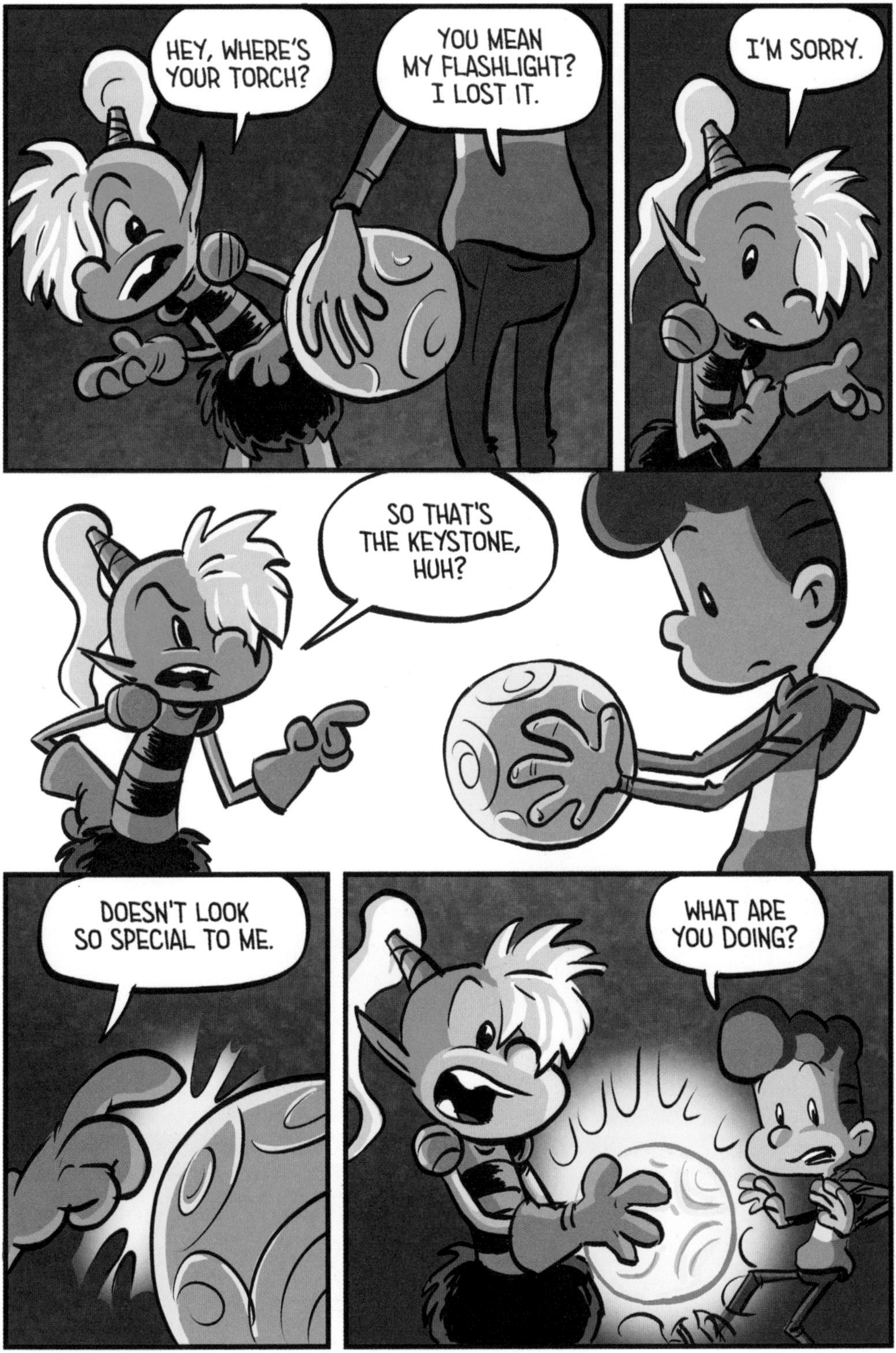
HEY, WHERE'S YOUR TORCH?
YOU MEAN MY FLASHLIGHT? I LOST IT.
I'M SORRY.
SO THAT'S THE KEYSTONE, HUH?
DOESN'T LOOK SO SPECIAL TO ME.
WHAT ARE YOU DOING?

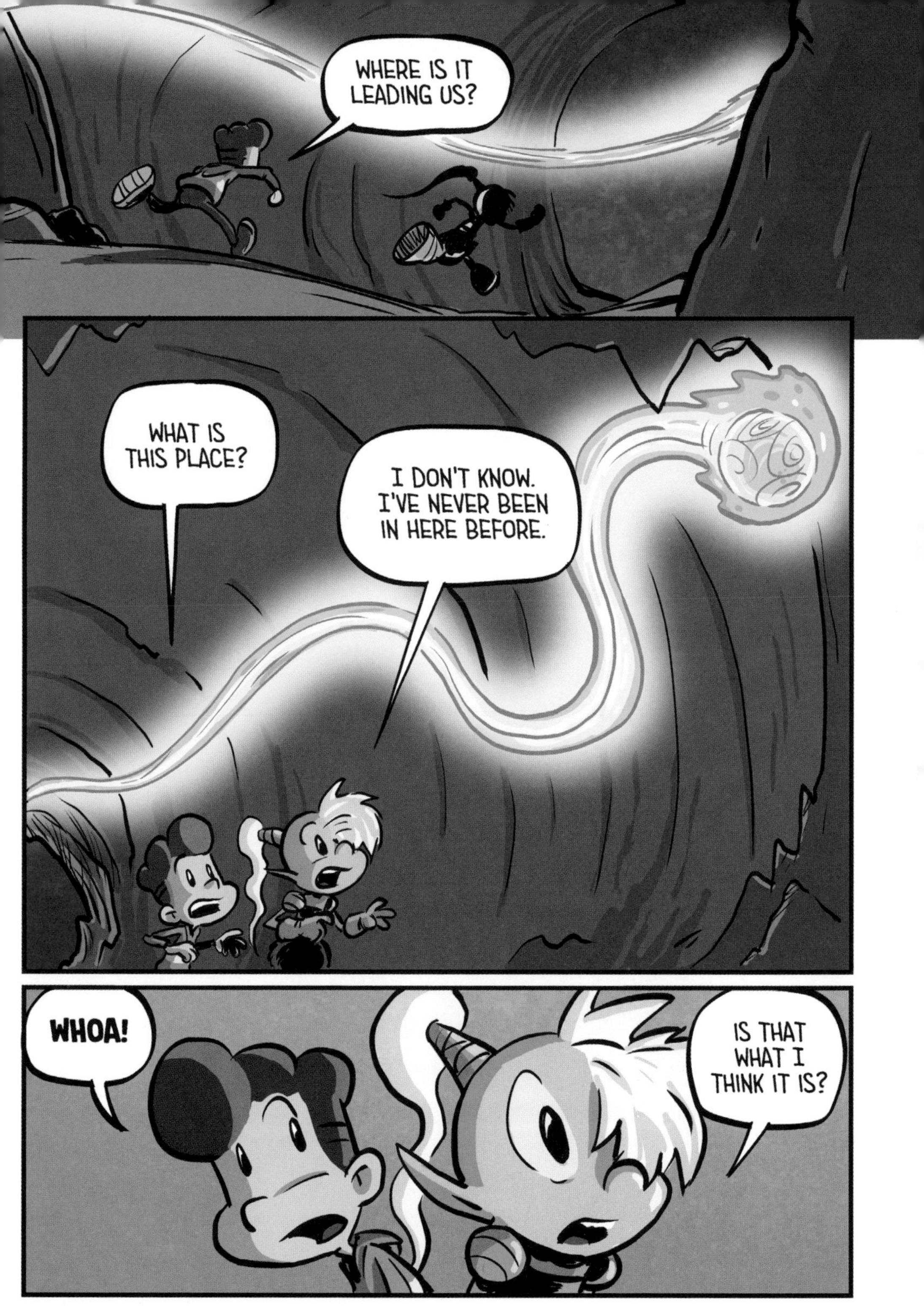

WHERE IS IT LEADING US?
WHAT IS THIS PLACE?
I DON'T KNOW. I'VE NEVER BEEN IN HERE BEFORE.
WHOA!
IS THAT WHAT I THINK IT IS?

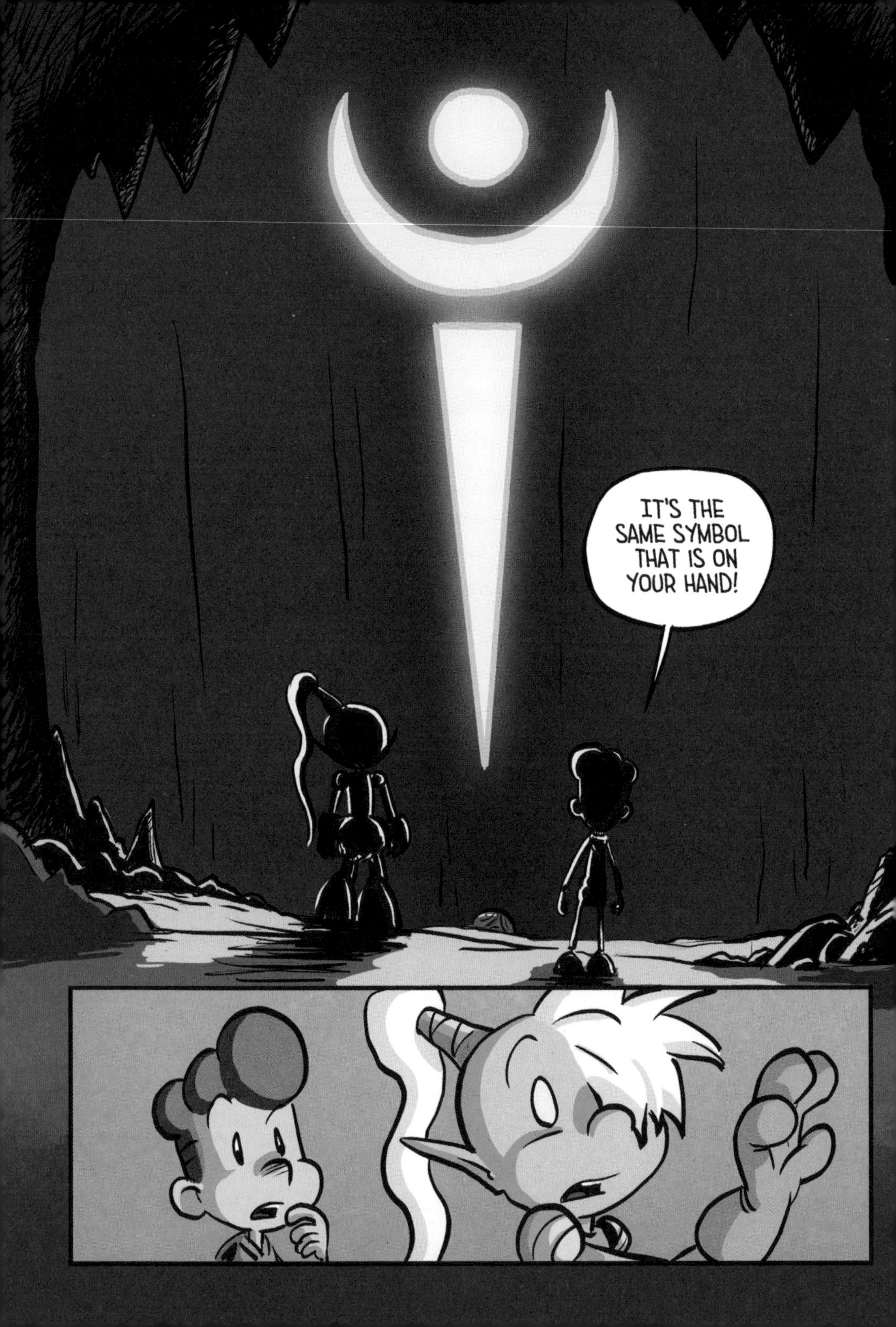
IT'S THE SAME SYMBOL THAT IS ON YOUR HAND!

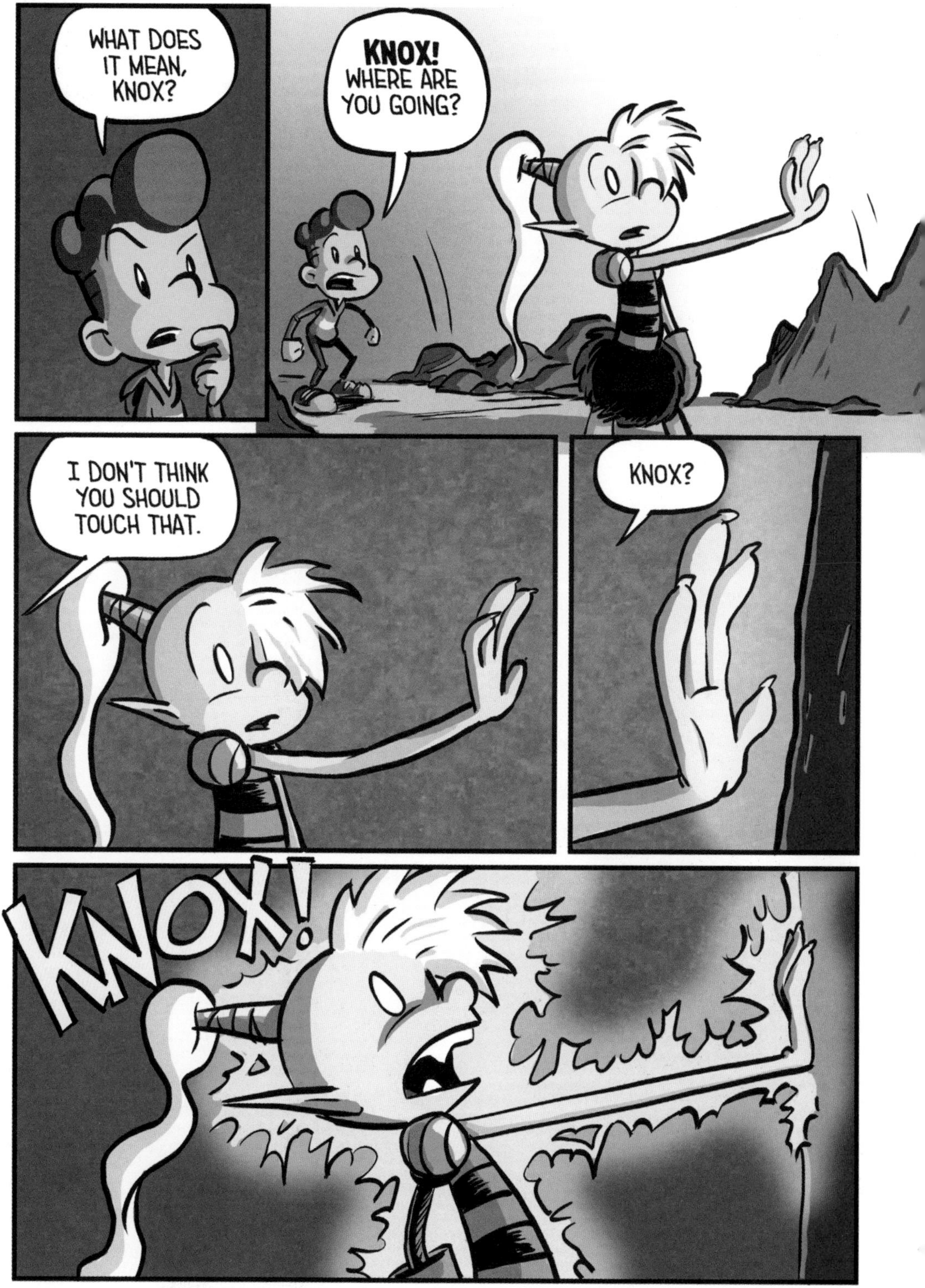
WHAT DOES IT MEAN, KNOX?
KNOX! WHERE ARE YOU GOING?
I DON'T THINK YOU SHOULD TOUCH THAT.
KNOX?
KNOX!

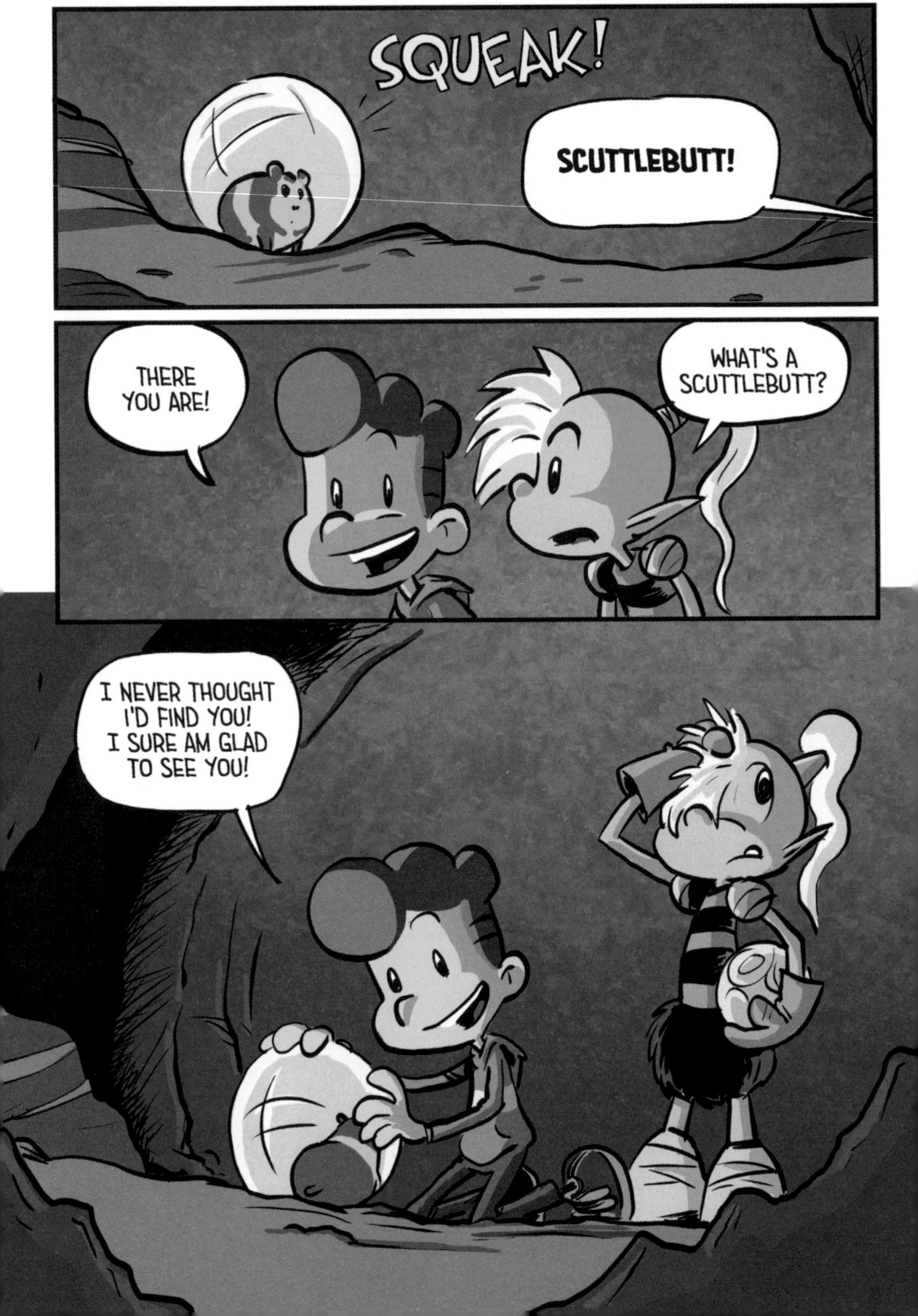
SQUEAK!
SCUTTLEBUTT!
THERE YOU ARE!
WHAT'S A SCUTTLEBUTT?
I NEVER THOUGHT I'D FIND YOU! I SURE AM GLAD TO SEE YOU!

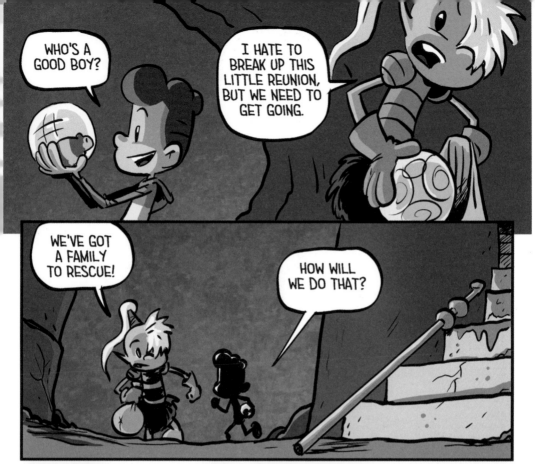

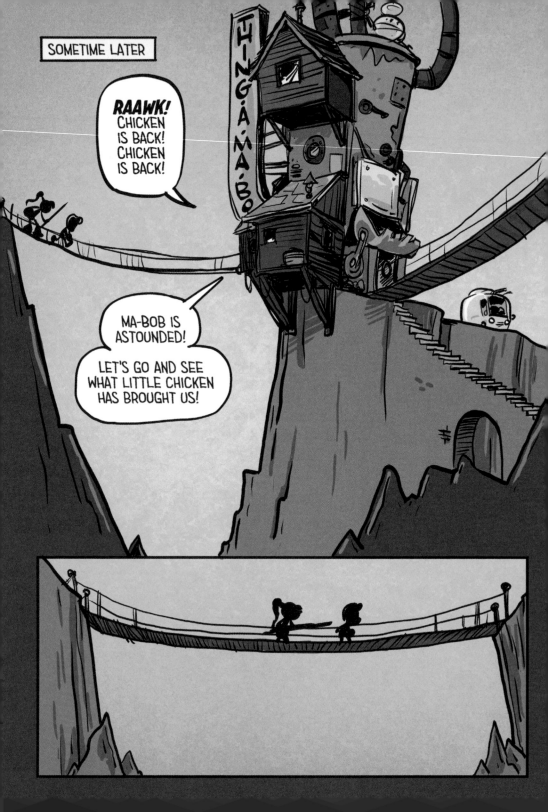

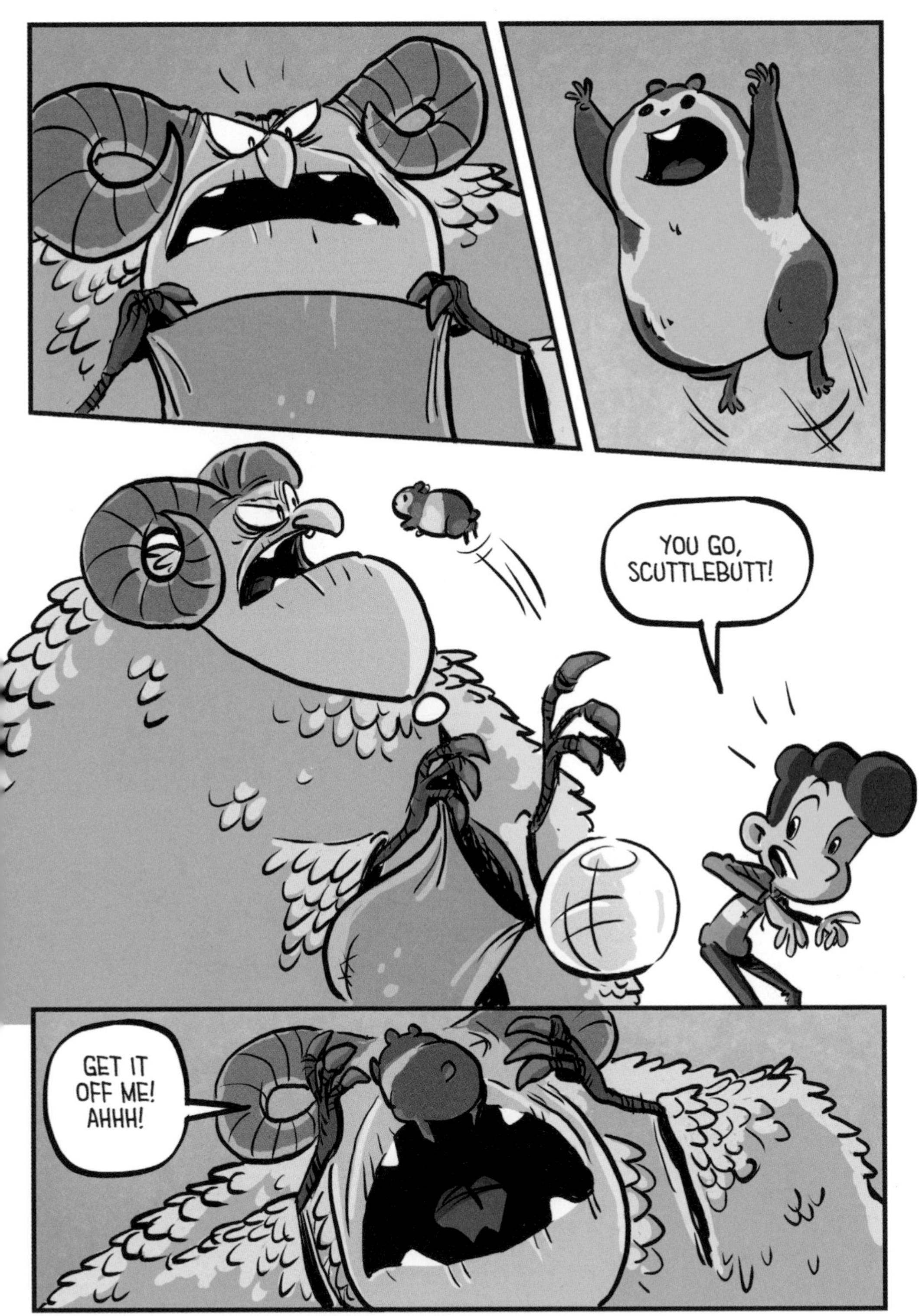
YOU GO, SCUTTLEBUTT!
GET IT OFF ME! AHHH!

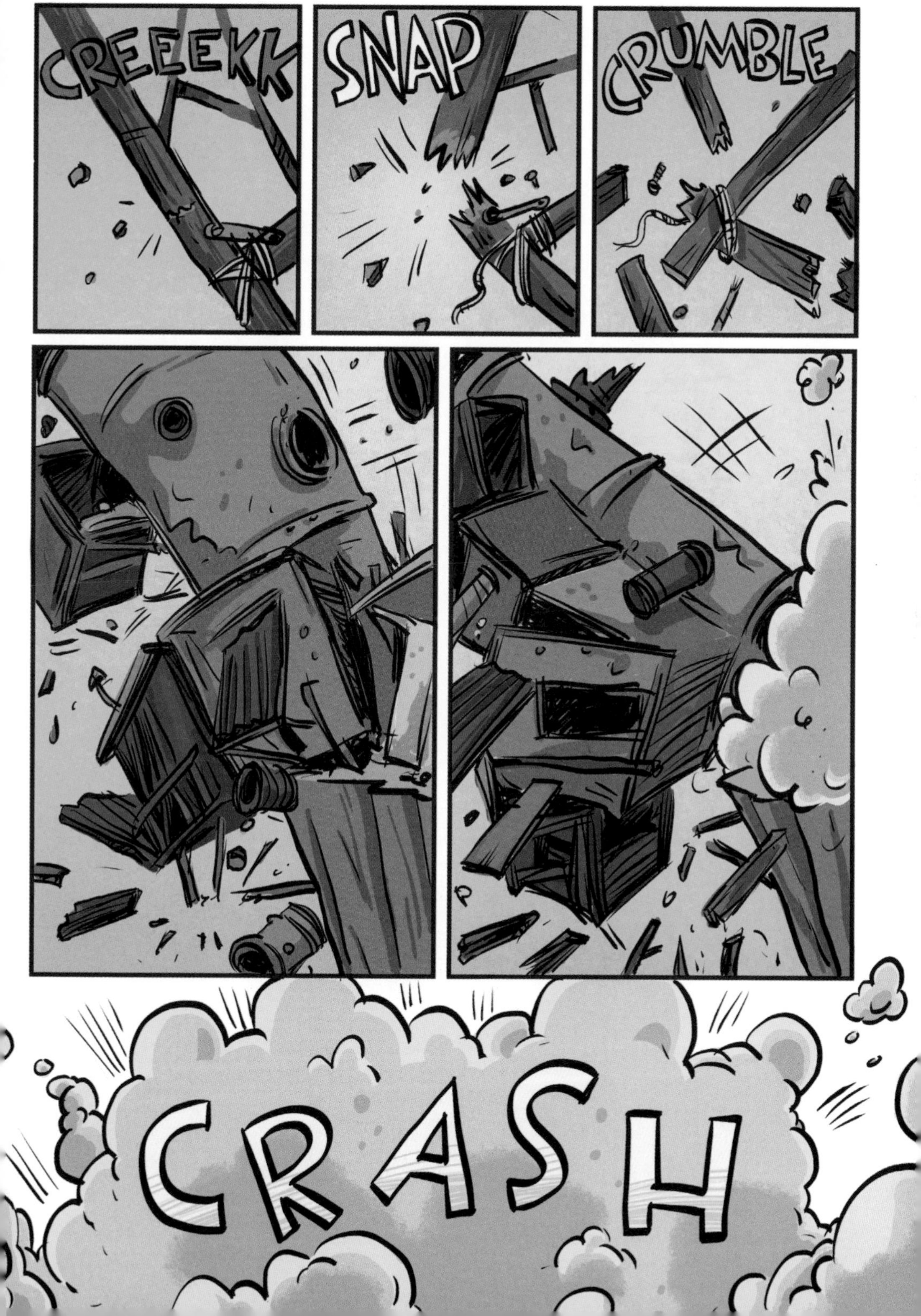
CREEEKK
SNAP
CRUMBLE
CRASH

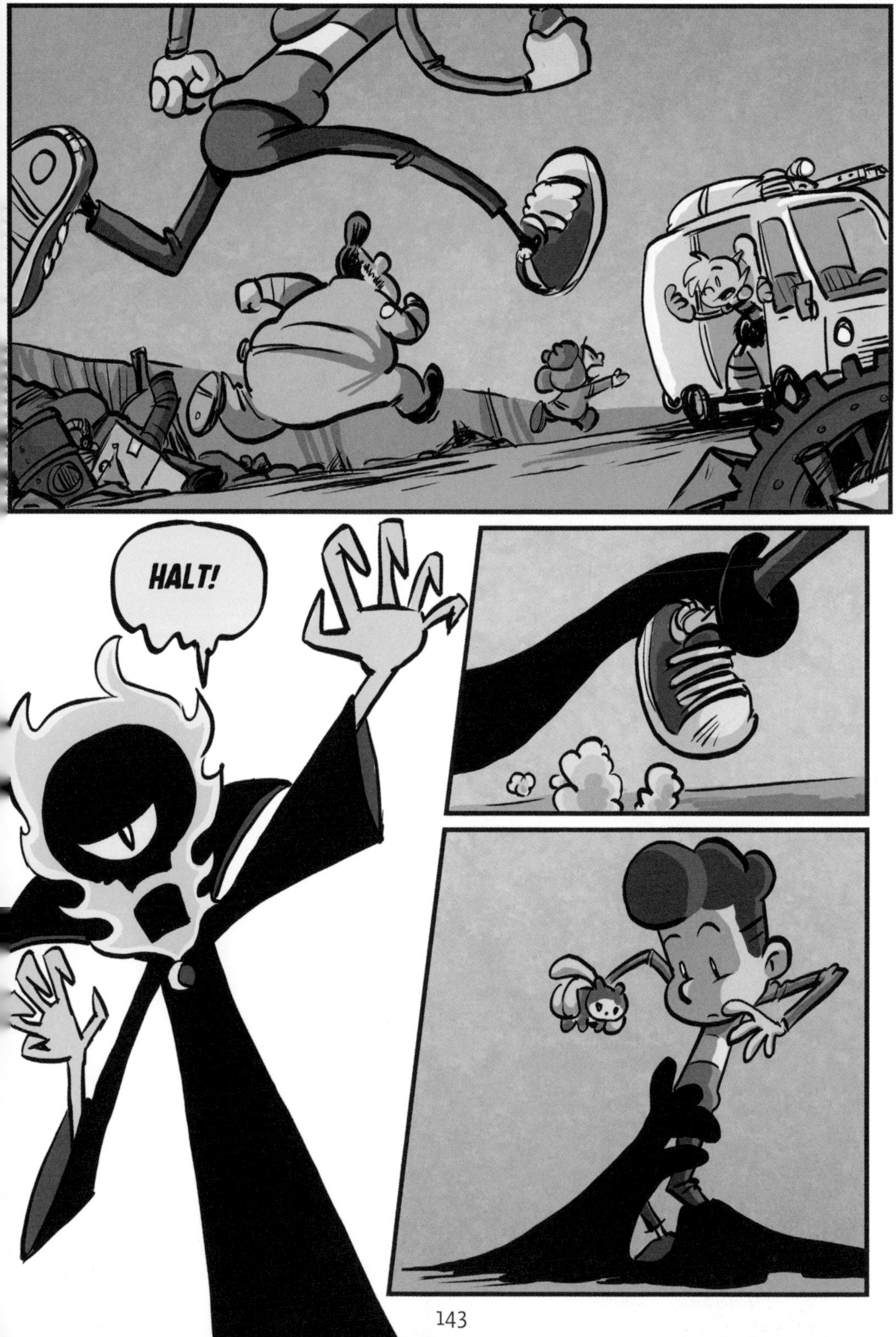
HALT!

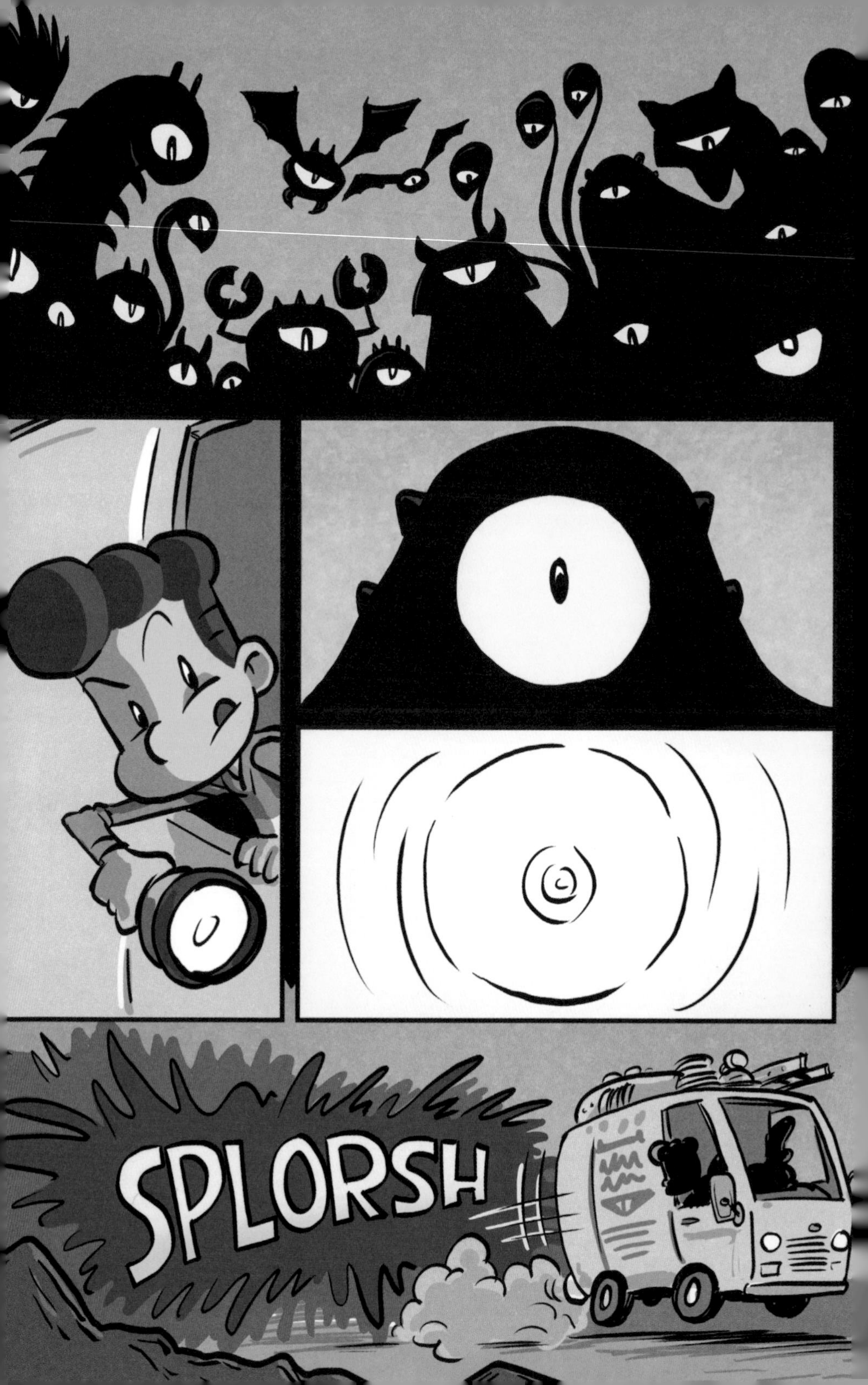
SPLORSH

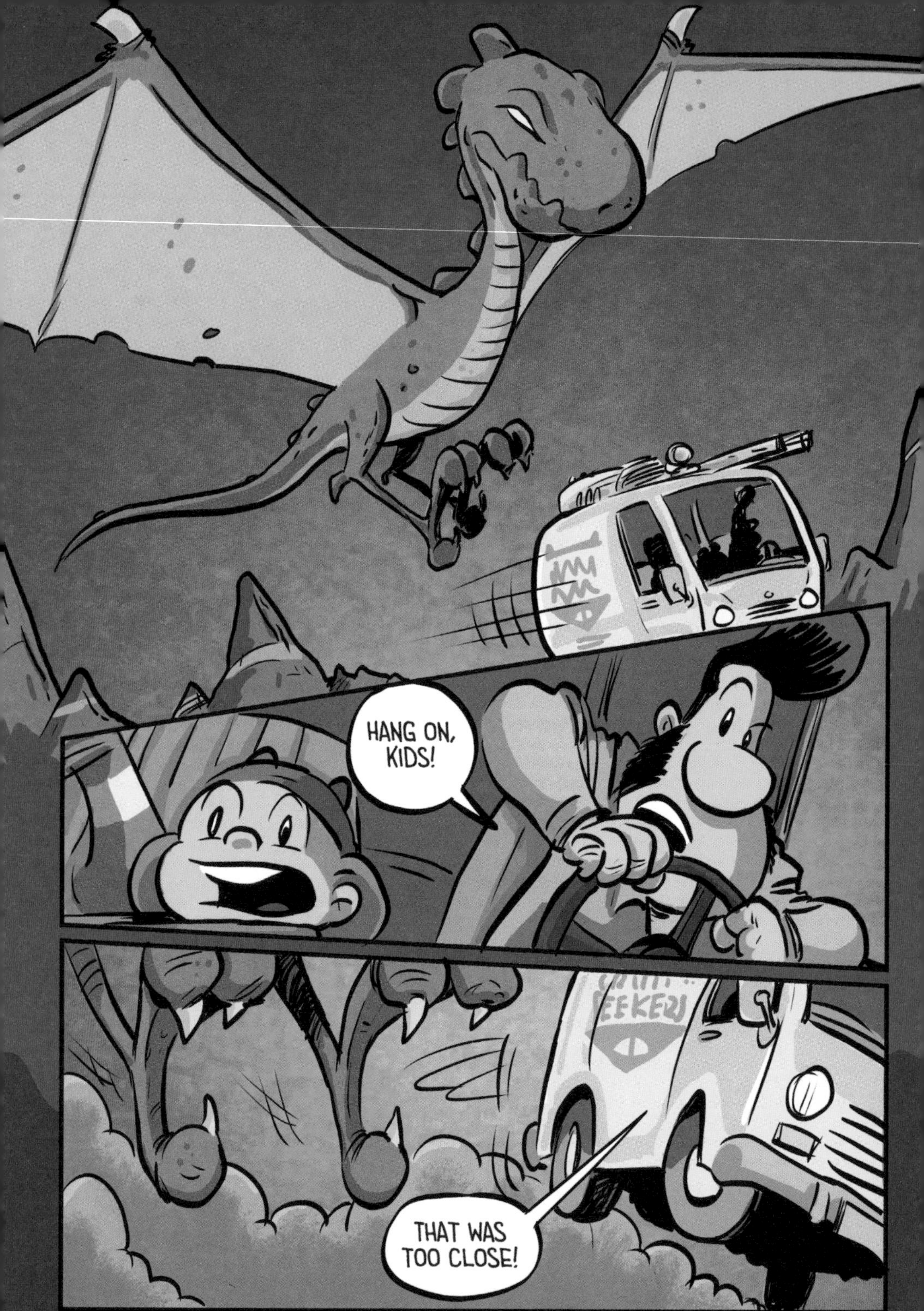
HANG ON, KIDS!
THAT WAS TOO CLOSE!

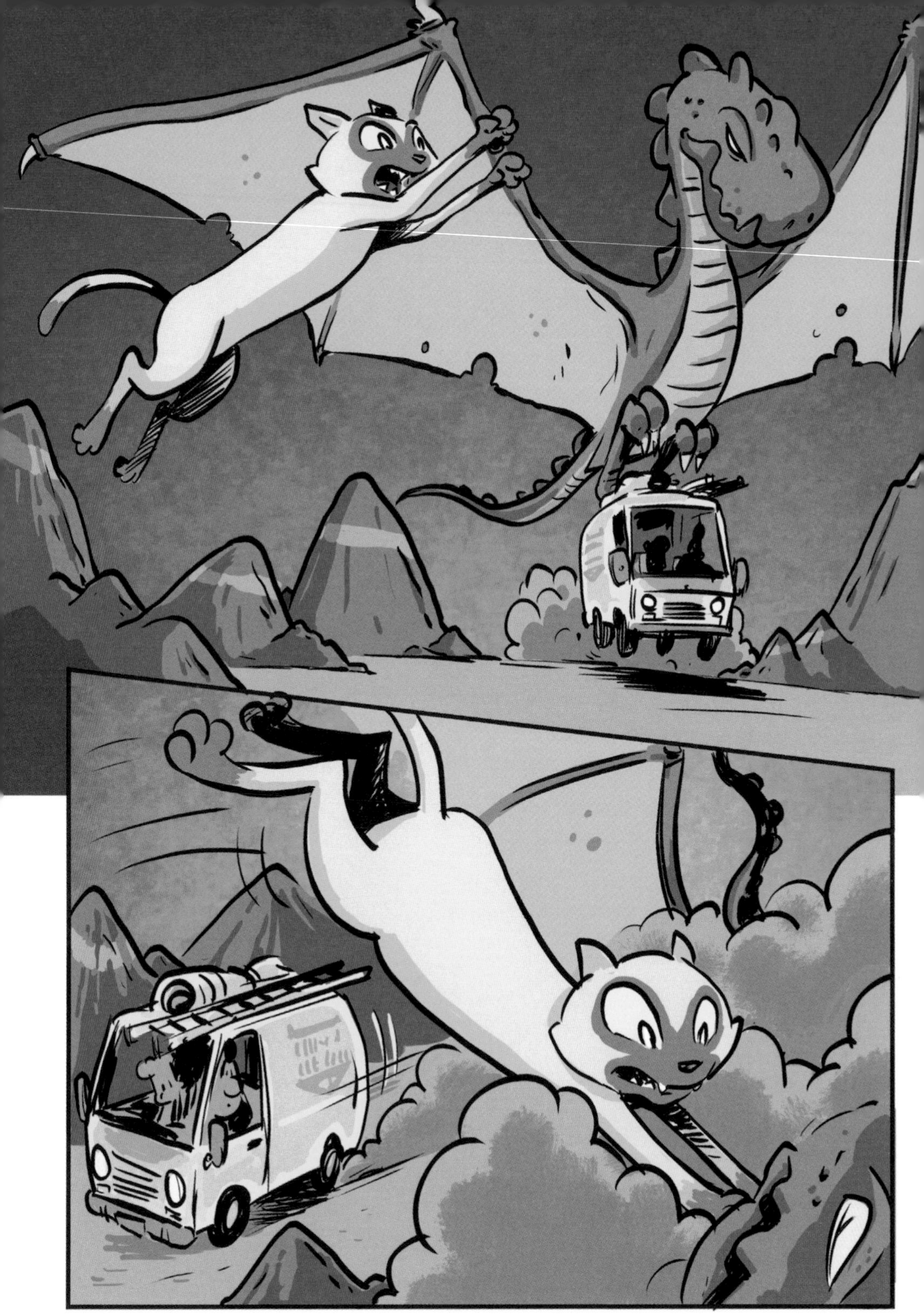

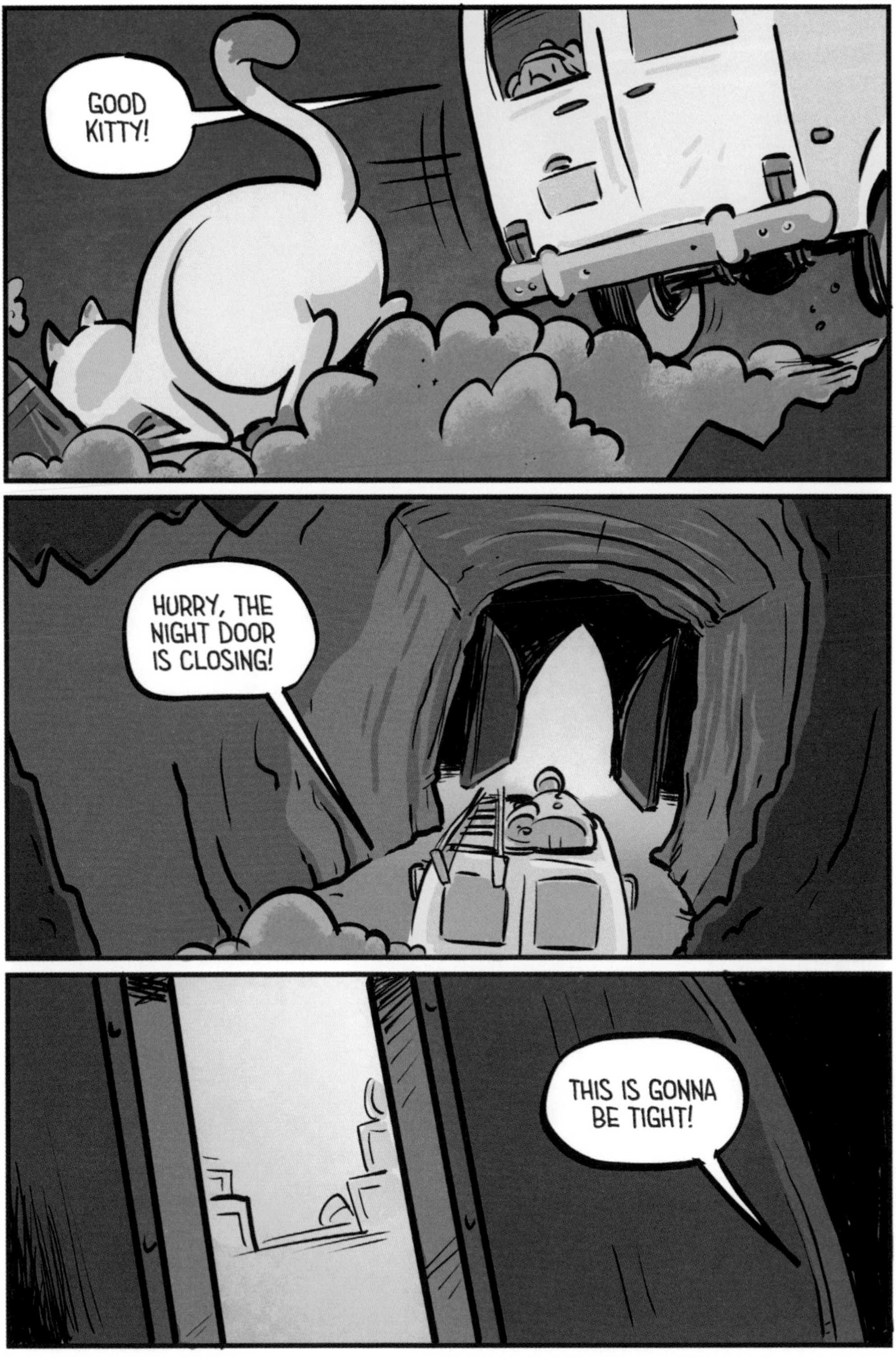
GOOD KITTY!
HURRY, THE NIGHT DOOR IS CLOSING!
THIS IS GONNA BE TIGHT!

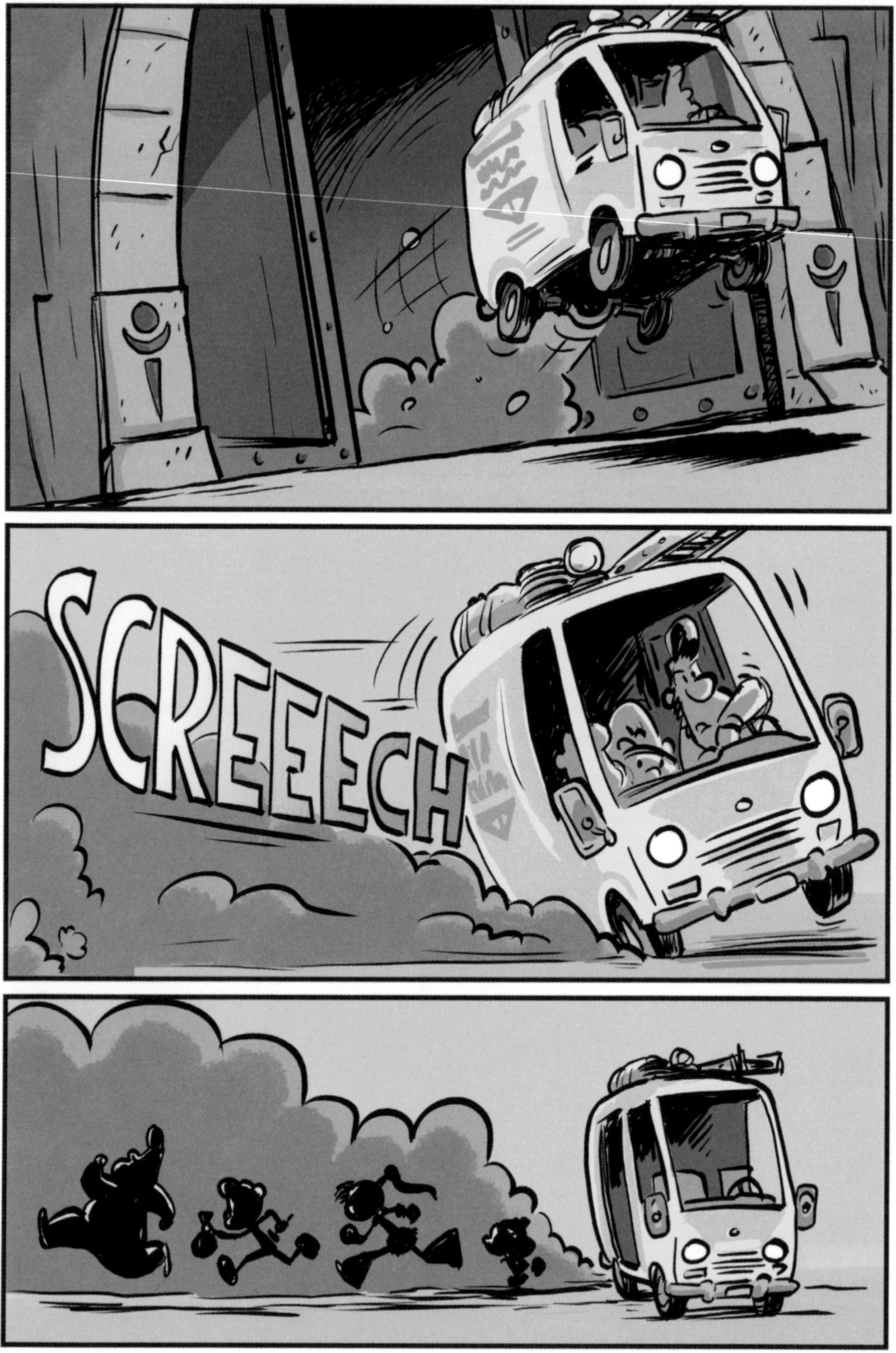
SCREEECH

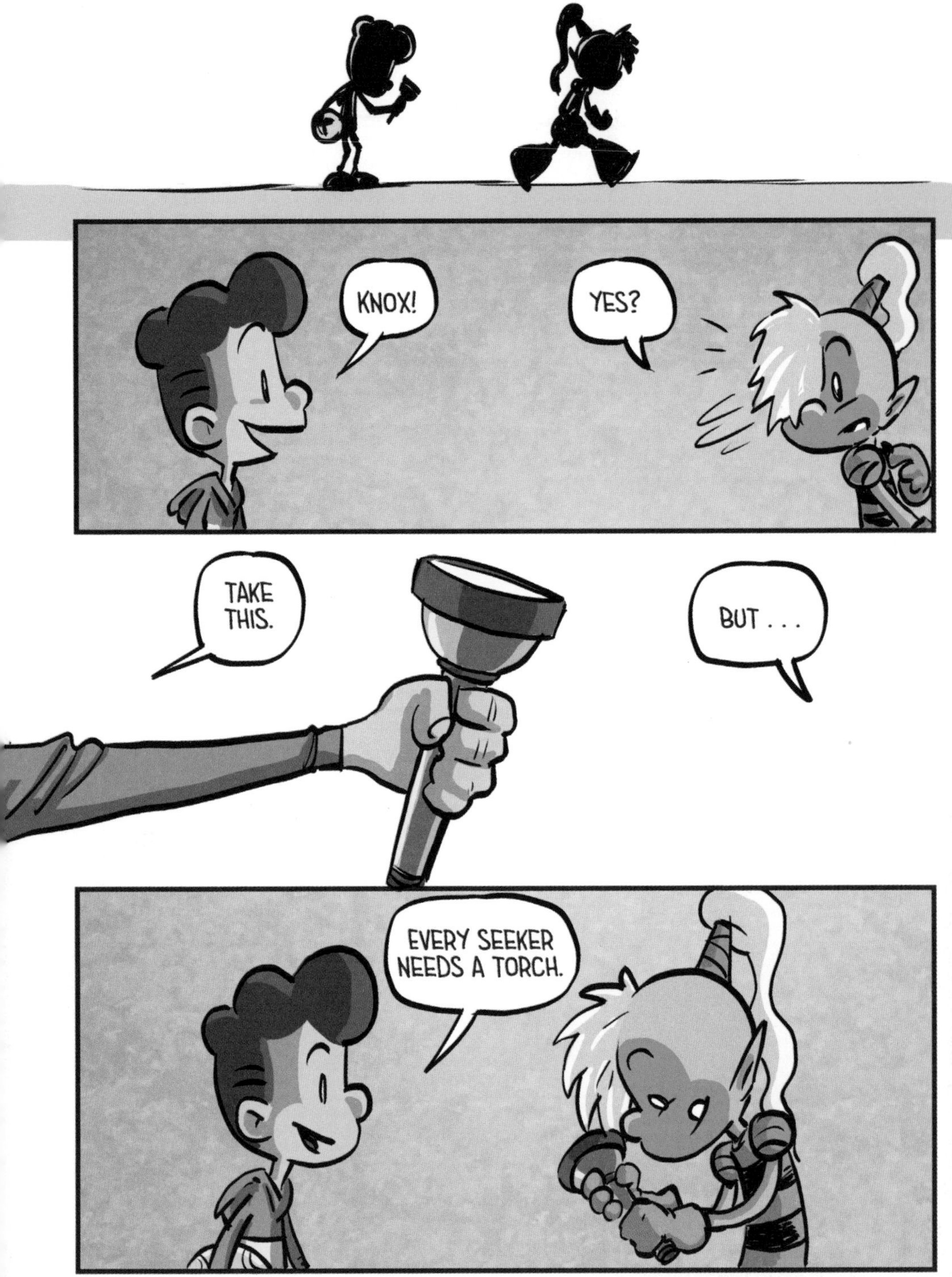
KNOX!
YES?
TAKE THIS.
BUT . . .
EVERY SEEKER NEEDS A TORCH.

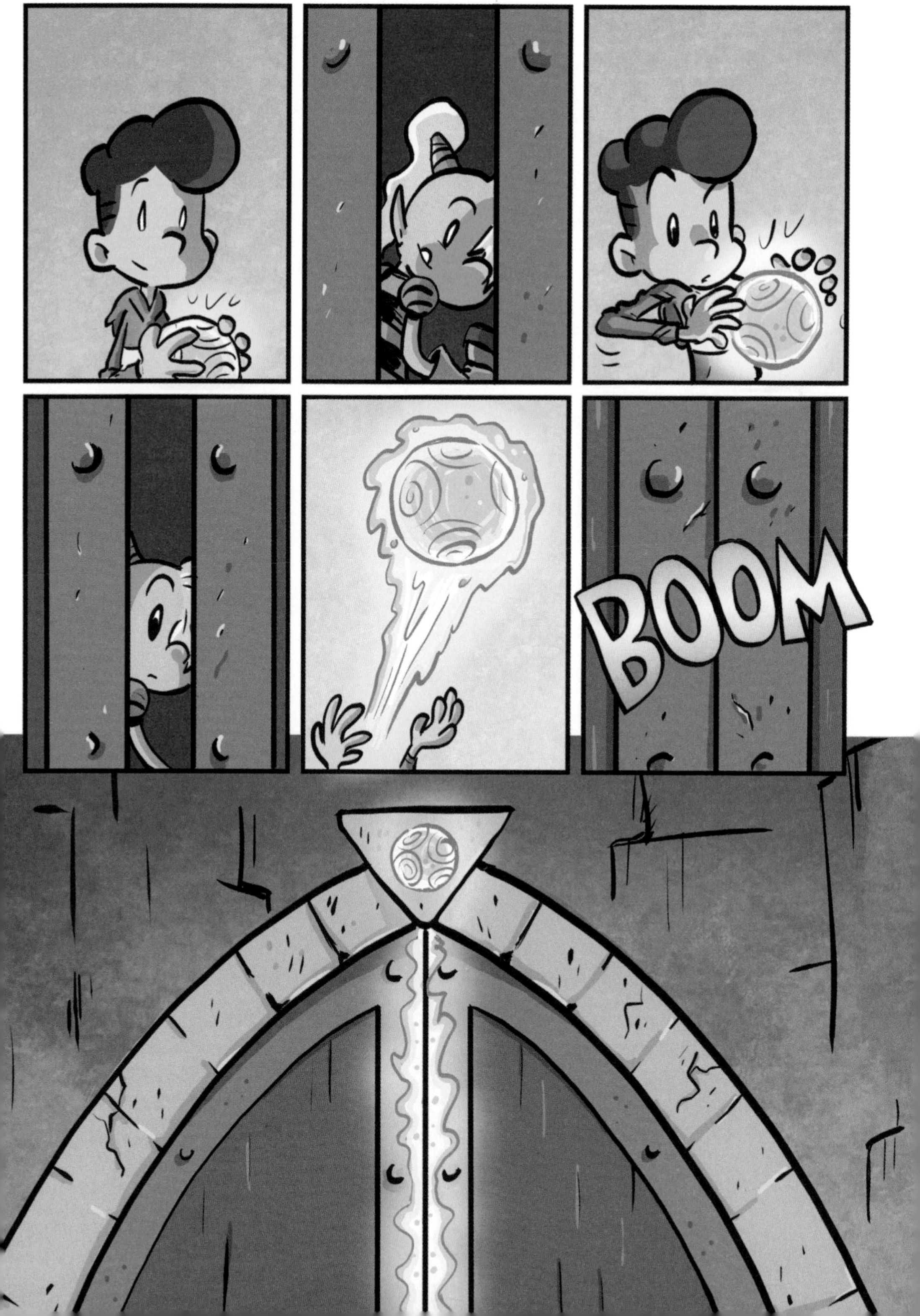
BOOM

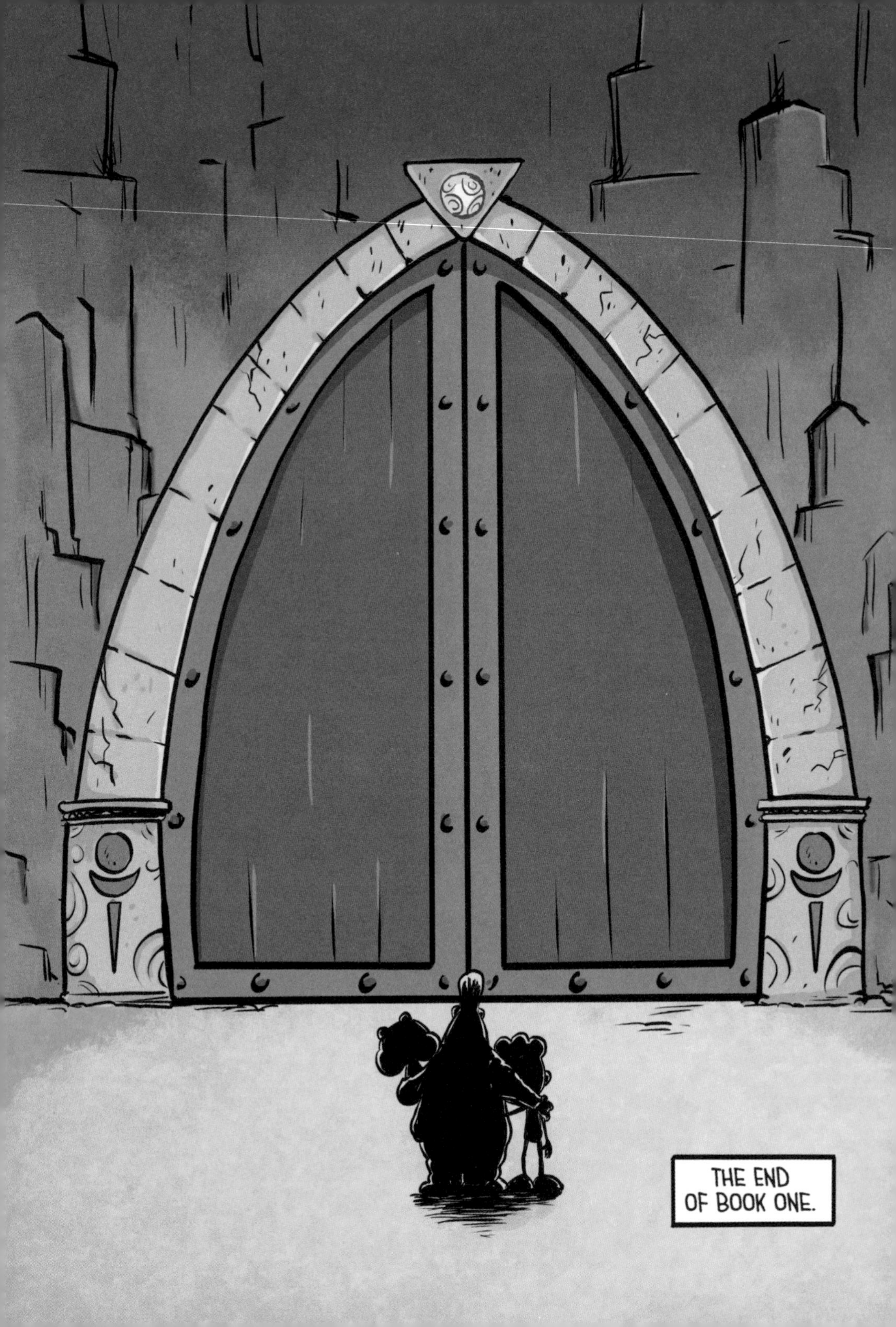
THE END
OF BOOK ONE.